THE LAST OF THE MOHICANS

VOLUME ONE OF TWO

The Last of the Mohicans

Cooper, James Fenimore 1789 – 1851

First Published by H.C. Carey & I. Lea in 1826

Text set in 18 point Helvetica.
Chapter headings set in Helvetica Neue.

ISBN: 978-1-83412-421-6 Volume One
ISBN: 978-1-83412-422-3 Volume Two

THE LAST OF THE MOHICANS

VOLUME ONE OF TWO

JAMES FENIMORE COOPER

GRAND TYPE CLASSICS

CONTENTS

VOLUME ONE

VOLUME TWO

Introduction

IT IS BELIEVED THAT the scene of this tale, and most of the information necessary to understand its allusions, are rendered sufficiently obvious to the reader in the text itself, or in the accompanying notes. Still there is so much obscurity in the Indian traditions, and so much confusion in the Indian names, as to render some explanation useful.

Few men exhibit greater diversity, or, if we may so express it, greater antithesis of character, than the native warrior of North

America. In war, he is daring, boastful, cunning, ruthless, self-denying, and self-devoted; in peace, just, generous, hospitable, revengeful, superstitious, modest, and commonly chaste. These are qualities, it is true, which do not distinguish all alike; but they are so far the predominating traits of these remarkable people as to be characteristic.

It is generally believed that the Aborigines of the American continent have an Asiatic origin. There are many physical as well as moral facts which corroborate this opinion, and some few that would seem to weigh against it.

The color of the Indian, the writer believes, is peculiar to himself, and while his cheek-bones have a very striking indication of a Tartar origin, his eyes have not. Climate may have had great influence on the former, but it is difficult to see how it can have produced the substantial difference which exists in the latter. The imagery of the Indian, both in his poetry and in his oratory, is oriental;

chastened, and perhaps improved, by the limited range of his practical knowledge. He draws his metaphors from the clouds, the seasons, the birds, the beasts, and the vegetable world. In this, perhaps, he does no more than any other energetic and imaginative race would do, being compelled to set bounds to fancy by experience; but the North American Indian clothes his ideas in a dress which is different from that of the African, and is oriental in itself. His language has the richness and sententious fullness of the Chinese. He will express a phrase in a word, and he will qualify the meaning of an entire sentence by a syllable; he will even convey different significations by the simplest inflections of the voice.

Philologists have said that there are but two or three languages, properly speaking, among all the numerous tribes which formerly occupied the country that now composes the United States. They ascribe the known difficulty one people have to understand another to corruptions and dialects. The writer remembers to have been present at an interview between two chiefs of the Great Prairies west of the Mississippi, and when an interpreter was in attendance who spoke both their languages. The warriors appeared to be on the most friendly terms, and seemingly conversed much together; yet, according to the account of the interpreter, each was absolutely ignorant of what the other said. They were of hostile tribes, brought together by the influence of the American government; and it is worthy of remark, that a common policy led them both to adopt the same subject. They mutually exhorted each other to be of use in the event of the chances of war throwing either of the parties into the hands of his enemies. Whatever may be the truth, as respects the root and the genius of the Indian tongues, it is quite certain they are now so distinct in their words as to possess most of the disadvantages of strange languages; hence much of the embarrassment that has arisen in learning their histories, and most of the uncertainty which exists in their traditions.

Like nations of higher pretensions, the American Indian gives a very different account of his own tribe or race from that which is given by other people. He is much addicted to overestimating his own perfections, and to undervaluing those of his rival or his enemy; a trait which may possibly be thought corroborative of the Mosaic account of the creation.

The whites have assisted greatly in rendering the traditions of the Aborigines more obscure by their own manner of corrupting names. Thus, the term used in the title of this book has undergone the changes of Mahicanni, Mohicans, and Mohegans; the latter being the word commonly used by the whites. When it is remembered that the Dutch (who first settled New York), the English, and the French, all gave appellations to the tribes that dwelt within the country which is the scene of this story, and that the Indians not only gave different names to their enemies, but frequently to themselves, the cause of the confusion will be understood.

In these pages, Lenni-Lenape, Lenope, Delawares, Wapanachki, and Mohicans, all mean the same people, or tribes of the same stock. The Mengwe, the Maquas, the Mingoes, and the Iroquois, though not all strictly the same, are identified frequently by the speakers, being politically confederated and opposed to those just named. Mingo was a term of peculiar reproach, as were Mengwe and Maqua in a less degree.

The Mohicans were the possessors of the country first occupied by the Europeans in this portion of the continent. They were, consequently, the first dispossessed; and the seemingly inevitable fate of all these people, who disappear before the advances, or it might be termed the inroads, of civilization, as the verdure of their native forests falls before the nipping frosts, is represented as having already befallen them. There is sufficient historical truth in the picture to justify the use that has been made of it.

In point of fact, the country which is the scene of the following tale has undergone as little change, since the historical events alluded to had place, as almost any other district of equal extent within the whole limits of the United States. There are fashionable and well-attended watering-places at and near the spring where Hawkeye halted to drink, and roads traverse the forests where he and his friends were compelled to journey without even a path. Glen's has a large village; and while William Henry, and even a fortress of later date, are only to be traced as ruins, there is another village on the shores of the Horican. But, beyond this, the enterprise and energy of a people who have done so much in other places have done little here. The whole of that wilderness, in which the latter incidents of the legend occurred, is nearly a wilderness still, though the red man has entirely deserted this part of the state. Of all the tribes named in these pages, there exist only a few half-civilized beings of the Oneidas, on the reservations of their people in New York. The rest have disappeared, either from the regions in which their fathers dwelt, or altogether from the earth.

There is one point on which we would wish to say a word before closing this preface. Hawkeye calls the Lac du Saint Sacrement, the "Horican." As we believe this to be an appropriation of the name that has its origin with ourselves, the time has arrived, perhaps, when the fact should be frankly admitted. While writing this book, fully a quarter of a century since, it occurred to us that the French name of this lake was too complicated, the American too commonplace, and the Indian too unpronounceable, for either to be used familiarly in a work of fiction. Looking over an ancient map, it was ascertained that a tribe of Indians, called “Les Horicans” by the French, existed in the neighborhood of this beautiful sheet of water. As every word uttered by Natty Bumppo was not to be received as rigid truth, we took the liberty of putting the “Horican” into his mouth, as the substitute for “Lake George.” The name has appeared to find favor, and all things considered, it may possibly be quite as well to let it stand, instead of going back to the House of Hanover for the appellation of our finest sheet of water. We relieve our conscience by the confession, at all events leaving it to exercise its authority as it may see fit.

Chapter One

"Mine ear is open, and my heart prepared:
The worst is wordly loss thou canst unfold: –
Say, is my kingdom lost?"
– Shakespeare

IT WAS A FEATURE peculiar to the colonial wars of North America, that the toils and dangers of the wilderness were to be encountered before the adverse hosts could meet. A wide and apparently an impervious boundary of forests severed the possessions of the hostile provinces of France and England. The hardy colonist, and the trained

European who fought at his side, frequently expended months in struggling against the rapids of the streams, or in effecting the rugged passes of the mountains, in quest of an opportunity to exhibit their courage in a more martial conflict. But, emulating the patience and self-denial of the practiced native warriors, they learned to overcome every difficulty; and it would seem that, in time, there was no recess of the woods so dark, nor any secret place so lovely, that it might claim exemption from the inroads of those who had pledged their blood to satiate their vengeance, or to uphold the cold and selfish policy of the distant monarchs of Europe.

Perhaps no district throughout the wide extent of the intermediate frontiers can furnish a livelier picture of the cruelty and fierceness of the savage warfare of those periods than the country which lies between the head waters of the Hudson and the adjacent lakes.

The facilities which nature had there offered to the march of the combatants were too obvious to be neglected. The lengthened sheet of the Champlain stretched from the frontiers of Canada, deep within the borders of the neighboring province of New York, forming a natural passage across half the distance that the French were compelled to master in order to strike their enemies. Near its southern termination, it received the contributions of another lake, whose waters were so limpid as to have been exclusively selected by the Jesuit missionaries to perform the typical purification of baptism, and to obtain for it the title of lake “du Saint Sacrement.” The less zealous English thought they conferred a sufficient honor on its unsullied fountains, when they bestowed the name of their reigning prince, the second of the house of Hanover. The two united to rob the untutored possessors of its wooded scenery of their native right to perpetuate its original appellation of "Horican."[1]

Winding its way among countless islands, and imbedded in mountains, the "holy lake" extended a dozen leagues still further to the south. With the high plain that there interposed itself to the further passage of the water, commenced a portage of as many miles, which conducted the adventurer to the banks of the Hudson, at a point where, with the usual obstructions of the rapids, or rifts, as they were then termed in the language of the country, the river became navigable to the tide.

---

1 As each nation of the Indians had its language or its dialect, they usually gave different names to the same places, though nearly all of their appellations were descriptive of thehd object. Thus a literal translation of the name of this beautiful sheet of water, used by the tribe that dwelt on its banks, would be "The Tail of the Lake." Lake George, as it is vulgarly, and now, indeed, legally, called, forms a sort of tail to Lake Champlain, when viewed on the map. Hence, the name.

While, in the pursuit of their daring plans of annoyance, the restless enterprise of the French even attempted the distant and difficult gorges of the Alleghany, it may easily be imagined that their proverbial acuteness would not overlook the natural advantages of the district we have just described. It became, emphatically, the bloody arena, in which most of the battles for the mastery of the colonies were contested. Forts were erected at the different points that commanded the facilities of the route, and were taken and retaken, razed and rebuilt, as victory alighted on the hostile banners. While the husbandman shrank back from the dangerous passes, within the safer boundaries of the more ancient settlements, armies larger than those that had often disposed of the scepters of the mother countries, were seen to bury themselves in these forests, whence they rarely returned but in skeleton bands, that were haggard with care or dejected by defeat. Though the arts of peace were unknown to this fatal region, its forests were alive with men; its shades and glens rang with the sounds of martial music, and the echoes of its mountains threw back the laugh, or repeated the wanton cry, of many a gallant and reckless youth, as he hurried by them, in the noontide of his spirits, to slumber in a long night of forgetfulness.

It was in this scene of strife and bloodshed that the incidents we shall attempt to relate occurred, during the third year of the war which England and France last waged for the possession of a country that neither was destined to retain.

The imbecility of her military leaders abroad, and the fatal want of energy in her councils at home, had lowered the character of Great Britain from the proud elevation on which it had been placed by the talents and enterprise of her former warriors and statesmen. No longer dreaded by her enemies, her servants were fast losing the confidence of self-respect. In this mortifying abasement, the colonists, though innocent of her imbecility, and too humble to be the agents of her blunders, were but the natural participators. They had recently seen a chosen army from that country, which, reverencing as a mother, they had blindly believed invincible – an army led by a chief who had been selected from a crowd of trained warriors, for his rare military endowments, disgracefully routed by a handful of French and Indians, and only saved from annihilation by the coolness and spirit of a Virginian boy, whose riper fame has since diffused itself, with the steady influence of moral truth, to the uttermost confines of Christendom.[2] A wide frontier had

---

2 Washington, who, after uselessly admonishing the European general of the danger into which he was heedlessly running, saved the remnants of the British army, on this occasion, by his decision and courage. The reputation earned by Washington in this battle

been laid naked by this unexpected disaster, and more substantial evils were preceded by a thousand fanciful and imaginary dangers. The alarmed colonists believed that the yells of the savages mingled with every fitful gust of wind that issued from the interminable forests of the west. The terrific character of their merciless enemies increased immeasurably the natural horrors of warfare. Numberless recent massacres were still vivid in their recollections; nor was there any ear in the provinces so deaf as not to have drunk in with avidity the narrative of some fearful tale of midnight

---

was the principal cause of his being selected to command the American armies at a later day. It is a circumstance worthy of observation, that while all America rang with his well-merited reputation, his name does not occur in any European account of the battle; at least the author has searched for it without success. In this manner does the mother country absorb even the fame, under that system of rule.

murder, in which the natives of the forests were the principal and barbarous actors. As the credulous and excited traveler related the hazardous chances of the wilderness, the blood of the timid curdled with terror, and mothers cast anxious glances even at those children which slumbered within the security of the largest towns. In short, the magnifying influence of fear began to set at naught the calculations of reason, and to render those who should have remembered their manhood, the slaves of the basest passions. Even the most confident and the stoutest hearts began to think the issue of the contest was becoming doubtful; and that abject class was hourly increasing in numbers, who thought they foresaw all the possessions of the English crown in America subdued by their Christian foes, or laid waste by the inroads of their relentless allies.

When, therefore, intelligence was received at the fort which covered the southern termination of the portage between the Hudson and the lakes, that Montcalm had been seen moving up the Champlain, with an army "numerous as the leaves on the trees," its truth was admitted with more of the craven reluctance of fear than with the stern joy that a warrior should feel, in finding an enemy within reach of his blow. The news had been brought, toward the decline of a day in midsummer, by an Indian runner, who also bore an urgent request from Munro, the commander of a work on the shore of the "holy lake," for a speedy and powerful reinforcement. It has already been mentioned that the distance between these two posts was less than five leagues. The rude path, which originally formed their line of communication, had been widened for the passage of wagons; so that the distance which had been traveled by the son of the forest in two hours, might easily be effected by a detachment of troops, with their necessary baggage, between the rising and setting of a summer sun. The loyal servants of the British crown had given to one of these forest-fastnesses the name of William Henry, and to the other that of Fort Edward, calling each after a favorite prince of the reigning family. The veteran Scotchman just named held the first, with a regiment of regulars and a few provincials; a force really by far too small to make head against the formidable power that Montcalm was leading to the foot of his earthen mounds. At the latter, however, lay General Webb, who commanded the armies of the king in the northern provinces, with a body of more than five thousand men. By uniting the several detachments of his command, this officer might have arrayed nearly double that number of combatants against the enterprising Frenchman, who had ventured so far from his reinforcements, with an army but little superior in numbers.

But under the influence of their degraded

fortunes, both officers and men appeared better disposed to await the approach of their formidable antagonists, within their works, than to resist the progress of their march, by emulating the successful example of the French at Fort du Quesne, and striking a blow on their advance.

After the first surprise of the intelligence had a little abated, a rumor was spread through the entrenched camp, which stretched along the margin of the Hudson, forming a chain of outworks to the body of the fort itself, that a chosen detachment of fifteen hundred men was to depart, with the dawn, for William Henry, the post at the northern extremity of the portage. That which at first was only rumor, soon became certainty, as orders passed from the quarters of the commander-in-chief to the several corps he had selected for this service, to prepare for their speedy departure. All doubts as to the intention of Webb now vanished, and an hour or two of hurried footsteps and anxious faces succeeded. The novice in the military art flew from point to point, retarding his own preparations by the excess of his violent and somewhat distempered zeal; while the more practiced veteran made his arrangements with a deliberation that scorned every appearance of haste; though his sober lineaments and anxious eye sufficiently betrayed that he had no very strong professional relish for the, as yet, untried and dreaded warfare of the wilderness. At length the sun set in a flood of glory, behind the distant western hills, and as darkness drew its veil around the secluded spot the sounds of preparation diminished; the last light finally disappeared from the log cabin of some officer; the trees cast their deeper shadows over the mounds and the rippling stream, and a silence soon pervaded the camp, as deep as that which reigned in the vast forest by which it was environed.

According to the orders of the preceding

night, the heavy sleep of the army was broken by the rolling of the warning drums, whose rattling echoes were heard issuing, on the damp morning air, out of every vista of the woods, just as day began to draw the shaggy outlines of some tall pines of the vicinity, on the opening brightness of a soft and cloudless eastern sky. In an instant the whole camp was in motion; the meanest soldier arousing from his lair to witness the departure of his comrades, and to share in the excitement and incidents of the hour. The simple array of the chosen band was soon completed. While the regular and trained hirelings of the king marched with haughtiness to the right of the line, the less pretending colonists took their humbler position on its left, with a docility that long practice had rendered easy. The scouts departed; strong guards preceded and followed the lumbering vehicles that bore the baggage; and before the gray light of the morning was mellowed by the rays of the sun, the main body of the combatants wheeled into column, and left the encampment with a show of high military bearing, that served to drown the slumbering apprehensions of many a novice, who was now about to make his first essay in arms. While in view of their admiring comrades, the same proud front and ordered array was observed, until the notes of their fifes growing fainter in distance, the forest at length appeared to swallow up the living mass which had slowly entered its bosom.

The deepest sounds of the retiring and invisible column had ceased to be borne on the breeze to the listeners, and the latest straggler had already disappeared in pursuit; but there still remained the signs of another departure, before a log cabin of unusual size and accommodations, in front of which those sentinels paced their rounds, who were known to guard the person of the English general. At this spot were gathered some half dozen horses, caparisoned in a manner which showed that two, at least, were destined to bear the persons of females, of a rank that it was not usual to meet so far in the wilds of the country. A third wore trappings and arms of an officer of the staff; while the rest, from the plainness of the housings, and the traveling mails with which they were encumbered, were evidently fitted for the reception of as many menials, who were, seemingly, already waiting the pleasure of those they served. At a respectful distance from this unusual show, were gathered divers groups of curious idlers; some admiring the blood and bone of the high-mettled military charger, and others gazing at the preparations, with the dull wonder of vulgar curiosity. There was one man, however, who, by his countenance and actions, formed a marked exception to those who composed the latter class of spectators, being neither idle, nor seemingly very ignorant.

The person of this individual was to the

last degree ungainly, without being in any particular manner deformed. He had all the bones and joints of other men, without any of their proportions. Erect, his stature surpassed that of his fellows; though seated, he appeared reduced within the ordinary limits of the race. The same contrariety in his members seemed to exist throughout the whole man. His head was large; his shoulders narrow; his arms long and dangling; while his hands were small, if not delicate. His legs and thighs were thin, nearly to emaciation, but of extraordinary length; and his knees would have been considered tremendous, had they not been outdone by the broader foundations on which this false superstructure of blended human orders was so profanely reared. The ill-assorted and injudicious attire of the individual only served to render his awkwardness more conspicuous. A sky-blue coat, with short and broad skirts and low cape, exposed a long, thin neck, and longer and thinner legs, to the worst animadversions of the evil-disposed. His nether garment was a yellow nankeen, closely fitted to the shape, and tied at his bunches of knees by large knots of white ribbon, a good deal sullied by use. Clouded cotton stockings, and shoes, on one of the latter of which was a plated spur, completed the costume of the lower extremity of this figure, no curve or angle of which was concealed, but, on the other hand, studiously exhibited, through the vanity or simplicity of its owner.

From beneath the flap of an enormous pocket of a soiled vest of embossed silk, heavily ornamented with tarnished silver lace, projected an instrument, which, from being seen in such martial company, might have been easily mistaken for some mischievous and unknown implement of war. Small as it was, this uncommon engine had excited the curiosity of most of the Europeans in the camp, though several of the provincials were seen to handle it, not only without fear, but with the utmost familiarity. A large, civil cocked hat, like those worn by clergymen within the last thirty years, surmounted the whole, furnishing dignity to a good-natured and somewhat vacant countenance, that apparently needed such artificial aid, to support the gravity of some high and extraordinary trust.

While the common herd stood aloof, in deference to the quarters of Webb, the figure we have described stalked into the center of the domestics, freely expressing his censures or commendations on the merits of the horses, as by chance they displeased or satisfied his judgment.

"This beast, I rather conclude, friend, is not of home raising, but is from foreign lands, or perhaps from the little island itself over the blue water?" he said, in a voice as remarkable for the softness and sweetness of its tones, as was his person for its rare proportions; "I may speak of these things, and be no braggart; for I have been down at both havens; that which is situate at the mouth of Thames, and is named after the capital of Old England, and that which is called 'Haven', with the addition of the word 'New'; and have seen the scows and brigantines collecting their droves, like the gathering to the ark, being outward bound to the Island of Jamaica, for the purpose of barter and traffic in four-footed animals; but never before have I beheld a beast which verified the true scripture war-horse like this: 'He paweth in the valley, and rejoiceth in his strength; he goeth on to meet the armed men. He saith among the trumpets, Ha, ha; and he smelleth the battle afar off, the thunder of the captains, and the shouting' It would seem that the stock of the horse of Israel had descended to our own time; would it not, friend?"

Receiving no reply to this extraordinary appeal, which in truth, as it was delivered with the vigor of full and sonorous tones, merited some sort of notice, he who had thus sung forth the language of the holy book turned to the silent figure to whom he had unwittingly addressed himself, and found a new and more powerful subject of admiration in the object that encountered his gaze. His eyes fell on the still, upright, and rigid form of the "Indian runner," who had borne to the camp the unwelcome tidings of the preceding evening. Although in a state of perfect repose, and apparently disregarding, with characteristic stoicism, the excitement and bustle around him, there was a sullen fierceness mingled with the quiet of the savage, that was likely to arrest the attention of much more experienced eyes than those which now scanned him, in unconcealed amazement. The native bore both the tomahawk and knife of his tribe; and yet his appearance was not altogether that of a warrior. On the contrary, there was an air of neglect about his person, like that which might have proceeded from great and recent exertion, which he had not yet found leisure to repair. The colors of the war-paint had blended in dark confusion about his fierce countenance, and rendered his swarthy lineaments still more savage and repulsive than if art had attempted an effect which had been thus produced by chance. His eye, alone, which glistened like a fiery star amid lowering clouds, was to be seen in its state of native wildness. For a single instant his searching and yet wary glance met the wondering look of the other, and then changing its direction, partly in cunning, and partly in disdain, it remained fixed, as if penetrating the distant air.

It is impossible to say what unlooked-for remark this short and silent communication, between two such singular men, might have elicited from the white man, had not his active curiosity been again drawn to other objects. A general movement among the domestics, and a low sound of gentle voices, announced the approach of those whose presence alone was wanted to enable the cavalcade to move. The simple admirer of the war-horse instantly fell back to a low, gaunt, switch-tailed mare, that was unconsciously gleaning the faded herbage of the camp nigh by; where, leaning with one elbow on the blanket that concealed an apology for a saddle, he became a spectator of the departure, while a foal was quietly making its morning repast, on the opposite side of the same animal.

A young man, in the dress of an officer, conducted to their steeds two females, who, as it was apparent by their dresses, were prepared to encounter the fatigues of a journey in the woods. One, and she was the more juvenile in her appearance, though both were young, permitted glimpses of her dazzling complexion, fair golden hair, and bright blue eyes, to be caught, as she artlessly suffered the morning air to blow aside the green veil which descended low from her beaver.

Chapter One

The flush which still lingered above the pines in the western sky was not more bright nor delicate than the bloom on her cheek; nor was the opening day more cheering than the animated smile which she bestowed on the youth, as he assisted her into the saddle. The other, who appeared to share equally in the attention of the young officer, concealed her charms from the gaze of the soldiery with a care that seemed better fitted to the experience of four or five additional years. It could be seen, however, that her person, though molded with the same exquisite proportions, of which none of the graces were lost by the traveling dress she wore, was rather fuller and more mature than that of her companion.

No sooner were these females seated, than their attendant sprang lightly into the saddle of the war-horse, when the whole three bowed to Webb, who in courtesy, awaited their parting on the threshold of his cabin and turning their horses' heads, they proceeded at a slow amble, followed by their train, toward the northern entrance of the encampment. As they traversed that short distance, not a voice was heard among them; but a slight exclamation proceeded from the younger of the females, as the Indian runner glided by her, unexpectedly, and led the way along the military road in her front. Though this sudden and startling movement of the Indian produced no sound from the other, in the surprise her veil also was allowed to open its folds, and betrayed an indescribable look of pity, admiration, and horror, as her dark eye followed the easy motions of the savage. The tresses of this lady were shining and black, like the plumage of the raven. Her complexion was not brown, but it rather appeared charged with the color of the rich blood, that seemed ready to burst its bounds. And yet there was neither coarseness nor want of shadowing in a countenance that was exquisitely regular, and dignified and surpassingly beautiful. She smiled, as if in pity at her own momentary forgetfulness, discovering by the act a row of teeth that would have shamed the purest ivory; when, replacing the veil, she bowed her face, and rode in silence, like one whose thoughts were abstracted from the scene around her.

Chapter Two

"Sola, sola, wo ha, ho, sola!"
– Shakespeare

WHILE ONE OF THE lovely beings we have so cursorily presented to the reader was thus lost in thought, the other quickly recovered from the alarm which induced the exclamation, and, laughing at her own weakness, she inquired of the youth who rode by her side:

"Are such specters frequent in the woods, Heyward, or is this sight an especial entertainment ordered on our behalf? If the latter, gratitude must close our mouths; but if the former, both Cora and I shall have need to draw largely on that stock of hereditary courage which we boast, even before we are made to encounter the redoubtable Montcalm."

"Yon Indian is a 'runner' of the army; and, after the fashion of his people, he may be accounted a hero," returned the officer. "He has volunteered to guide us to the lake, by a path but little known, sooner than if we followed the tardy movements of the column; and, by consequence, more agreeably."

"I like him not," said the lady, shuddering, partly in assumed, yet more in real terror. "You know him, Duncan, or you would not trust yourself so freely to his keeping?"

"Say, rather, Alice, that I would not trust you. I do know him, or he would not have my confidence, and least of all at this moment. He is said to be a Canadian too; and yet he served with our friends the Mohawks, who, as you know, are one of the six allied nations. He was brought among us, as I have heard, by some strange accident in which your father was interested, and in which the savage was rigidly dealt by; but I forget the idle tale, it is enough, that he is now our friend."

"If he has been my father's enemy, I like him still less!" exclaimed the now really anxious girl. "Will you not speak to him, Major Heyward, that I may hear his tones? Foolish though it may be, you have often heard me avow my faith in the tones of the human voice!"

"It would be in vain; and answered, most probably, by an ejaculation. Though he may understand it, he affects, like most of his people, to be ignorant of the English; and least of all will he condescend to speak it, now that the war demands the utmost exercise of his dignity. But he stops; the private path by which we are to journey is, doubtless, at hand."

The conjecture of Major Heyward was true. When they reached the spot where the Indian stood, pointing into the thicket that fringed the military road; a narrow and blind path, which might, with some little inconvenience, receive one person at a time, became visible.

"Here, then, lies our way," said the young man, in a low voice. "Manifest no distrust, or you may invite the danger you appear to apprehend."

"Cora, what think you?" asked the reluctant fair one. "If we journey with the troops, though we may find their presence irksome, shall we not feel better assurance of our safety?"

"Being little accustomed to the practices of the savages, Alice, you mistake the place of real danger," said Heyward. "If enemies have reached the portage at all, a thing by no means probable, as our scouts are abroad, they will surely be found skirting the column, where scalps abound the most. The route of the detachment is known, while ours, having been determined within the hour, must still be secret."

"Should we distrust the man because his manners are not our manners, and that his skin is dark?" coldly asked Cora.

Alice hesitated no longer; but giving her Narragansett[3] a smart cut of the whip, she was the first to dash aside the slight branches of the bushes, and to follow the runner along the dark and tangled pathway. The young man regarded the

---

3 In the state of Rhode Island there is a bay called Narragansett, so named after a powerful tribe of Indians, which formerly dwelt on its banks. Accident, or one of those unaccountable freaks which nature sometimes plays in the animal world, gave rise to a breed of horses which were once well known in America, and distinguished by their habit of pacing. Horses of this race were, and are still, in much request as saddle horses, on account of their hardiness and the ease of their movements. As they were also sure of foot, the Narragansetts were greatly sought for by females who were obliged to travel over the roots and holes in the "new countries."

last speaker in open admiration, and even permitted her fairer, though certainly not more beautiful companion, to proceed unattended, while he sedulously opened the way himself for the passage of her who has been called Cora. It would seem that the domestics had been previously instructed; for, instead of penetrating the thicket, they followed the route of the column; a measure which Heyward stated had been dictated by the sagacity of their guide, in order to diminish the marks of their trail, if, haply, the Canadian savages should be lurking so far in advance of their army. For many minutes the intricacy of the route admitted of no further dialogue; after which they emerged from the broad border of underbrush which grew along the line of the highway, and entered under the high but dark arches of the forest. Here their progress was less interrupted; and the instant the guide perceived that the females could command their steeds, he moved on, at a pace between a trot and a walk, and at a rate which kept the sure-footed and peculiar animals they rode at a fast yet easy amble. The youth had turned to speak to the dark-eyed Cora, when the distant sound of horses hoofs, clattering over the roots of the broken way in his rear, caused him to check his charger; and, as his companions drew their reins at the same instant, the whole party came to a halt, in order to obtain an explanation of the unlooked-for interruption.

In a few moments a colt was seen gliding, like a fallow deer, among the straight trunks of the pines; and, in another instant, the person of the ungainly man, described in the preceding chapter, came into view, with as much rapidity as he could excite his meager beast to endure without coming to an open rupture. Until now this personage had escaped the observation of the travelers. If he possessed the power to arrest any wandering eye when exhibiting the glories of his altitude on foot, his equestrian graces were still more likely to attract attention.

Notwithstanding a constant application of his one armed heel to the flanks of the mare, the most confirmed gait that he could establish was a Canterbury gallop with the hind legs, in which those more forward assisted for doubtful moments, though generally content to maintain a loping trot. Perhaps the rapidity of the changes from one of these paces to the other created an optical illusion, which might thus magnify the powers of the beast; for it is certain that Heyward, who possessed a true eye for the merits of a horse, was unable, with his utmost ingenuity, to decide by what sort of movement his pursuer worked his sinuous way on his footsteps with such persevering hardihood.

The industry and movements of the rider were not less remarkable than those of the ridden. At each change in the evolutions of the latter, the former raised his tall person in the stirrups; producing, in this manner, by the undue elongation of his legs, such sudden growths and diminishings of the stature, as baffled every conjecture that might be made as to his dimensions. If to this be added the fact that, in consequence of the ex parte application of the spur, one side of the mare appeared to journey faster than the other; and that the aggrieved flank was resolutely indicated by unremitted flourishes of a bushy tail, we finish the picture of both horse and man.

The frown which had gathered around the handsome, open, and manly brow of Heyward, gradually relaxed, and his lips curled into a slight smile, as he regarded the stranger. Alice made no very powerful effort to control her merriment; and even the dark, thoughtful eye of Cora lighted with a humor that it would seem, the habit, rather than the nature, of its mistress repressed.

"Seek you any here?" demanded Heyward, when the other had arrived sufficiently nigh to abate his speed; "I trust you are no messenger of evil tidings?"

"Even so," replied the stranger, making diligent use of his triangular castor, to produce a circulation in the close air of the woods, and leaving his hearers in doubt to which of the young man's questions he responded; when, however, he had cooled his face, and recovered his breath, he continued, "I hear you are riding to William Henry; as I am journeying thitherward myself, I concluded good company would seem consistent to the wishes of both parties."

"You appear to possess the privilege of a casting vote," returned Heyward; "we are three, while you have consulted no one but yourself."

"Even so. The first point to be obtained is to know one's own mind. Once sure of that, and where women are concerned it is not easy, the next is, to act up to the decision. I have endeavored to do both, and here I am."

"If you journey to the lake, you have mistaken your route," said Heyward, haughtily; "the highway thither is at least half a mile behind you."

"Even so," returned the stranger, nothing daunted by this cold reception; "I have tarried at 'Edward' a week, and I should be dumb not to have inquired the road I was to journey; and if dumb there would be an end to my calling." After simpering in a small way, like one whose modesty prohibited a more open expression of his admiration of a witticism that was perfectly unintelligible to his hearers, he continued, "It is not prudent for any one of my profession to be too familiar with those he has to instruct; for which reason I follow not the line of the army; besides which, I conclude that a gentleman of your character has the best judgment in matters of wayfaring; I have, therefore, decided to join company, in order that the ride may be made agreeable, and partake of social communion."

"A most arbitrary, if not a hasty decision!" exclaimed Heyward, undecided whether to give vent to his growing anger, or to laugh in the other's face. "But you speak of instruction, and of a profession; are you an adjunct to the provincial corps, as a master of the noble science of defense and offense; or, perhaps, you are one who draws lines and angles, under the pretense of expounding the mathematics?"

The stranger regarded his interrogator a moment in wonder; and then, losing every mark of self-satisfaction in an expression of solemn humility, he answered:

"Of offense, I hope there is none, to either party: of defense, I make none – by God's good mercy, having committed no palpable sin since last entreating his pardoning grace. I understand not your allusions about lines and angles; and I leave expounding to those who have been called and set apart for that holy office. I lay claim to no higher gift than a small insight into the glorious art of petitioning and thanksgiving, as practiced in psalmody."

"The man is, most manifestly, a disciple of Apollo," cried the amused Alice, "and I take him under my own especial protection. Nay, throw aside that frown, Heyward, and in pity to my longing ears, suffer him to journey in our train. Besides," she added, in a low and hurried voice, casting a glance at the distant Cora, who slowly followed the footsteps of their silent, but sullen guide, "it may be a friend added to our strength, in time of need."

"Think you, Alice, that I would trust those I love by this secret path, did I imagine such need could happen?"

"Nay, nay, I think not of it now; but this strange man amuses me; and if he 'hath music in his soul', let us not churlishly reject his company." She pointed persuasively along the path with her riding whip, while their eyes met in a look which the young man lingered a moment to prolong; then, yielding to her gentle influence, he clapped his spurs into his charger, and in a few bounds was again at the side of Cora.

"I am glad to encounter thee, friend," continued the maiden, waving her hand to the stranger to proceed, as she urged her Narragansett to renew its amble. "Partial relatives have almost persuaded me that I am not entirely worthless in a duet myself; and we may enliven our wayfaring by indulging in our favorite pursuit. It might be of signal advantage to one, ignorant as I, to hear the opinions and experience of a master in the art."

"It is refreshing both to the spirits and to the body to indulge in psalmody, in befitting seasons," returned the master of song, unhesitatingly complying with her intimation to follow; "and nothing would relieve the mind more than such a consoling communion. But four parts are altogether necessary to the perfection of melody. You have all the manifestations of a soft and rich treble; I can, by especial aid, carry a full tenor to the highest letter; but we lack counter and bass! Yon officer of the king, who hesitated to admit me to his company, might fill the latter, if one may judge from the intonations of his voice in common dialogue."

"Judge not too rashly from hasty and deceptive appearances," said the lady, smiling; "though Major Heyward can assume such deep notes on occasion, believe me, his natural tones are better fitted for a mellow tenor than the bass you heard."

"Is he, then, much practiced in the art of psalmody?" demanded her simple companion.

Alice felt disposed to laugh, though she succeeded in suppressing her merriment, ere she answered:

"I apprehend that he is rather addicted to profane song. The chances of a soldier's life are but little fitted for the encouragement of more sober inclinations."

"Man's voice is given to him, like his other talents, to be used, and not to be abused. None can say they have ever known me to neglect my gifts! I am thankful that, though my boyhood may be said to have been set apart, like the youth of the royal David, for the purposes of music, no syllable of rude verse has ever profaned my lips."

"You have, then, limited your efforts to sacred song?"

"Even so. As the psalms of David exceed all other language, so does the psalmody that has been fitted to them by the divines and sages of the land, surpass all vain poetry. Happily, I may say that I utter nothing but the thoughts and the wishes of the King of Israel himself; for though the times may call for some slight changes, yet does this version which we use in the colonies of New England so much exceed all other versions, that, by its richness, its exactness, and its spiritual simplicity, it approacheth, as near as may be, to the great work of the inspired writer. I never abide in any place, sleeping or waking, without an example of this gifted work. 'Tis the six-and-twentieth edition, promulgated at Boston, Anno Domini 1744; and is entitled, 'The Psalms, Hymns, and Spiritual Songs of the Old and New Testaments; faithfully translated into English Metre, for the Use, Edification, and Comfort of the Saints, in Public and Private, especially in New England'."

During this eulogium on the rare production of his native poets, the stranger had drawn the book from his pocket, and fitting a pair of iron-rimmed spectacles to his nose, opened the volume with a care and veneration suited to its sacred purposes. Then, without circumlocution or apology, first pronounced the word "Standish," and placing the unknown engine, already described, to his mouth, from which he drew a high, shrill sound, that was followed by an octave below, from his own voice, he commenced singing the following words, in full, sweet, and melodious tones, that set the music, the poetry, and even the uneasy motion of his ill-trained beast at defiance; "How good it is, O see, And how it pleaseth well, Together e'en in unity, For brethren so to dwell. It's like the choice ointment, From the head to the beard did go; Down Aaron's head, that downward went His garment's skirts unto."

The delivery of these skillful rhymes was accompanied, on the part of the stranger, by a regular rise and fall of his right hand, which terminated at the descent, by suffering the fingers to dwell a moment on the leaves of the little volume; and on the ascent, by such a flourish of the member as none but the initiated may ever hope to imitate. It would seem long practice had rendered this manual accompaniment necessary; for it did not cease until the preposition which the poet had selected for the close of his verse had been duly delivered like a word of two syllables.

Such an innovation on the silence and

retirement of the forest could not fail to enlist the ears of those who journeyed at so short a distance in advance. The Indian muttered a few words in broken English to Heyward, who, in his turn, spoke to the stranger; at once interrupting, and, for the time, closing his musical efforts.

"Though we are not in danger, common prudence would teach us to journey through this wilderness in as quiet a manner as possible. You will then, pardon me, Alice, should I diminish your enjoyments, by requesting this gentleman to postpone his chant until a safer opportunity."

"You will diminish them, indeed," returned the arch girl; "for never did I hear a more unworthy conjunction of execution and language than that to which I have been listening; and I was far gone in a learned inquiry into the causes of such an unfitness between sound and sense, when you broke the charm of my musings by that bass of yours, Duncan!"

"I know not what you call my bass," said Heyward, piqued at her remark, "but I know that your safety, and that of Cora, is far dearer to me than could be any orchestra of Handel's music." He paused and turned his head quickly toward a thicket, and then bent his eyes suspiciously on their guide, who continued his steady pace, in undisturbed gravity. The young man smiled to himself, for he believed he had mistaken some shining berry of the woods for the glistening eyeballs of a prowling savage, and he rode forward, continuing the conversation which had been interrupted by the passing thought.

Major Heyward was mistaken only in suffering his youthful and generous pride to suppress his active watchfulness. The cavalcade had not long passed, before the branches of the bushes that formed the thicket were cautiously moved asunder, and a human visage, as fiercely wild as savage art and unbridled passions could make it, peered out on the retiring footsteps of the travelers. A gleam of exultation shot across the darkly-painted lineaments of the inhabitant of the forest, as he traced the route of his intended victims, who rode unconsciously onward, the light and graceful forms of the females waving among the trees, in the curvatures of their path, followed at each bend by the manly figure of Heyward, until, finally, the shapeless person of the singing master was concealed behind the numberless trunks of trees, that rose, in dark lines, in the intermediate space.

Chapter Three

"Before these fields were shorn and
till'd,
Full to the brim our rivers flow'd;
The melody of waters fill'd
The fresh and boundless wood;
And torrents dash'd, and rivulets play'd,
And fountains spouted in the shade."
– Bryant

LEAVING THE UNSUSPECTING Heyward and his confiding companions to penetrate still deeper into a forest that contained such treacherous inmates, we must use an author's privilege, and shift the scene a few miles to the westward of the place where we have last seen them.

On that day, two men were lingering on the banks of a small but rapid stream, within an hour's journey of the encampment of Webb, like those who awaited the appearance of an absent person, or the approach of some expected event. The vast canopy of woods spread itself to the margin of the river, overhanging the water, and shadowing its dark current with a deeper hue. The rays of the sun were beginning to grow less fierce, and the intense heat of the day was lessened, as the cooler vapors of the springs and fountains rose above their leafy beds, and rested in the atmosphere. Still that breathing silence, which marks the drowsy sultriness of an American landscape in July, pervaded the secluded spot, interrupted only by the low voices of the men, the occasional and lazy tap of a woodpecker, the discordant cry of some gaudy jay, or a swelling on the ear, from the dull roar of a distant waterfall. These feeble and broken sounds were, however, too familiar to the foresters to draw their attention from the more interesting matter of their dialogue. While one of these loiterers showed the red skin and wild accouterments of a native of the woods, the other exhibited, through the mask of his rude and nearly savage equipments, the brighter, though sun-burned and long-faced complexion of one who might claim descent from a European parentage. The former was seated on the end of a mossy log, in a posture that permitted him to heighten the effect of his earnest language, by the calm but expressive gestures of an Indian engaged in debate. His body, which was nearly naked, presented a terrific emblem of death, drawn in intermingled colors of white and black. His closely-shaved head, on which no other hair than the well-known and chivalrous scalping tuft[4] was preserved,

4 The North American warrior caused the hair to be plucked from his whole body; a small tuft was left on the crown of his head, in order

was without ornament of any kind, with the exception of a solitary eagle's plume, that crossed his crown, and depended over the left shoulder. A tomahawk and scalping knife, of English manufacture, were in his girdle; while a short military rifle, of that sort with which the policy of the whites armed their savage allies, lay carelessly across his bare and sinewy knee. The expanded chest, full formed limbs, and grave countenance of this warrior, would denote that he had reached the vigor of his days, though no symptoms of decay appeared to have yet weakened his manhood.

---

that his enemy might avail himself of it, in wrenching off the scalp in the event of his fall. The scalp was the only admissible trophy of victory. Thus, it was deemed more important to obtain the scalp than to kill the man. Some tribes lay great stress on the honor of striking a dead body. These practices have nearly disappeared among the Indians of the Atlantic states.

The frame of the white man, judging by such parts as were not concealed by his clothes, was like that of one who had known hardships and exertion from his earliest youth. His person, though muscular, was rather attenuated than full; but every nerve and muscle appeared strung and indurated by unremitted exposure and toil. He wore a hunting shirt of forest-green, fringed with faded yellow,[5] and a summer cap of skins which had been shorn of their fur. He also bore a knife in a girdle of wampum, like that which confined the scanty garments of the Indian, but no tomahawk. His moccasins were ornamented after the gay fashion of

---

5 The hunting-shirt is a picturesque smock-frock, being shorter, and ornamented with fringes and tassels. The colors are intended to imitate the hues of the wood, with a view to concealment. Many corps of American riflemen have been thus attired, and the dress is one of the most striking of modern times. The hunting-shirt is frequently white.

the natives, while the only part of his under dress which appeared below the hunting-frock was a pair of buckskin leggings, that laced at the sides, and which were gartered above the knees, with the sinews of a deer. A pouch and horn completed his personal accouterments, though a rifle of great length,[6] which the theory of the more ingenious whites had taught them was the most dangerous of all firearms, leaned against a neighboring sapling. The eye of the hunter, or scout, whichever he might be, was small, quick, keen, and restless, roving while he spoke, on every side of him, as if in quest of game, or distrusting the sudden approach of some lurking enemy. Notwithstanding the symptoms of habitual suspicion, his countenance was not only without guile, but at the moment at which he is introduced, it was charged with an expression of sturdy honesty.

---

6 The rifle of the army is short; that of the hunter is always long.

"Even your traditions make the case in my favor, Chingachgook," he said, speaking in the tongue which was known to all the natives who formerly inhabited the country between the Hudson and the Potomac, and of which we shall give a free translation for the benefit of the reader; endeavoring, at the same time, to preserve some of the peculiarities, both of the individual and of the language. "Your fathers came from the setting sun, crossed the big river,[7] fought the people of the country, and took the land; and mine came from the red sky of the morning, over the salt lake, and did their work much after the fashion that had been set them by yours; then let God judge the matter between us, and friends spare their

7 The Mississippi. The scout alludes to a tradition which isvery popular among the tribes of the Atlantic states.Evidence of their Asiatic origin is deduced from thecircumstances, though great uncertainty hangs over the wholehistory of the Indians.

words!"

"My fathers fought with the naked red man!" returned the Indian, sternly, in the same language. "Is there no difference, Hawkeye, between the stone-headed arrow of the warrior, and the leaden bullet with which you kill?"

"There is reason in an Indian, though nature has made him with a red skin!" said the white man, shaking his head like one on whom such an appeal to his justice was not thrown away. For a moment he appeared to be conscious of having the worst of the argument, then, rallying again, he answered the objection of his antagonist in the best manner his limited information would allow:

"I am no scholar, and I care not who knows it; but, judging from what I have seen, at deer chases and squirrel hunts, of the sparks below, I should think a rifle in the hands of their grandfathers was not so dangerous as a hickory bow and a good flint-head might be, if drawn with Indian judgment, and sent by an Indian eye."

"You have the story told by your fathers," returned the other, coldly waving his hand. "What say your old men? Do they tell the young warriors that the pale faces met the red men, painted for war and armed with the stone hatchet and wooden gun?"

"I am not a prejudiced man, nor one who vaunts himself on his natural privileges, though the worst enemy I have on earth, and he is an Iroquois, daren't deny that I am genuine white," the scout replied, surveying, with secret satisfaction, the faded color of his bony and sinewy hand, "and I am willing to own that my people have many ways, of which, as an honest man, I can't approve. It is one of their customs to write in books what they have done and seen, instead of telling them in their villages, where the lie can be given to the face of a cowardly boaster, and the brave soldier can call on his comrades to witness for the truth of his words. In consequence of this bad fashion, a man, who is too conscientious to misspend his days among the women, in learning the names of black marks, may never hear of the deeds of his fathers, nor feel a pride in striving to outdo them. For myself, I conclude the Bumppos could shoot, for I have a natural turn with a rifle, which must have been handed down from generation to generation, as, our holy commandments tell us, all good and evil gifts are bestowed; though I should be loath to answer for other people in such a matter. But every story has its two sides; so I ask you, Chingachgook, what passed, according to the traditions of the red men, when our fathers first met?"

A silence of a minute succeeded, during which the Indian sat mute; then, full of the dignity of his office, he commenced his brief tale, with a solemnity that served to heighten its appearance of truth.

"Listen, Hawkeye, and your ear shall drink no lie. 'Tis what my fathers have said, and what the Mohicans have done." He hesitated a single instant, and bending a cautious glance toward his companion, he continued, in a manner that was divided between interrogation and assertion. “Does not this stream at our feet run toward the summer, until its waters grow salt, and the current flows upward?”

“It can’t be denied that your traditions tell you true in both these matters,” said the white man; “for I have been there, and have seen them, though why water, which is so sweet in the shade, should become bitter in the sun, is an alteration for which I have never been able to account.”

“And the current!” demanded the Indian, who expected his reply with that sort of interest that a man feels in the confirmation of testimony, at which he marvels even while he respects it; “the fathers of Chingachgook have not lied!”

“The holy Bible is not more true, and that is the truest thing in nature. They call this up-stream current the tide, which is a thing soon explained, and clear enough. Six hours the waters run in, and six hours they run out, and the reason is this: when there is higher water in the sea than in the river, they run in until the river gets to be highest, and then it runs out again."

"The waters in the woods, and on the great lakes, run downward until they lie like my hand," said the Indian, stretching the limb horizontally before him, "and then they run no more."

"No honest man will deny it," said the scout, a little nettled at the implied distrust of his explanation of the mystery of the tides; "and I grant that it is true on the small scale, and where the land is level. But everything depends on what scale you look at things. Now, on the small scale, the 'arth is level; but on the large scale it is round. In this manner, pools and ponds, and even the great fresh-water lakes, may be stagnant, as you and I both know they are, having seen them; but when you come to spread water over a great tract, like the sea, where the earth is round, how in reason can the water be quiet? You might as well expect the river to lie still on the brink of those black rocks a mile above us, though your own ears tell you that it is tumbling over them at this very moment."

If unsatisfied by the philosophy of his companion, the Indian was far too dignified to betray his unbelief. He listened like one who was convinced, and resumed his narrative in his former solemn manner.

"We came from the place where the sun is hid at night, over great plains where the buffaloes live, until we reached the big river. There we fought the Alligewi, till the ground was red with their blood. From the banks of the big river to the shores of the salt lake, there was none to meet us. The Maquas followed at a distance. We said the country should be ours from the place where the water runs up no longer on this stream, to a river twenty sun's journey toward the summer. We drove the Maquas into the woods with the bears. They only tasted salt at the licks; they drew no fish from the great lake; we threw them the bones."

"All this I have heard and believe," said the white man, observing that the Indian paused; "but it was long before the English came into the country."

"A pine grew then where this chestnut now stands. The first pale faces who came among us spoke no English. They came in a large canoe, when my fathers had buried the tomahawk with the red men around them. Then, Hawkeye," he continued, betraying his deep emotion, only by permitting his voice to fall to those low, guttural tones, which render his language, as spoken at times, so very musical; "then, Hawkeye, we were one people, and we were happy. The salt lake gave us its fish, the wood its deer, and the air its birds. We took wives who bore us children; we worshipped the Great

Spirit; and we kept the Maquas beyond the sound of our songs of triumph."

"Know you anything of your own family at that time?" demanded the white. "But you are just a man, for an Indian; and as I suppose you hold their gifts, your fathers must have been brave warriors, and wise men at the council-fire."

"My tribe is the grandfather of nations, but I am an unmixed man. The blood of chiefs is in my veins, where it must stay forever. The Dutch landed, and gave my people the fire-water; they drank until the heavens and the earth seemed to meet, and they foolishly thought they had found the Great Spirit. Then they parted with their land. Foot by foot, they were driven back from the shores, until I, that am a chief and a Sagamore, have never seen the sun shine but through the trees, and have never visited the graves of my fathers."

"Graves bring solemn feelings over the mind," returned the scout, a good deal touched at the calm suffering of his companion; "and they often aid a man in his good intentions; though, for myself, I expect to leave my own bones unburied, to bleach in the woods, or to be torn asunder by the wolves. But where are to be found those of your race who came to their kin in the Delaware country, so many summers since?"

"Where are the blossoms of those summers! – fallen, one by one; so all of my family departed, each in his turn, to the land of spirits. I am on the hilltop and must go down into the valley; and when Uncas follows in my footsteps there will no longer be any of the blood of the Sagamores, for my boy is the last of the Mohicans."

"Uncas is here," said another voice, in the same soft, guttural tones, near his elbow; "who speaks to Uncas?"

The white man loosened his knife in his leathern sheath, and made an involuntary movement of the hand toward his rifle, at this sudden interruption; but the Indian sat composed, and without turning his head at the unexpected sounds.

At the next instant, a youthful warrior passed between them, with a noiseless step, and seated himself on the bank of the rapid stream. No exclamation of surprise escaped the father, nor was any question asked, or reply given, for several minutes; each appearing to await the moment when he might speak, without betraying womanish curiosity or childish impatience. The white man seemed to take counsel from their customs, and, relinquishing his grasp of the rifle, he also remained silent and reserved. At length Chingachgook turned his eyes slowly toward his son, and demanded:

"Do the Maquas dare to leave the print of their moccasins in these woods?"

"I have been on their trail," replied the young Indian, "and know that they number as many as the fingers of my two hands; but they lie hid like cowards."

"The thieves are outlying for scalps and

plunder," said the white man, whom we shall call Hawkeye, after the manner of his companions. "That busy Frenchman, Montcalm, will send his spies into our very camp, but he will know what road we travel!"

"'Tis enough," returned the father, glancing his eye toward the setting sun; "they shall be driven like deer from their bushes. Hawkeye, let us eat to-night, and show the Maquas that we are men to-morrow."

"I am as ready to do the one as the other; but to fight the Iroquois 'tis necessary to find the skulkers; and to eat, 'tis necessary to get the game – talk of the devil and he will come; there is a pair of the biggest antlers I have seen this season, moving the bushes below the hill! Now, Uncas," he continued, in a half whisper, and laughing with a kind of inward sound, like one who had learned to be watchful, "I will bet my charger three times full of powder, against a foot of wampum, that I take him atwixt the eyes, and nearer to the right than to the left."

"It cannot be!" said the young Indian, springing to his feet with youthful eagerness; "all but the tips of his horns are hid!"

"He's a boy!" said the white man, shaking his head while he spoke, and addressing the father. "Does he think when a hunter sees a part of the creature', he can't tell where the rest of him should be!"

Adjusting his rifle, he was about to make an exhibition of that skill on which he so much valued himself, when the warrior struck up the piece with his hand, saying:

"Hawkeye! will you fight the Maquas?"

"These Indians know the nature of the woods, as it might be by instinct!" returned the scout, dropping his rifle, and turning away like a man who was convinced of his error. "I must leave the buck to your arrow, Uncas, or we may kill a deer for them thieves, the Iroquois, to eat."

The instant the father seconded this intimation by an expressive gesture of the hand, Uncas threw himself on the ground, and approached the animal with wary movements. When within a few yards of the cover, he fitted an arrow to his bow with the utmost care, while the antlers moved, as if their owner snuffed an enemy in the tainted air. In another moment the twang of the cord was heard, a white streak was seen glancing into the bushes, and the wounded buck plunged from the cover, to the very feet of his hidden enemy. Avoiding the horns of the infuriated animal, Uncas darted to his side, and passed his knife across the throat, when bounding to the edge of the river it fell, dyeing the waters with its blood.

"'Twas done with Indian skill," said the scout laughing inwardly, but with vast satisfaction; "and 'twas a pretty sight to behold! Though an arrow is a near shot, and needs a knife to finish the work."

"Hugh!" ejaculated his companion, turning quickly, like a hound who scented game.

"By the Lord, there is a drove of them!" exclaimed the scout, whose eyes began to glisten with the ardor of his usual occupation; "if they come within range of a bullet I will drop one, though the whole Six Nations should be lurking within sound! What do you hear, Chingachgook? for to my ears the woods are dumb."

"There is but one deer, and he is dead," said the Indian, bending his body till his ear nearly touched the earth. "I hear the sounds of feet!"

"Perhaps the wolves have driven the buck to shelter, and are following on his trail."

"No. The horses of white men are coming!" returned the other, raising himself with dignity, and resuming his seat on the log with his former composure. "Hawkeye, they are your brothers; speak to them."

"That I will, and in English that the king needn't be ashamed to answer," returned the hunter, speaking in the language of which he boasted; "but I see nothing, nor do I hear the sounds of man or beast; 'tis strange that an Indian should understand white sounds better than a man who, his very enemies will own, has no cross in his blood, although he may have lived with the red skins long enough to be suspected! Ha! there goes something like the cracking of a dry stick, too – now I hear the bushes move – yes, yes, there is a trampling that I mistook for the falls – and – but here they come themselves; God keep them from the Iroquois!"

Chapter Four

"Well go thy way: thou shalt not from
this grove
Till I torment thee for this injury."
– Midsummer Night's Dream.

THE WORDS WERE STILL in the mouth of the scout, when the leader of the party, whose approaching footsteps had caught the vigilant ear of the Indian, came openly into view. A beaten path, such as those made by the periodical passage of the deer, wound through a little glen at no great distance, and struck the river at the point where the white man and his red companions had posted themselves. Along this track the travelers, who had produced a surprise so unusual in the depths of the forest, advanced slowly toward the hunter, who was in front of his associates, in readiness to receive them.

"Who comes?" demanded the scout, throwing his rifle carelessly across his left arm, and keeping the forefinger of his right hand on the trigger, though he avoided all appearance of menace in the act. "Who comes hither, among the beasts and dangers of the wilderness?"

"Believers in religion, and friends to the law and to the king," returned he who rode foremost. "Men who have journeyed since the rising sun, in the shades of this forest, without nourishment, and are sadly tired of their wayfaring."

"You are, then, lost," interrupted the hunter, "and have found how helpless 'tis not to know whether to take the right hand or the left?"

"Even so; sucking babes are not more dependent on those who guide them than we who are of larger growth, and who may now be said to possess the stature without the knowledge of men. Know you the distance to a post of the crown called William Henry?"

"Hoot!" shouted the scout, who did not spare his open laughter, though instantly checking the dangerous sounds he indulged his merriment at less risk of being overheard by any lurking enemies. "You are as much off the scent as a hound would be, with Horican atwixt him and the deer! William Henry, man! if you are friends to the king and have business with the army, your way would be to follow the river down to Edward, and lay the matter before Webb, who tarries there, instead of pushing into the defiles, and driving this saucy Frenchman back across Champlain, into his den again."

Before the stranger could make any reply to this unexpected proposition, another horseman dashed the bushes aside, and leaped his charger into the pathway, in front of his companion.

"What, then, may be our distance from Fort Edward?" demanded a new speaker; "the place you advise us to seek we left this morning, and our destination is the head of the lake."

"Then you must have lost your eyesight afore losing your way, for the road across the portage is cut to a good two rods, and is as grand a path, I calculate, as any that runs into London, or even before the palace of the king himself."

"We will not dispute concerning the excellence of the passage," returned Heyward, smiling; for, as the reader has anticipated, it was he. "It is enough, for the present, that we trusted to an Indian guide to take us by a nearer, though blinder path, and that we are deceived in his knowledge. In plain words, we know not where we are."

"An Indian lost in the woods!" said the scout, shaking his head doubtingly; "When the sun is scorching the tree tops, and the water courses are full; when the moss on every beech he sees will tell him in what quarter the north star will shine at night. The woods are full of deer-paths which run to the streams and licks, places well known to everybody; nor have the geese done their flight to the Canada waters altogether! 'Tis strange that an Indian should be lost atwixt Horican and the bend in the river! Is he a Mohawk?"

"Not by birth, though adopted in that tribe; I think his birthplace was farther north, and he is one of those you call a Huron."

"Hugh!" exclaimed the two companions of the scout, who had continued until this part of the dialogue, seated immovable, and apparently indifferent to what passed, but who now sprang to their feet with an activity and interest that had evidently got the better of their reserve by surprise.

"A Huron!" repeated the sturdy scout, once more shaking his head in open distrust; "they are a thievish race, nor do I care by whom they are adopted; you can never make anything of them but skulks and vagabonds. Since you trusted yourself to the care of one of that nation, I only wonder that you have not fallen in with more."

"Of that there is little danger, since William Henry is so many miles in our front. You forget that I have told you our guide is now a Mohawk, and that he serves with our forces as a friend."

"And I tell you that he who is born a Mingo will die a Mingo," returned the other positively. "A Mohawk! No, give me a Delaware or a Mohican for honesty; and when they will fight, which they won't all do, having suffered their cunning enemies, the Maquas, to make them women – but when they will fight at all, look to a Delaware, or a Mohican, for a warrior!"

"Enough of this," said Heyward, impatiently; "I wish not to inquire into the character of a man that I know, and to whom you must be a stranger. You have not yet answered my question; what is our distance from the main army at Edward?"

"It seems that may depend on who is your guide. One would think such a horse as that might get over a good deal of ground atwixt sun-up and sun-down."

"I wish no contention of idle words with you, friend," said Heyward, curbing his dissatisfied manner, and speaking in a more gentle voice; "if you will tell me the distance to Fort Edward, and conduct me thither, your labor shall not go without its reward."

"And in so doing, how know I that I don't guide an enemy and a spy of Montcalm, to the works of the army? It is not every man who can speak the English tongue that is an honest subject."

"If you serve with the troops, of whom I judge you to be a scout, you should know of such a regiment of the king as the Sixtieth."

"The Sixtieth! you can tell me little of the Royal Americans that I don't know, though I do wear a hunting-shirt instead of a scarlet jacket."

"Well, then, among other things, you may know the name of its major?"

"Its major!" interrupted the hunter, elevating his body like one who was proud of his trust. "If there is a man in the country who knows Major Effingham, he stands before you."

"It is a corps which has many majors; the gentleman you name is the senior, but I speak of the junior of them all; he who commands the companies in garrison at William Henry."

"Yes, yes, I have heard that a young gentleman of vast riches, from one of the provinces far south, has got the place. He is over young, too, to hold such rank, and to be put above men whose heads are beginning to bleach; and yet they say he is a soldier in his knowledge, and a gallant gentleman!"

"Whatever he may be, or however he may be qualified for his rank, he now speaks to you and, of course, can be no enemy to dread."

The scout regarded Heyward in surprise, and then lifting his cap, he answered, in a tone less confident than before – though still expressing doubt.

"I have heard a party was to leave the encampment this morning for the lake shore?"

"You have heard the truth; but I preferred a nearer route, trusting to the knowledge of the Indian I mentioned."

"And he deceived you, and then deserted?"

"Neither, as I believe; certainly not the latter, for he is to be found in the rear."

"I should like to look at the creature; if it is a true Iroquois I can tell him by his knavish look, and by his paint," said the scout; stepping past the charger of Heyward, and entering the path behind the mare of the singing master, whose foal had taken advantage of the halt to exact the maternal contribution. After shoving aside the bushes, and proceeding a few paces, he encountered the females, who awaited the result of the conference with anxiety, and not entirely without apprehension. Behind these, the runner leaned against a tree, where he stood the close examination of the scout with an air unmoved, though with a look so dark and savage, that it might in itself excite fear. Satisfied with his scrutiny, the hunter soon left him. As he repassed the females, he paused a moment to gaze upon their beauty, answering to the smile and nod of Alice with a look of open pleasure. Thence he went to the side of the motherly animal, and spending a minute in a fruitless inquiry into the character of her rider, he shook his head and returned to Heyward.

"A Mingo is a Mingo, and God having made him so, neither the Mohawks nor any other tribe can alter him," he said, when he had regained his former position. "If we were alone, and you would leave that noble horse at the mercy of the wolves to-night, I could show you the way to Edward myself, within an hour, for it lies only about an hour's journey hence; but with such ladies in your company 'tis impossible!"

"And why? They are fatigued, but they are quite equal to a ride of a few more miles."

"'Tis a natural impossibility!" repeated the scout; "I wouldn't walk a mile in these woods after night gets into them, in company with that runner, for the best rifle in the colonies. They are full of outlying Iroquois, and your mongrel Mohawk knows where to find them too well to be my companion."

"Think you so?" said Heyward, leaning forward in the saddle, and dropping his voice nearly to a whisper; "I confess I have not been without my own suspicions, though I have endeavored to conceal them, and affected a confidence I have not always felt, on account of my companions. It was because I suspected him that I would follow no longer; making him, as you see, follow me."

"I knew he was one of the cheats as soon as I laid eyes on him!" returned the scout, placing a finger on his nose, in sign of caution.

"The thief is leaning against the foot of the sugar sapling, that you can see over them bushes; his right leg is in a line with the bark of the tree, and," tapping his rifle, "I can take him from where I stand, between the angle and the knee, with a single shot, putting an end to his tramping through the woods, for at least a month to come. If I should go back to him, the cunning varmint would suspect something, and be dodging through the trees like a frightened deer."

"It will not do. He may be innocent, and I dislike the act. Though, if I felt confident of his treachery – "

"'Tis a safe thing to calculate on the knavery of an Iroquois," said the scout, throwing his rifle forward, by a sort of instinctive movement.

"Hold!" interrupted Heyward, "it will not do – we must think of some other scheme – and yet, I have much reason to believe the rascal has deceived me."

The hunter, who had already abandoned

his intention of maiming the runner, mused a moment, and then made a gesture, which instantly brought his two red companions to his side. They spoke together earnestly in the Delaware language, though in an undertone; and by the gestures of the white man, which were frequently directed towards the top of the sapling, it was evident he pointed out the situation of their hidden enemy. His companions were not long in comprehending his wishes, and laying aside their firearms, they parted, taking opposite sides of the path, and burying themselves in the thicket, with such cautious movements, that their steps were inaudible.

"Now, go you back," said the hunter, speaking again to Heyward, "and hold the imp in talk; these Mohicans here will take him without breaking his paint."

"Nay," said Heyward, proudly, "I will seize him myself."

"Hist! what could you do, mounted, against an Indian in the bushes!"

"I will dismount."

"And, think you, when he saw one of your feet out of the stirrup, he would wait for the other to be free? Whoever comes into the woods to deal with the natives, must use Indian fashions, if he would wish to prosper in his undertakings. Go, then; talk openly to the miscreant, and seem to believe him the truest friend you have on 'arth."

Heyward prepared to comply, though with strong disgust at the nature of the office he was compelled to execute. Each moment, however, pressed upon him a conviction of the critical situation in which he had suffered his invaluable trust to be involved through his own confidence. The sun had already disappeared, and the woods, suddenly deprived of his light,[8] were assuming a dusky hue, which keenly reminded him that the hour the savage usually chose for his

8 The scene of this tale was in the 42d degree of latitude, where the twilight is never of long continuation.

most barbarous and remorseless acts of vengeance or hostility, was speedily drawing near. Stimulated by apprehension, he left the scout, who immediately entered into a loud conversation with the stranger that had so unceremoniously enlisted himself in the party of travelers that morning. In passing his gentler companions Heyward uttered a few words of encouragement, and was pleased to find that, though fatigued with the exercise of the day, they appeared to entertain no suspicion that their present embarrassment was other than the result of accident. Giving them reason to believe he was merely employed in a consultation concerning the future route, he spurred his charger, and drew the reins again when the animal had carried him within a few yards of the place where the sullen runner still stood, leaning against the tree.

"You may see, Magua," he said, endeavoring to assume an air of freedom and confidence, "that the night is closing around us, and yet we are no nearer to William Henry than when we left the encampment of Webb with the rising sun.

"You have missed the way, nor have I been more fortunate. But, happily, we have fallen in with a hunter, he whom you hear talking to the singer, that is acquainted with the deerpaths and by-ways of the woods, and who promises to lead us to a place where we may rest securely till the morning."

The Indian riveted his glowing eyes on Heyward as he asked, in his imperfect English, "Is he alone?"

"Alone!" hesitatingly answered Heyward, to whom deception was too new to be assumed without embarrassment. "Oh! not alone, surely, Magua, for you know that we are with him."

"Then Le Renard Subtil will go," returned the runner, coolly raising his little wallet from the place where it had lain at his feet; "and the pale faces will see none but their own color."

"Go! Whom call you Le Renard?"

"'Tis the name his Canada fathers have given to Magua," returned the runner, with an air that manifested his pride at the distinction. "Night is the same as day to Le Subtil, when Munro waits for him."

"And what account will Le Renard give the chief of William Henry concerning his daughters? Will he dare to tell the hot-blooded Scotsman that his children are left without a guide, though Magua promised to be one?"

"Though the gray head has a loud voice, and a long arm, Le Renard will not hear him, nor feel him, in the woods."

"But what will the Mohawks say? They will make him petticoats, and bid him stay in the wigwam with the women, for he is no longer to be trusted with the business of a man."

"Le Subtil knows the path to the great lakes, and he can find the bones of his fathers," was the answer of the unmoved runner.

"Enough, Magua," said Heyward; "are

we not friends? Why should there be bitter words between us? Munro has promised you a gift for your services when performed, and I shall be your debtor for another. Rest your weary limbs, then, and open your wallet to eat. We have a few moments to spare; let us not waste them in talk like wrangling women. When the ladies are refreshed we will proceed."

"The pale faces make themselves dogs to their women," muttered the Indian, in his native language, "and when they want to eat, their warriors must lay aside the tomahawk to feed their laziness."

"What say you, Renard?"

"Le Subtil says it is good."

The Indian then fastened his eyes keenly on the open countenance of Heyward, but meeting his glance, he turned them quickly away, and seating himself deliberately on the ground, he drew forth the remnant of some former repast, and began to eat, though not without first bending his looks slowly and cautiously around him.

"This is well," continued Heyward; "and Le Renard will have strength and sight to find the path in the morning"; he paused, for sounds like the snapping of a dried stick, and the rustling of leaves, rose from the adjacent bushes, but recollecting himself instantly, he continued, "we must be moving before the sun is seen, or Montcalm may lie in our path, and shut us out from the fortress."

The hand of Magua dropped from his mouth to his side, and though his eyes were fastened on the ground, his head was turned aside, his nostrils expanded, and his ears seemed even to stand more erect than usual, giving to him the appearance of a statue that was made to represent intense attention.

Heyward, who watched his movements with a vigilant eye, carelessly extricated one of his feet from the stirrup, while he passed a hand toward the bear-skin covering of his holsters.

Every effort to detect the point most regarded by the runner was completely frustrated by the tremulous glances of his organs, which seemed not to rest a single instant on any particular object, and which, at the same time, could be hardly said to move. While he hesitated how to proceed, Le Subtil cautiously raised himself to his feet, though with a motion so slow and guarded, that not the slightest noise was produced by the change. Heyward felt it had now become incumbent on him to act. Throwing his leg over the saddle, he dismounted, with a determination to advance and seize his treacherous companion, trusting the result to his own manhood. In order, however, to prevent unnecessary alarm, he still preserved an air of calmness and friendship.

"Le Renard Subtil does not eat," he said, using the appellation he had found most flattering to the vanity of the Indian. "His corn is not well parched, and it seems dry. Let me examine; perhaps something may be found among my own provisions that will help his appetite."

Magua held out the wallet to the proffer of the other. He even suffered their hands to meet, without betraying the least emotion, or varying his riveted attitude of attention. But when he felt the fingers of Heyward moving gently along his own naked arm, he struck up the limb of the young man, and, uttering a piercing cry, he darted beneath it, and plunged, at a single bound, into the opposite thicket. At the next instant the form of Chingachgook appeared from the bushes, looking like a specter in its paint, and glided across the path in swift pursuit. Next followed the shout of Uncas, when the woods were lighted by a sudden flash, that was accompanied by the sharp report of the hunter's rifle.

Chapter Five

..."In such a night
Did This be fearfully o'ertrip the dew;
And saw the lion's shadow ere himself."
– Merchant of Venice

THE SUDDENNESS OF THE flight of his guide, and the wild cries of the pursuers, caused Heyward to remain fixed, for a few moments, in inactive surprise. Then recollecting the importance of securing the fugitive, he dashed aside the surrounding bushes, and pressed eagerly forward to lend his aid in the chase. Before he had, however, proceeded a hundred yards, he met the three foresters already returning from their unsuccessful pursuit.

"Why so soon disheartened!" he exclaimed; "the scoundrel must be concealed behind some of these trees, and may yet be secured. We are not safe while he goes at large."

"Would you set a cloud to chase the wind?" returned the disappointed scout; "I heard the imp brushing over the dry leaves, like a black snake, and blinking a glimpse of him, just over ag'in yon big pine, I pulled as it might be on the scent; but 'twouldn't do! and yet for a reasoning aim, if anybody but myself had touched the trigger, I should call it a quick sight; and I may be accounted to have experience in these matters, and one who ought to know. Look at this sumach; its leaves are red, though everybody knows the fruit is in the yellow blossom in the month of July!"

"'Tis the blood of Le Subtil! he is hurt, and may yet fall!"

"No, no," returned the scout, in decided disapprobation of this opinion, "I rubbed the bark off a limb, perhaps, but the creature leaped the longer for it. A rifle bullet acts on a running animal, when it barks him, much the same as one of your spurs on a horse; that is, it quickens motion, and puts life into the flesh, instead of taking it away. But when it cuts the ragged hole, after a bound or two, there is, commonly, a stagnation of further leaping, be it Indian or be it deer!"

"We are four able bodies, to one wounded man!"

"Is life grievous to you?" interrupted the scout. "Yonder red devil would draw you within swing of the tomahawks of his comrades, before you were heated in the chase. It was an unthoughtful act in a man who has so often slept with the war-whoop ringing in the air, to let off his piece within sound of an ambushment! But then it was a natural temptation! 'twas very natural! Come, friends, let us move our station, and in such fashion, too, as will throw the cunning of a Mingo on a wrong scent, or our scalps will be drying in the wind in front of Montcalm's marquee, ag'in this hour to-morrow."

This appalling declaration, which the scout uttered with the cool assurance of a man who fully comprehended, while he did not fear to face the danger, served to remind Heyward of the importance of the charge with which he himself had been intrusted. Glancing his eyes around, with a vain effort to pierce the gloom that was thickening beneath the leafy arches of the forest, he felt as if, cut off from human aid, his unresisting companions would soon lie at the entire mercy of those barbarous enemies, who, like beasts of prey, only waited till the gathering darkness might render their blows more fatally certain. His awakened imagination, deluded by the deceptive light, converted each waving bush, or the fragment of some fallen tree, into human forms, and twenty times he fancied he could distinguish the horrid visages of his lurking foes, peering from their hiding places, in never ceasing watchfulness of the movements of his party. Looking upward, he found that the thin fleecy clouds, which evening had painted on the blue sky, were already losing their faintest tints of rose-color, while the imbedded stream, which glided past the spot where he stood, was to be traced only by the dark boundary of its wooded banks.

"What is to be done!" he said, feeling the utter helplessness of doubt in such a pressing strait; "desert me not, for God's sake! remain to defend those I escort, and freely name your own reward!"

His companions, who conversed apart in the language of their tribe, heeded not this sudden and earnest appeal. Though their dialogue was maintained in low and cautious sounds, but little above a whisper, Heyward, who now approached, could easily distinguish the earnest tones of the younger warrior from the more deliberate speeches of his seniors. It was evident that they debated on the propriety of some measure, that nearly concerned the welfare of the travelers. Yielding to his powerful interest in the subject, and impatient of a delay that seemed fraught with so much additional danger, Heyward drew still nigher to the dusky group, with an intention of making his offers of compensation more definite, when the white man, motioning with his hand, as if he conceded the disputed point, turned away, saying in a sort of soliloquy, and in the English tongue:

"Uncas is right! it would not be the act of men to leave such harmless things to their fate, even though it breaks up the harboring place forever. If you would save these tender blossoms from the fangs of the worst of serpents, gentleman, you have neither time to lose nor resolution to throw away!"

"How can such a wish be doubted! Have I not already offered – "

"Offer your prayers to Him who can give us wisdom to circumvent the cunning of the devils who fill these woods," calmly interrupted the scout, "but spare your offers of money, which neither you may live to realize, nor I to profit by. These Mohicans and I will do what man's thoughts can invent, to keep such flowers, which, though so sweet, were never made for the wilderness, from harm, and that without hope of any other recompense but such as God always gives to upright dealings. First, you must promise two things, both in your own name and for your friends, or without serving you we shall only injure ourselves!"

"Name them."

"The one is, to be still as these sleeping woods, let what will happen and the other is, to keep the place where we shall take you, forever a secret from all mortal men."

"I will do my utmost to see both these conditions fulfilled."

"Then follow, for we are losing moments

that are as precious as the heart's blood to a stricken deer!"

Heyward could distinguish the impatient gesture of the scout, through the increasing shadows of the evening, and he moved in his footsteps, swiftly, toward the place where he had left the remainder of the party. When they rejoined the expecting and anxious females, he briefly acquainted them with the conditions of their new guide, and with the necessity that existed for their hushing every apprehension in instant and serious exertions. Although his alarming communication was not received without much secret terror by the listeners, his earnest and impressive manner, aided perhaps by the nature of the danger, succeeded in bracing their nerves to undergo some unlooked-for and unusual trial. Silently, and without a moment's delay, they permitted him to assist them from their saddles, and when they descended quickly to the water's edge, where the scout had collected the rest of the party, more by the agency of expressive gestures than by any use of words.

"What to do with these dumb creatures!" muttered the white man, on whom the sole control of their future movements appeared to devolve; "it would be time lost to cut their throats, and cast them into the river; and to leave them here would be to tell the Mingoes that they have not far to seek to find their owners!"

"Then give them their bridles, and let them range the woods," Heyward ventured to suggest.

"No; it would be better to mislead the imps, and make them believe they must equal a horse's speed to run down their chase. Ay, ay, that will blind their fireballs of eyes! Chingach – Hist! what stirs the bush?"

"The colt."

"That colt, at least, must die," muttered the scout, grasping at the mane of the nimble beast, which easily eluded his hand; "Uncas, your arrows!"

"Hold!" exclaimed the proprietor of the condemned animal, aloud, without regard to the whispering tones used by the others; "spare the foal of Miriam! it is the comely offspring of a faithful dam, and would willingly injure naught."

"When men struggle for the single life God has given them," said the scout, sternly, "even their own kind seem no more than the beasts of the wood. If you speak again, I shall leave you to the mercy of the Maquas! Draw to your arrow's head, Uncas; we have no time for second blows."

The low, muttering sounds of his threatening voice were still audible, when the wounded foal, first rearing on its hinder legs, plunged forward to its knees. It was met by Chingachgook, whose knife passed across its throat quicker than thought, and then precipitating the motions of the struggling victim, he dashed into the river, down whose stream it glided away, gasping audibly for breath with its ebbing life. This deed of apparent cruelty, but of real necessity, fell upon the spirits of the travelers like a terrific warning of the peril in which they stood, heightened as it was by the calm though steady resolution of the actors in the scene. The sisters shuddered and clung closer to each other, while Heyward instinctively laid his hand on one of the pistols he had just drawn from their holsters, as he placed himself between his charge and those dense shadows that seemed to draw an impenetrable veil before the bosom of the forest.

The Indians, however, hesitated not a moment, but taking the bridles, they led the frightened and reluctant horses into the bed of the river.

At a short distance from the shore they turned, and were soon concealed by the projection of the bank, under the brow of which they moved, in a direction opposite to the course of the waters. In the meantime, the scout drew a canoe of bark from its place of concealment beneath some low bushes, whose branches were waving with the eddies of the current, into which he silently motioned for the females to enter. They complied without hesitation, though many a fearful and anxious glance was thrown behind them, toward the thickening gloom, which now lay like a dark barrier along the margin of the stream.

So soon as Cora and Alice were seated, the scout, without regarding the element, directed Heyward to support one side of the frail vessel, and posting himself at the other, they bore it up against the stream, followed by the dejected owner of the dead foal. In this manner they proceeded, for many rods, in a silence that was only interrupted by the rippling of the water, as its eddies played around them, or the low dash made by their own cautious footsteps. Heyward yielded the guidance of the canoe implicitly to the scout, who approached or receded from the shore, to avoid the fragments of rocks, or deeper parts of the river, with a readiness that showed his knowledge of the route they held. Occasionally he would stop; and in the midst of a breathing stillness, that the dull but increasing roar of the waterfall only served to render more impressive, he would listen with painful intenseness, to catch any sounds that might arise from the slumbering forest. When assured that all was still, and unable to detect, even by the aid of his practiced senses, any sign of his approaching foes, he would deliberately resume his slow and guarded progress. At length they reached a point in the river where the roving eye of Heyward became riveted on a cluster of black objects, collected at a spot where the high bank threw a deeper shadow than usual on the dark waters. Hesitating to advance, he pointed out the place to the attention of his companion.

"Ay," returned the composed scout, "the Indians have hid the beasts with the judgment of natives! Water leaves no trail, and an owl's eyes would be blinded by the darkness of such a hole."

The whole party was soon reunited, and another consultation was held between the scout and his new comrades, during which, they, whose fates depended on the faith and ingenuity of these unknown foresters, had a little leisure to observe their situation more minutely.

The river was confined between high and cragged rocks, one of which impended above the spot where the canoe rested. As these, again, were surmounted by tall trees, which appeared to totter on the brows of the precipice, it gave the stream the appearance of running through a deep and narrow dell. All beneath the fantastic limbs and ragged tree tops, which were, here and there, dimly painted against the starry zenith, lay alike in shadowed obscurity. Behind them, the curvature of the banks soon bounded the view by the same dark and wooded outline; but in front, and apparently at no great distance, the water seemed piled against the heavens, whence it tumbled into caverns, out of which issued those sullen sounds that had loaded the evening atmosphere. It seemed, in truth, to be a spot devoted to seclusion, and the sisters imbibed a soothing impression of security, as they gazed upon its romantic though not unappalling beauties. A general movement among their conductors, however, soon recalled them from a contemplation of the wild charms that night had assisted to lend the place to a painful sense of their real peril.

The horses had been secured to some scattering shrubs that grew in the fissures of the rocks, where, standing in the water, they were left to pass the night. The scout directed Heyward and his disconsolate fellow travelers to seat themselves in the forward end of the canoe, and took possession of the other himself, as erect and steady as if he floated in a vessel of much firmer materials. The Indians warily retraced their steps toward the place they had left, when the scout, placing his pole against a rock, by a powerful shove, sent his frail bark directly into the turbulent stream. For many minutes the struggle between the light bubble in which they floated and the swift current was severe and doubtful. Forbidden to stir even a hand, and almost afraid to breath, lest they should expose the frail fabric to the fury of the stream, the passengers watched the glancing waters in feverish suspense. Twenty times they thought the whirling eddies were sweeping them to destruction, when the master-hand of their pilot would bring the bows of the canoe to stem the rapid. A long, a vigorous, and, as it appeared to the females, a desperate effort, closed the struggle. Just as Alice veiled her eyes in horror, under the impression that they were about to be swept within the vortex at the foot of the cataract, the canoe floated, stationary, at the side of a flat rock, that lay on a level with the water.

"Where are we, and what is next to be done!" demanded Heyward, perceiving that the exertions of the scout had ceased.

"You are at the foot of Glenn's," returned the other, speaking aloud, without fear of consequences within the roar of the cataract; "and the next thing is to make a steady landing, lest the canoe upset, and you should go down again the hard road we have traveled faster than you came up; 'tis a hard rift to stem, when the river is a little swelled; and five is an unnatural number to keep dry, in a hurry-skurry, with a little birchen bark and gum. There, go you all on the rock, and I will bring up the Mohicans with the venison. A man had better sleep without his scalp, than famish in the midst of plenty."

His passengers gladly complied with these directions. As the last foot touched the rock, the canoe whirled from its station, when the tall form of the scout was seen, for an instant, gliding above the waters, before it disappeared in the impenetrable darkness that rested on the bed of the river. Left by their guide, the travelers remained a few minutes in helpless ignorance, afraid even to move along the broken rocks, lest a false step should precipitate them down some one of the many deep and roaring caverns, into which the water seemed to tumble, on every side of them. Their suspense, however, was soon relieved; for, aided by the skill of the natives, the canoe shot back into the eddy, and floated again at the side of the low rock, before they thought the scout had even time to rejoin his companions.

"We are now fortified, garrisoned, and provisioned," cried Heyward cheerfully, "and may set Montcalm and his allies at defiance. How, now, my vigilant sentinel, can see anything of those you call the Iroquois, on the main land!"

"I call them Iroquois, because to me every native, who speaks a foreign tongue, is accounted an enemy, though he may pretend to serve the king! If Webb wants faith and honesty in an Indian, let him bring out the tribes of the Delawares, and send these greedy and lying Mohawks and Oneidas, with their six nations of varlets, where in nature they belong, among the French!"

"We should then exchange a warlike for a useless friend! I have heard that the Delawares have laid aside the hatchet, and are content to be called women!"

"Aye, shame on the Hollanders and Iroquois, who circumvented them by their deviltries, into such a treaty! But I have known them for twenty years, and I call him liar that says cowardly blood runs in the veins of a Delaware. You have driven their tribes from the seashore, and would now believe what their enemies say, that you may sleep at night upon an easy pillow. No, no; to me, every Indian who speaks a foreign tongue is an Iroquois, whether the castle[9] of his tribe be in Canada, or be in York."

Heyward, perceiving that the stubborn adherence of the scout to the cause of his friends the Delawares, or Mohicans, for they were branches of the same numerous people, was likely to prolong a useless discussion, changed the subject.

"Treaty or no treaty, I know full well that your two companions are brave and cautious warriors! have they heard or seen anything of our enemies!"

"An Indian is a mortal to be felt afore he is seen," returned the scout, ascending the rock, and throwing the deer carelessly down. "I trust to other signs than such as come in at the eye, when I am outlying on the trail of the Mingoes."

"Do your ears tell you that they have traced

---

9 The principal villages of the Indians are still called "castles" by the whites of New York. "Oneida castle" is no more than a scattered hamlet; but the name is in general use.

our retreat?"

"I should be sorry to think they had, though this is a spot that stout courage might hold for a smart scrimmage. I will not deny, however, but the horses cowered when I passed them, as though they scented the wolves; and a wolf is a beast that is apt to hover about an Indian ambushment, craving the offals of the deer the savages kill."

"You forget the buck at your feet! or, may we not owe their visit to the dead colt? Ha! what noise is that?"

"Poor Miriam!" murmured the stranger; "thy foal was foreordained to become a prey to ravenous beasts!" Then, suddenly lifting up his voice, amid the eternal din of the waters, he sang aloud: "First born of Egypt, smite did he, Of mankind, and of beast also: O, Egypt! wonders sent 'midst thee, On Pharaoh and his servants too!"

"The death of the colt sits heavy on the heart of its owner," said the scout; "but it's a good sign to see a man account upon his dumb friends. He has the religion of the matter, in believing what is to happen will happen; and with such a consolation, it won't be long afore he submits to the rationality of killing a four-footed beast to save the lives of human men. It may be as you say," he continued, reverting to the purport of Heyward's last remark; "and the greater the reason why we should cut our steaks, and let the carcass drive down the stream, or we shall have the pack howling along the cliffs, begrudging every mouthful we swallow. Besides, though the Delaware tongue is the same as a book to the Iroquois, the cunning varlets are quick enough at understanding the reason of a wolf's howl."

The scout, while making his remarks, was busied in collecting certain necessary implements; as he concluded, he moved silently by the group of travelers, accompanied by the Mohicans, who seemed to comprehend his intentions with instinctive readiness, when the whole three disappeared in succession, seeming to vanish against the dark face of a perpendicular rock that rose to the height of a few yards, within as many feet of the water's edge.

Chapter Six

"Those strains that once did sweet in
Zion glide;
He wales a portion with judicious care;
And 'Let us worship God', he says, with
solemn air."

– Burns

HEYWARD AND HIS FEMALE companions witnessed this mysterious movement with secret uneasiness; for, though the conduct of the white man had hitherto been above reproach, his rude equipments, blunt address, and strong antipathies, together with the character of his silent associates, were all causes for exciting distrust in minds that had been so recently alarmed by Indian treachery.

The stranger alone disregarded the passing incidents. He seated himself on a projection of the rocks, whence he gave no other signs of consciousness than by the struggles of his spirit, as manifested in frequent and heavy sighs. Smothered voices were next heard, as though men called to each other in the bowels of the earth, when a sudden light flashed upon those without, and laid bare the much-prized secret of the place.

At the further extremity of a narrow, deep cavern in the rock, whose length appeared much extended by the perspective and the nature of the light by which it was seen, was seated the scout, holding a blazing knot of pine. The strong glare of the fire fell full upon his sturdy, weather-beaten countenance and forest attire, lending an air of romantic wildness to the aspect of an individual, who, seen by the sober light of day, would have exhibited the peculiarities of a man remarkable for the strangeness of his dress, the iron-like inflexibility of his frame, and the singular compound of quick, vigilant sagacity, and of exquisite simplicity, that by turns usurped the possession of his muscular features. At a little distance in advance stood Uncas, his whole person thrown powerfully into view. The travelers anxiously regarded the upright, flexible figure of the young Mohican, graceful and unrestrained in the attitudes and movements of nature. Though his person was more than usually screened by a green and fringed hunting-shirt, like that of the white man, there was no concealment to his dark, glancing, fearless eye, alike terrible and calm; the bold outline of his high, haughty features, pure in their native red; or to the dignified elevation of his receding forehead, together with all the finest proportions of a noble head, bared to the generous scalping tuft. It was the first opportunity possessed by Duncan and his companions to view the marked lineaments of either of their Indian attendants, and each individual of the party felt relieved from a burden of doubt, as the proud and determined, though wild expression of the features of the young warrior forced itself on their notice. They felt it might be a being partially benighted in the vale of ignorance, but it could not be one who would willingly devote his rich natural gifts to the purposes of wanton treachery. The ingenuous Alice gazed at his free air and proud carriage, as she would have looked upon some precious relic of the Grecian chisel, to which life had been imparted by the intervention of a miracle; while Heyward, though accustomed to see the perfection of form which abounds among the uncorrupted natives, openly expressed his admiration at such an unblemished specimen of the noblest proportions of man.

"I could sleep in peace," whispered Alice,

in reply, "with such a fearless and generous-looking youth for my sentinel. Surely, Duncan, those cruel murders, those terrific scenes of torture, of which we read and hear so much, are never acted in the presence of such as he!"

"This certainly is a rare and brilliant instance of those natural qualities in which these peculiar people are said to excel," he answered. "I agree with you, Alice, in thinking that such a front and eye were formed rather to intimidate than to deceive; but let us not practice a deception upon ourselves, by expecting any other exhibition of what we esteem virtue than according to the fashion of the savage. As bright examples of great qualities are but too uncommon among Christians, so are they singular and solitary with the Indians; though, for the honor of our common nature, neither are incapable of producing them. Let us then hope that this Mohican may not disappoint our wishes, but prove what his looks assert him to be, a brave and constant friend."

"Now Major Heyward speaks as Major Heyward should," said Cora; "who that looks at this creature of nature, remembers the shade of his skin?"

A short and apparently an embarrassed silence succeeded this remark, which was interrupted by the scout calling to them, aloud, to enter.

"This fire begins to show too bright a flame," he continued, as they complied, "and might light the Mingoes to our undoing. Uncas, drop the blanket, and show the knaves its dark side. This is not such a supper as a major of the Royal Americans has a right to expect, but I've known stout detachments of the corps glad to eat their venison raw, and without a relish, too.[10] Here, you see, we have plenty of salt, and can make a quick broil. There's fresh sassafras boughs for the ladies to sit on, which may not be as proud as their my-hog-guinea chairs, but which sends up a sweeter flavor, than the skin of any hog can do, be it of Guinea, or be it of any other land. Come, friend, don't be mournful for the colt; 'twas an innocent thing, and had not seen much hardship. Its death will save the creature many a sore back and weary foot!"

Uncas did as the other had directed, and when the voice of Hawkeye ceased,

10 In vulgar parlance the condiments of a repast are called by the American "a relish," substituting the thing for its effect. These provincial terms are frequently put in the mouths of the speakers, according to their several conditions in life. Most of them are of local use, and others quite peculiar to the particular class of men to which the character belongs. In the present instance, the scout uses the word with immediate reference to the "salt," with which his own party was so fortunate as to be provided.

the roar of the cataract sounded like the rumbling of distant thunder.

"Are we quite safe in this cavern?" demanded Heyward. "Is there no danger of surprise? A single armed man, at its entrance, would hold us at his mercy."

A spectral-looking figure stalked from out of the darkness behind the scout, and seizing a blazing brand, held it toward the further extremity of their place of retreat. Alice uttered a faint shriek, and even Cora rose to her feet, as this appalling object moved into the light; but a single word from Heyward calmed them, with the assurance it was only their attendant, Chingachgook, who, lifting another blanket, discovered that the cavern had two outlets. Then, holding the brand, he crossed a deep, narrow chasm in the rocks which ran at right angles with the passage they were in, but which, unlike that, was open to the heavens, and entered another cave, answering to the description of the first, in every essential particular.

"Such old foxes as Chingachgook and myself are not often caught in a barrow with one hole," said Hawkeye, laughing; "you can easily see the cunning of the place – the rock is black limestone, which everybody knows is soft; it makes no uncomfortable pillow, where brush and pine wood is scarce; well, the fall was once a few yards below us, and I dare to say was, in its time, as regular and as handsome a sheet of water as any along the Hudson. But old age is a great injury to good looks, as these sweet young ladies have yet to l'arn! The place is sadly changed! These rocks are full of cracks, and in some places they are softer than at othersome, and the water has worked out deep hollows for itself, until it has fallen back, ay, some hundred feet, breaking here and wearing there, until the falls have neither shape nor consistency."

"In what part of them are we?" asked Heyward.

"Why, we are nigh the spot that Providence first placed them at, but where, it seems, they were too rebellious to stay. The rock proved softer on each side of us, and so they left the center of the river bare and dry, first working out these two little holes for us to hide in."

"We are then on an island!"

"Ay! there are the falls on two sides of us, and the river above and below. If you had daylight, it would be worth the trouble to step up on the height of this rock, and look at the perversity of the water. It falls by no rule at all; sometimes it leaps, sometimes it tumbles; there it skips; here it shoots; in one place 'tis white as snow, and in another 'tis green as grass; hereabouts, it pitches into deep hollows, that rumble and crush the 'arth; and thereaways, it ripples and sings like a brook, fashioning whirlpools and gullies in the old stone, as if 'twas no harder than trodden clay. The whole design of the river seems disconcerted. First it runs smoothly, as if meaning to go down the descent as things were ordered; then it angles about and faces the shores;

nor are there places wanting where it looks backward, as if unwilling to leave the wilderness, to mingle with the salt. Ay, lady, the fine cobweb-looking cloth you wear at your throat is coarse, and like a fishnet, to little spots I can show you, where the river fabricates all sorts of images, as if having broke loose from order, it would try its hand at everything. And yet what does it amount to! After the water has been suffered so to have its will, for a time, like a headstrong man, it is gathered together by the hand that made it, and a few rods below you may see it all, flowing on steadily toward the sea, as was foreordained from the first foundation of the 'arth!"

While his auditors received a cheering assurance of the security of their place of concealment from this untutored description of Glenn's,[11] they were much inclined to

---

11 Glenn's Falls are on the Hudson, some forty or fifty miles above the head of tide, or that place where the river becomes navigable for sloops. The description of this picturesque and remarkable little cataract, as given by the scout, is sufficiently correct, though the application of the water to uses of civilized life has materially injured its beauties. The rocky island and the two caverns are known to every traveler, since the former sustains the pier of a bridge, which is now thrown across the river, immediately above the fall. In explanation of the taste of Hawkeye, it should be remembered that men always prize that most which is least enjoyed. Thus, in a new country, the woods and other objects, which in an old country would be maintained at great cost, are got rid of, simply with a view of "improving" as it is called.

judge differently from Hawkeye, of its wild beauties. But they were not in a situation to suffer their thoughts to dwell on the charms of natural objects; and, as the scout had not found it necessary to cease his culinary labors while he spoke, unless to point out, with a broken fork, the direction of some particularly obnoxious point in the rebellious stream, they now suffered their attention to be drawn to the necessary though more vulgar consideration of their supper.

The repast, which was greatly aided by the addition of a few delicacies that Heyward had the precaution to bring with him when they left their horses, was exceedingly refreshing to the weary party. Uncas acted as attendant to the females, performing all the little offices within his power, with a mixture of dignity and anxious grace, that served to amuse Heyward, who well knew that it was an utter innovation on the Indian customs, which forbid their warriors to descend to any menial employment, especially in favor of their women. As the rights of hospitality were, however, considered sacred among them, this little departure from the dignity of manhood excited no audible comment. Had there been one there sufficiently disengaged to become a close observer, he might have fancied that the services of the young chief were not entirely impartial. That while he tendered to Alice the gourd of sweet water, and the venison in a trencher, neatly carved from the knot of the pepperidge, with sufficient courtesy, in performing the same offices to her sister, his dark eye lingered on her rich, speaking countenance. Once or twice he was compelled to speak, to command her attention of those he served. In such cases he made use of English, broken and imperfect, but sufficiently intelligible, and which he rendered so mild and musical, by his deep, guttural voice, that it never failed to cause both ladies to look up in admiration and astonishment. In the course of these civilities, a few sentences were exchanged, that served to establish the appearance of an amicable intercourse between the parties.

In the meanwhile, the gravity of Chingcachgook remained immovable. He had seated himself more within the circle of light, where the frequent, uneasy glances of his guests were better enabled to separate the natural expression of his face from the artificial terrors of the war paint. They found a strong resemblance between father and son, with the difference that might be expected from age and hardships. The fierceness of his countenance now seemed to slumber, and in its place was to be seen the quiet, vacant composure which distinguishes an Indian warrior, when his faculties are not required for any of the greater purposes of his existence. It was, however, easy to be seen, by the occasional gleams that shot across his swarthy visage, that it was only necessary to arouse his passions, in order to give full effect to the terrific device which he had adopted to intimidate his enemies. On the other hand, the quick, roving eye of the scout seldom rested. He ate and drank with an appetite that no sense of danger could disturb, but his vigilance seemed never to desert him. Twenty times the gourd or the venison was suspended before his lips, while his head was turned aside, as though he listened to some distant and distrusted sounds – a movement that never failed to recall his guests from regarding the novelties of their situation, to a recollection of the alarming reasons that had driven them to seek it. As these frequent pauses were never followed by any remark, the momentary uneasiness they created quickly passed away, and for a time was forgotten.

“Come, friend,” said Hawkeye, drawing out a keg from beneath a cover of leaves, toward the close of the repast, and addressing the stranger who sat at his elbow, doing great justice to his culinary skill, “try a little spruce; ‘twill wash away all thoughts of the colt, and quicken the life in your bosom. I drink to our better friendship, hoping that a little horse-flesh may leave no heart-burnings atween us. How do you name yourself?"

"Gamut – David Gamut," returned the singing master, preparing to wash down his sorrows in a powerful draught of the woodsman's high-flavored and well-laced compound.

"A very good name, and, I dare say, handed down from honest forefathers. I'm an admirator of names, though the Christian fashions fall far below savage customs in this particular. The biggest coward I ever knew as called Lyon; and his wife, Patience, would scold you out of hearing in less time than a hunted deer would run a rod. With an Indian 'tis a matter of conscience; what he calls himself, he generally is – not that Chingachgook, which signifies Big Sarpent, is really a snake, big or little; but that he understands the windings and turnings of human natur', and is silent, and strikes his enemies when they least expect him. What may be your calling?"

"I am an unworthy instructor in the art of psalmody."

"Anan!"

"I teach singing to the youths of the Connecticut levy."

"You might be better employed. The young hounds go laughing and singing too much already through the woods, when they ought not to breathe louder than a fox in his cover. Can you use the smoothbore, or handle the rifle?"

"Praised be God, I have never had occasion to meddle with murderous implements!"

"Perhaps you understand the compass, and lay down the watercourses and mountains of the wilderness on paper, in order that they who follow may find places by their given names?"

"I practice no such employment."

"You have a pair of legs that might make a

long path seem short! you journey sometimes, I fancy, with tidings for the general."

"Never; I follow no other than my own high vocation, which is instruction in sacred music!"

"'Tis a strange calling!" muttered Hawkeye, with an inward laugh, "to go through life, like a catbird, mocking all the ups and downs that may happen to come out of other men's throats. Well, friend, I suppose it is your gift, and mustn't be denied any more than if 'twas shooting, or some other better inclination. Let us hear what you can do in that way; 'twill be a friendly manner of saying good-night, for 'tis time that these ladies should be getting strength for a hard and a long push, in the pride of the morning, afore the Maquas are stirring."

"With joyful pleasure do I consent", said David, adjusting his iron-rimmed spectacles, and producing his beloved little volume, which he immediately tendered to Alice. "What can be more fitting and consolatory, than to offer up evening praise, after a day of such exceeding jeopardy!"

Alice smiled; but, regarding Heyward, she blushed and hesitated.

"Indulge yourself," he whispered; "ought not the suggestion of the worthy namesake of the Psalmist to have its weight at such a moment?"

Encouraged by his opinion, Alice did what her pious inclinations, and her keen relish for gentle sounds, had before so strongly urged. The book was open at a hymn not ill adapted to their situation, and in which the poet, no longer goaded by his desire to excel the inspired King of Israel, had discovered some chastened and respectable powers. Cora betrayed a disposition to support her sister, and the sacred song proceeded, after the indispensable preliminaries of the pitchpipe, and the tune had been duly attended to by the methodical David.

The air was solemn and slow. At times it rose to the fullest compass of the rich voices of the females, who hung over their little book in holy excitement, and again it sank so low, that the rushing of the waters ran through their melody, like a hollow accompaniment. The natural taste and true ear of David governed and modified the sounds to suit the confined cavern, every crevice and cranny of which was filled with the thrilling notes of their flexible voices. The Indians riveted their eyes on the rocks, and listened with an attention that seemed to turn them into stone. But the scout, who had placed his chin in his hand, with an expression of cold indifference, gradually suffered his rigid features to relax, until, as verse succeeded verse, he felt his iron nature subdued, while his recollection was carried back to boyhood, when his ears had been accustomed to listen to similar sounds of praise, in the settlements of the colony. His roving eyes began to moisten, and before the hymn was ended scalding tears rolled out of fountains that had long seemed dry, and followed each other down those cheeks, that had oftener felt the storms of heaven than any testimonials of weakness. The singers were dwelling on one of those low, dying chords, which the ear devours with such greedy rapture, as if conscious that it is about to lose them, when a cry, that seemed neither human nor earthly, rose in the outward air, penetrating not only the recesses of the cavern, but to the inmost hearts of all who heard it. It was followed by a stillness apparently as deep as if the waters had been checked in their furious progress, at such a horrid and unusual interruption.

"What is it?" murmured Alice, after a few moments of terrible suspense.

"What is it?" repeated Hewyard aloud.

Neither Hawkeye nor the Indians made any reply. They listened, as if expecting the sound would be repeated, with a manner that expressed their own astonishment. At length they spoke together, earnestly, in the

Delaware language, when Uncas, passing by the inner and most concealed aperture, cautiously left the cavern. When he had gone, the scout first spoke in English.

"What it is, or what it is not, none here can tell, though two of us have ranged the woods for more than thirty years. I did believe there was no cry that Indian or beast could make, that my ears had not heard; but this has proved that I was only a vain and conceited mortal."

"Was it not, then, the shout the warriors make when they wish to intimidate their enemies?" asked Cora who stood drawing her veil about her person, with a calmness to which her agitated sister was a stranger.

"No, no; this was bad, and shocking, and had a sort of unhuman sound; but when you once hear the war-whoop, you will never mistake it for anything else. Well, Uncas!" speaking in Delaware to the young chief as he re-entered, "what see you? do our lights shine through the blankets?"

The answer was short, and apparently decided, being given in the same tongue.

"There is nothing to be seen without," continued Hawkeye, shaking his head in discontent; "and our hiding-place is still in darkness. Pass into the other cave, you that need it, and seek for sleep; we must be afoot long before the sun, and make the most of our time to get to Edward, while the Mingoes are taking their morning nap."

Cora set the example of compliance, with a steadiness that taught the more timid Alice the necessity of obedience. Before leaving the place, however, she whispered a request to Duncan, that he would follow. Uncas raised the blanket for their passage, and as the sisters turned to thank him for this act of attention, they saw the scout seated again before the dying embers, with his face resting on his hands, in a manner which showed how deeply he brooded on the unaccountable interruption which had broken up their evening devotions.

Heyward took with him a blazing knot, which threw a dim light through the narrow vista of their new apartment. Placing it in a favorable position, he joined the females, who now found themselves alone with him for the first time since they had left the friendly ramparts of Fort Edward.

"Leave us not, Duncan," said Alice: "we cannot sleep in such a place as this, with that horrid cry still ringing in our ears."

"First let us examine into the security of your fortress," he answered, "and then we will speak of rest."

He approached the further end of the cavern, to an outlet, which, like the others, was concealed by blankets; and removing the thick screen, breathed the fresh and reviving air from the cataract. One arm of the river flowed through a deep, narrow ravine, which its current had worn in the soft rock, directly beneath his feet, forming an effectual defense, as he believed, against any danger from that quarter; the water, a few rods above them, plunging, glancing, and sweeping along in its most violent and broken manner.

"Nature has made an impenetrable barrier on this side," he continued, pointing down the perpendicular declivity into the dark current before he dropped the blanket; "and as you know that good men and true are on guard in front I see no reason why the advice of our honest host should be disregarded. I am certain Cora will join me in saying that sleep is necessary to you both."

"Cora may submit to the justice of your opinion though she cannot put it in practice," returned the elder sister, who had placed herself by the side of Alice, on a couch of sassafras; "there would be other causes to chase away sleep, though we had been spared the shock of this mysterious noise. Ask yourself, Heyward, can daughters forget the anxiety a father must endure, whose children lodge he knows not where or how, in such a wilderness, and in the midst of so many perils?"

"He is a soldier, and knows how to estimate the chances of the woods."

"He is a father, and cannot deny his nature."

"How kind has he ever been to all my follies, how tender and indulgent to all my wishes!" sobbed Alice. "We have been selfish, sister, in urging our visit at such hazard."

"I may have been rash in pressing his consent in a moment of much embarrassment, but I would have proved to him, that however others might neglect him in his strait his children at least were faithful."

"When he heard of your arrival at Edward," said Heyward, kindly, "there was a powerful struggle in his bosom between fear and love; though the latter, heightened, if possible, by so long a separation, quickly prevailed. 'It is the spirit of my noble-minded Cora that leads them, Duncan', he said, 'and I will not balk it. Would to God, that he who holds the honor of our royal master in his guardianship, would show but half her firmness!'"

"And did he not speak of me, Heyward?" demanded Alice, with jealous affection; "surely, he forgot not altogether his little Elsie?"

"That were impossible," returned the young man; "he called you by a thousand endearing epithets, that I may not presume to use, but to the justice of which, I can warmly testify. Once, indeed, he said – "

Duncan ceased speaking; for while his eyes were riveted on those of Alice, who had turned toward him with the eagerness of filial affection, to catch his words, the same strong, horrid cry, as before, filled the air, and rendered him mute. A long, breathless silence succeeded, during which each looked at the others in fearful expectation of hearing the sound repeated. At length, the blanket was slowly raised, and the scout stood in the aperture with a countenance whose firmness evidently began to give way before a mystery that seemed to threaten some danger, against which all his cunning and experience might prove of no avail.

Chapter Seven

"They do not sleep,
On yonder cliffs, a grizzly band,
I see them sit."

– Gray

"'TWOULD BE NEGLECTING A warning that is given for our good to lie hid any longer," said Hawkeye "when such sounds are raised in the forest. These gentle ones may keep close, but the Mohicans and I will watch upon the rock, where I suppose a major of the Sixtieth would wish to keep us company."

"Is, then, our danger so pressing?" asked

Cora.

"He who makes strange sounds, and gives them out for man's information, alone knows our danger. I should think myself wicked, unto rebellion against His will, was I to burrow with such warnings in the air! Even the weak soul who passes his days in singing is stirred by the cry, and, as he says, is 'ready to go forth to the battle' If 'twere only a battle, it would be a thing understood by us all, and easily managed; but I have heard that when such shrieks are atween heaven and 'arth, it betokens another sort of warfare!"

"If all our reasons for fear, my friend, are confined to such as proceed from supernatural causes, we have but little occasion to be alarmed," continued the undisturbed Cora, "are you certain that our enemies have not invented some new and ingenious method to strike us with terror, that their conquest may become more easy?"

"Lady," returned the scout, solemnly, "I

have listened to all the sounds of the woods for thirty years, as a man will listen whose life and death depend on the quickness of his ears. There is no whine of the panther, no whistle of the catbird, nor any invention of the devilish Mingoes, that can cheat me! I have heard the forest moan like mortal men in their affliction; often, and again, have I listened to the wind playing its music in the branches of the girdled trees; and I have heard the lightning cracking in the air like the snapping of blazing brush as it spitted forth sparks and forked flames; but never have I thought that I heard more than the pleasure of him who sported with the things of his hand. But neither the Mohicans, nor I, who am a white man without a cross, can explain the cry just heard. We, therefore, believe it a sign given for our good."

"It is extraordinary!" said Heyward, taking his pistols from the place where he had laid them on entering; "be it a sign of peace or a signal of war, it must be looked to. Lead the way, my friend; I follow."

On issuing from their place of confinement, the whole party instantly experienced a grateful renovation of spirits, by exchanging the pent air of the hiding-place for the cool and invigorating atmosphere which played around the whirlpools and pitches of the cataract. A heavy evening breeze swept along the surface of the river, and seemed to drive the roar of the falls into the recesses of their own cavern, whence it issued heavily and constant, like thunder rumbling beyond the distant hills. The moon had risen, and its light was already glancing here and there on the waters above them; but the extremity of the rock where they stood still lay in shadow. With the exception of the sounds produced by the rushing waters, and an occasional breathing of the air, as it murmured past them in fitful currents, the scene was as still as night and solitude could make it. In vain were the eyes of each individual bent along the opposite shores, in quest of some signs of life, that might explain the nature of the interruption they had heard. Their anxious and eager looks were baffled by the deceptive light, or rested only on naked rocks, and straight and immovable trees.

"Here is nothing to be seen but the gloom and quiet of a lovely evening," whispered Duncan; "how much should we prize such a scene, and all this breathing solitude, at any other moment, Cora! Fancy yourselves in security, and what now, perhaps, increases your terror, may be made conducive to enjoyment – "

"Listen!" interrupted Alice.

The caution was unnecessary. Once more the same sound arose, as if from the bed of the river, and having broken out of the narrow bounds of the cliffs, was heard undulating through the forest, in distant and dying cadences.

"Can any here give a name to such a cry?" demanded Hawkeye, when the last echo was lost in the woods; "if so, let him speak;

for myself, I judge it not to belong to 'arth!"

"Here, then, is one who can undeceive you," said Duncan; "I know the sound full well, for often have I heard it on the field of battle, and in situations which are frequent in a soldier's life. 'Tis the horrid shriek that a horse will give in his agony; oftener drawn from him in pain, though sometimes in terror. My charger is either a prey to the beasts of the forest, or he sees his danger, without the power to avoid it. The sound might deceive me in the cavern, but in the open air I know it too well to be wrong."

The scout and his companions listened to this simple explanation with the interest of men who imbibe new ideas, at the same time that they get rid of old ones, which had proved disagreeable inmates. The two latter uttered their usual expressive exclamation, "hugh!" as the truth first glanced upon their minds, while the former, after a short, musing pause, took upon himself to reply.

"I cannot deny your words," he said, "for I

am little skilled in horses, though born where they abound. The wolves must be hovering above their heads on the bank, and the timorsome creatures are calling on man for help, in the best manner they are able. Uncas" – he spoke in Delaware – "Uncas, drop down in the canoe, and whirl a brand among the pack; or fear may do what the wolves can't get at to perform, and leave us without horses in the morning, when we shall have so much need to journey swiftly!"

The young native had already descended to the water to comply, when a long howl was raised on the edge of the river, and was borne swiftly off into the depths of the forest, as though the beasts, of their own accord, were abandoning their prey in sudden terror. Uncas, with instinctive quickness, receded, and the three foresters held another of their low, earnest conferences.

"We have been like hunters who have lost the points of the heavens, and from whom the sun has been hid for days," said Hawkeye, turning away from his companions; "now we begin again to know the signs of our course, and the paths are cleared from briers! Seat yourselves in the shade which the moon throws from yonder beech – 'tis thicker than that of the pines – and let us wait for that which the Lord may choose to send next. Let all your conversation be in whispers; though it would be better, and, perhaps, in the end, wiser, if each one held discourse with his own thoughts, for a time."

The manner of the scout was seriously impressive, though no longer distinguished by any signs of unmanly apprehension. It was evident that his momentary weakness had vanished with the explanation of a mystery which his own experience had not served to fathom; and though he now felt all the realities of their actual condition, that he was prepared to meet them with the energy of his hardy nature. This feeling seemed also common to the natives, who placed themselves in positions which commanded a full view of both shores, while their own persons were effectually concealed from observation. In such circumstances, common prudence dictated that Heyward and his companions should imitate a caution that proceeded from so intelligent a source. The young man drew a pile of the sassafras from the cave, and placing it in the chasm which separated the two caverns, it was occupied by the sisters, who were thus protected by the rocks from any missiles, while their anxiety was relieved by the assurance that no danger could approach without a warning. Heyward himself was posted at hand, so near that he might communicate with his companions without raising his voice to a dangerous elevation; while David, in imitation of the woodsmen, bestowed his person in such a manner among the fissures of the rocks, that his ungainly limbs were no longer offensive to the eye.

In this manner hours passed without further interruption. The moon reached the zenith, and shed its mild light perpendicularly on the lovely sight of the sisters slumbering peacefully in each other's arms. Duncan cast the wide shawl of Cora before a spectacle he so much loved to contemplate, and then suffered his own head to seek a pillow on the rock. David began to utter sounds that would have shocked his delicate organs in more wakeful moments; in short, all but Hawkeye and the Mohicans lost every idea of consciousness, in uncontrollable drowsiness. But the watchfulness of these vigilant protectors neither tired nor slumbered. Immovable as that rock, of which each appeared to form a part, they lay, with their eyes roving, without intermission, along the dark margin of trees, that bounded the adjacent shores of the narrow stream. Not a sound escaped them; the most subtle examination could not have told they breathed. It was evident that this excess of caution proceeded from an experience that no subtlety on the part of their enemies could deceive. It was, however, continued without any apparent consequences, until the moon had set, and a pale streak above the treetops, at the bend of the river a little below, announced the approach of day.

Then, for the first time, Hawkeye was seen to stir. He crawled along the rock and shook Duncan from his heavy slumbers.

"Now is the time to journey," he whispered; "awake the gentle ones, and be ready to get into the canoe when I bring it to the landing-place."

"Have you had a quiet night?" said Heyward; "for myself, I believe sleep has got the better of my vigilance."

"All is yet still as midnight. Be silent, but be quick."

By this time Duncan was thoroughly awake, and he immediately lifted the shawl from the sleeping females. The motion caused Cora to raise her hand as if to repulse him, while Alice murmured, in her soft, gentle voice,

"No, no, dear father, we were not deserted; Duncan was with us!"

"Yes, sweet innocence," whispered the youth; "Duncan is here, and while life continues or danger remains, he will never quit thee. Cora! Alice! awake! The hour has come to move!"

A loud shriek from the younger of the sisters, and the form of the other standing upright before him, in bewildered horror, was the unexpected answer he received.

While the words were still on the lips of Heyward, there had arisen such a tumult of yells and cries as served to drive the swift currents of his own blood back from its bounding course into the fountains of his heart. It seemed, for near a minute, as if the demons of hell had possessed themselves of the air about them, and were venting their savage humors in barbarous sounds. The cries came from no particular direction, though it was evident they filled the woods, and, as the appalled listeners easily imagined, the caverns of the falls, the rocks, the bed of the river, and the upper air. David raised his tall person in the midst of the infernal din, with a hand on either ear, exclaiming:

"Whence comes this discord! Has hell broke loose, that man should utter sounds like these!"

The bright flashes and the quick reports of a dozen rifles, from the opposite banks of the stream, followed this incautious exposure of his person, and left the unfortunate singing master senseless on that rock where he had been so long slumbering. The Mohicans boldly sent back the intimidating yell of their enemies, who raised a shout of savage triumph at the fall of Gamut. The flash of rifles was then quick and close between them, but either party was too well skilled to leave even a limb exposed to the hostile aim. Duncan listened with intense anxiety for the strokes of the paddle, believing that flight was now their only refuge. The river glanced by with its ordinary velocity, but the canoe was nowhere to be seen on its dark waters. He had just fancied they were cruelly deserted by their scout, as a stream of flame issued from the rock beneath them, and a fierce yell, blended with a shriek of agony, announced that the messenger of death sent from the fatal weapon of Hawkeye, had found a victim. At this slight repulse the assailants instantly withdrew, and gradually the place became as still as before the sudden tumult.

Duncan seized the favorable moment to spring to the body of Gamut, which he bore within the shelter of the narrow chasm that protected the sisters. In another minute the whole party was collected in this spot of comparative safety.

"The poor fellow has saved his scalp," said Hawkeye, coolly passing his hand over the head of David; "but he is a proof that a man may be born with too long a tongue! 'Twas downright madness to show six feet of flesh and blood, on a naked rock, to the raging savages. I only wonder he has escaped with life."

"Is he not dead?" demanded Cora, in a voice whose husky tones showed how powerfully natural horror struggled with her assumed firmness. "Can we do aught to assist the wretched man?"

"No, no! the life is in his heart yet, and after he has slept awhile he will come to himself, and be a wiser man for it, till the hour of his real time shall come," returned Hawkeye, casting another oblique glance at the insensible body, while he filled his charger with admirable nicety. "Carry him in, Uncas, and lay him on the sassafras. The longer his nap lasts the better it will be for him, as I doubt whether he can find a proper cover for such a shape on these rocks; and singing won't do any good with the Iroquois."

"You believe, then, the attack will be renewed?" asked Heyward.

"Do I expect a hungry wolf will satisfy his craving with a mouthful! They have lost a man, and 'tis their fashion, when they meet a loss, and fail in the surprise, to fall back; but we shall have them on again, with new expedients to circumvent us, and master our scalps. Our main hope," he continued, raising his rugged countenance, across which a shade of anxiety just then passed like a darkening cloud, "will be to keep the rock until Munro can send a party to our help! God send it may be soon and under a leader that knows the Indian customs!"

"You hear our probable fortunes, Cora," said Duncan, "and you know we have everything to hope from the anxiety and experience of your father. Come, then, with Alice, into this cavern, where you, at least, will be safe from the murderous rifles of our enemies, and where you may bestow a care suited to your gentle natures on our unfortunate comrade."

The sisters followed him into the outer cave, where David was beginning, by his sighs, to give symptoms of returning consciousness, and then commending the wounded man to their attention, he immediately prepared to leave them.

"Duncan!" said the tremulous voice of Cora, when he had reached the mouth of the cavern. He turned and beheld the speaker, whose color had changed to a deadly paleness, and whose lips quivered, gazing after him, with an expression of interest which immediately recalled him to her side. "Remember, Duncan, how necessary your safety is to our own – how you bear a father's sacred trust – how much depends on your discretion and care – in short," she added, while the telltale blood stole over her features, crimsoning her very temples, "how very deservedly dear you are to all of the name of Munro."

"If anything could add to my own base

love of life," said Heyward, suffering his unconscious eyes to wander to the youthful form of the silent Alice, "it would be so kind an assurance. As major of the Sixtieth, our honest host will tell you I must take my share of the fray; but our task will be easy; it is merely to keep these blood-hounds at bay for a few hours."

Without waiting for a reply, he tore himself from the presence of the sisters, and joined the scout and his companions, who still lay within the protection of the little chasm between the two caves.

"I tell you, Uncas," said the former, as Heyward joined them, "you are wasteful of your powder, and the kick of the rifle disconcerts your aim! Little powder, light lead, and a long arm, seldom fail of bringing the death screech from a Mingo! At least, such has been my experience with the creatur's. Come, friends: let us to our covers, for no man can tell when or where a Maqua[12] will strike his blow."

The Indians silently repaired to their appointed stations, which were fissures in the rocks, whence they could command the approaches to the foot of the falls. In the center of the little island, a few short and stunted pines had found root, forming a thicket, into which Hawkeye darted with the swiftness of a deer, followed by the active Duncan. Here they secured themselves, as well as circumstances would permit, among the shrubs and fragments of stone that were scattered about the place. Above them was a bare, rounded rock, on each side of which the water played its gambols, and plunged into the abysses beneath, in the manner already described. As the day had now dawned, the opposite shores no longer

---

12 Mingo was the Delaware term of the Five Nations. Maquas was the name given them by the Dutch. The French, from their first intercourse with them, called them Iroquois.

presented a confused outline, but they were able to look into the woods, and distinguish objects beneath a canopy of gloomy pines.

A long and anxious watch succeeded, but without any further evidences of a renewed attack; and Duncan began to hope that their fire had proved more fatal than was supposed, and that their enemies had been effectually repulsed. When he ventured to utter this impression to his companions, it was met by Hawkeye with an incredulous shake of the head.

"You know not the nature of a Maqua, if you think he is so easily beaten back without a scalp!" he answered. "If there was one of the imps yelling this morning, there were forty! and they know our number and quality too well to give up the chase so soon. Hist! look into the water above, just where it breaks over the rocks. I am no mortal, if the risky devils haven't swam down upon the very pitch, and, as bad luck would have it, they have hit the head of the island. Hist! man, keep close! or the hair will be off your crown in the turning of a knife!"

Heyward lifted his head from the cover, and beheld what he justly considered a prodigy of rashness and skill. The river had worn away the edge of the soft rock in such a manner as to render its first pitch less abrupt and perpendicular than is usual at waterfalls. With no other guide than the ripple of the stream where it met the head of the island, a party of their insatiable foes had ventured into the current, and swam down upon this point, knowing the ready access it would give, if successful, to their intended victims.

As Hawkeye ceased speaking, four human heads could be seen peering above a few logs of drift-wood that had lodged on these naked rocks, and which had probably suggested the idea of the practicability of the hazardous undertaking. At the next moment, a fifth form was seen floating over the green edge of the fall, a little from the line of the island.

The savage struggled powerfully to gain the point of safety, and, favored by the glancing water, he was already stretching forth an arm to meet the grasp of his companions, when he shot away again with the shirling current, appeared to rise into the air, with uplifted arms and starting eyeballs, and fell, with a sudden plunge, into that deep and yawning abyss over which he hovered. A single, wild, despairing shriek rose from the cavern, and all was hushed again as the grave.

The first generous impulse of Duncan was to rush to the rescue of the hapless wretch; but he felt himself bound to the spot by the iron grasp of the immovable scout.

"Would ye bring certain death upon us, by telling the Mingoes where we lie?" demanded Hawkeye, sternly; "'Tis a charge of powder saved, and ammunition is as precious now as breath to a worried deer! Freshen the priming of your pistols – the midst of the falls is apt to dampen the brimstone – and stand firm for a close struggle, while I fire on their rush."

He placed a finger in his mouth, and drew a long, shrill whistle, which was answered from the rocks that were guarded by the Mohicans. Duncan caught glimpses of heads above the scattered drift-wood, as this signal rose on the air, but they disappeared again as suddenly as they had glanced upon his sight. A low, rustling sound next drew his attention behind him, and turning his head, he beheld Uncas within a few feet, creeping to his side. Hawkeye spoke to him in Delaware, when the young chief took his position with singular caution and undisturbed coolness. To Heyward this was a moment of feverish and impatient suspense; though the scout saw fit to select it as a fit occasion to read a lecture to his more youthful associates on the art of using firearms with discretion.

"Of all we'pons," he commenced, "the long barreled, true-grooved, soft-metaled rifle is the most dangerous in skillful hands, though it wants a strong arm, a quick eye, and great judgment in charging, to put forth all its beauties. The gunsmiths can have but little insight into their trade when they make their fowling-pieces and short horsemen's – "

He was interrupted by the low but expressive "hugh" of Uncas.

"I see them, boy, I see them!" continued Hawkeye; "they are gathering for the rush, or they would keep their dingy backs below the logs. Well, let them," he added, examining his flint; "the leading man certainly comes on to his death, though it should be Montcalm himself!"

At that moment the woods were filled with another burst of cries, and at the signal four savages sprang from the cover of the driftwood. Heyward felt a burning desire to rush forward to meet them, so intense was the delirious anxiety of the moment; but he was restrained by the deliberate examples of the scout and Uncas.

When their foes, who had leaped over

the black rocks that divided them, with long bounds, uttering the wildest yells, were within a few rods, the rifle of Hawkeye slowly rose among the shrubs, and poured out its fatal contents. The foremost Indian bounded like a stricken deer, and fell headlong among the clefts of the island.

"Now, Uncas!" cried the scout, drawing his long knife, while his quick eyes began to flash with ardor, "take the last of the screeching imps; of the other two we are sartain!"

He was obeyed; and but two enemies remained to be overcome. Heyward had given one of his pistols to Hawkeye, and together they rushed down a little declivity toward their foes; they discharged their weapons at the same instant, and equally without success.

"I know'd it! and I said it!" muttered the scout, whirling the despised little implement over the falls with bitter disdain. "Come on, ye bloody minded hell-hounds! ye meet a man without a cross!"

The words were barely uttered, when he encountered a savage of gigantic stature, of the fiercest mien. At the same moment, Duncan found himself engaged with the other, in a similar contest of hand to hand. With ready skill, Hawkeye and his antagonist each grasped that uplifted arm of the other which held the dangerous knife. For near a minute they stood looking one another in the eye, and gradually exerting the power of their muscles for the mastery.

At length, the toughened sinews of the white man prevailed over the less practiced limbs of the native. The arm of the latter slowly gave way before the increasing force of the scout, who, suddenly wresting his armed hand from the grasp of the foe, drove the sharp weapon through his naked bosom to the heart. In the meantime, Heyward had been pressed in a more deadly struggle. His slight sword was snapped in the first encounter. As he was destitute of any other means of defense, his safety now depended entirely on bodily strength and resolution. Though deficient in neither of these qualities, he had met an enemy every way his equal. Happily, he soon succeeded in disarming his adversary, whose knife fell on the rock at their feet; and from this moment it became a fierce struggle who should cast the other over the dizzy height into a neighboring cavern of the falls. Every successive struggle brought them nearer to the verge, where Duncan perceived the final and conquering effort must be made. Each of the combatants threw all his energies into that effort, and the result was, that both tottered on the brink of the precipice. Heyward felt the grasp of the other at his throat, and saw the grim smile the savage gave, under the revengeful hope that he hurried his enemy to a fate similar to his own, as he felt his body slowly yielding to a resistless power, and the young man experienced the passing agony of such a moment in all its horrors. At that instant of extreme danger, a dark hand and glancing knife appeared before him; the Indian released his hold, as the blood flowed freely from around the severed tendons of the wrist; and while Duncan was drawn backward by the saving hand of Uncas, his charmed eyes still were riveted on the fierce and disappointed countenance of his foe, who fell sullenly and disappointed down the irrecoverable precipice.

"To cover! to cover!" cried Hawkeye, who just then had despatched the enemy; "to cover, for your lives! the work is but half ended!"

The young Mohican gave a shout of triumph, and followed by Duncan, he glided up the acclivity they had descended to the combat, and sought the friendly shelter of the rocks and shrubs.

Chapter Eight

"They linger yet,
Avengers of their native land."
– Gray

THE WARNING CALL OF the scout was not uttered without occasion. During the occurrence of the deadly encounter just related, the roar of the falls was unbroken by any human sound whatever. It would seem that interest in the result had kept the natives on the opposite shores in breathless suspense, while the quick evolutions and swift changes in the positions of the combatants effectually prevented a fire that might prove dangerous alike to friend and enemy. But the moment the struggle was decided, a yell arose as fierce and savage as wild and revengeful passions could throw into the air. It was followed by the swift flashes of the rifles, which sent their leaden messengers across the rock in volleys, as though the assailants would pour out their impotent fury on the insensible scene of the fatal contest.

A steady, though deliberate return was made from the rifle of Chingachgook, who had maintained his post throughout the fray with unmoved resolution. When the triumphant shout of Uncas was borne to his ears, the gratified father raised his voice in a single responsive cry, after which his busy piece alone proved that he still guarded his pass with unwearied diligence. In this manner many minutes flew by with the swiftness of thought; the rifles of the assailants speaking, at times, in rattling volleys, and at others in occasional, scattering shots. Though the rock, the trees, and the shrubs, were cut and torn in a hundred places around the besieged, their cover was so close, and so rigidly maintained, that, as yet, David had been the only sufferer in their little band.

"Let them burn their powder," said the deliberate scout, while bullet after bullet whizzed by the place where he securely lay; "there will be a fine gathering of lead when it is over, and I fancy the imps will tire of the sport afore these old stones cry out for mercy! Uncas, boy, you waste the kernels by overcharging; and a kicking rifle never carries a true bullet. I told you to take that loping miscreant under the line of white point; now, if your bullet went a hair's breadth it went two inches above it. The life lies low in a Mingo, and humanity teaches us to make a quick end to the sarpents."

A quiet smile lighted the haughty features of the young Mohican, betraying his knowledge of the English language as well as of the other's meaning; but he suffered it to pass away without vindication of reply.

"I cannot permit you to accuse Uncas of want of judgment or of skill," said Duncan; "he saved my life in the coolest and readiest manner, and he has made a friend who never will require to be reminded of the debt he owes."

Uncas partly raised his body, and offered his hand to the grasp of Heyward. During this act of friendship, the two young men exchanged looks of intelligence which caused Duncan to forget the character and condition of his wild associate. In the meanwhile, Hawkeye, who looked on this burst of youthful feeling with a cool but kind regard made the following reply:

"Life is an obligation which friends often owe each other in the wilderness. I dare say I may have served Uncas some such turn myself before now; and I very well remember that he has stood between me and death five different times; three times from the Mingoes, once in crossing Horican, and – ”

“That bullet was better aimed than common!” exclaimed Duncan, involuntarily shrinking from a shot which struck the rock at his side with a smart rebound.

Hawkeye laid his hand on the shapeless metal, and shook his head, as he examined it, saying, “Falling lead is never flattened, had it come from the clouds this might have happened.”

But the rifle of Uncas was deliberately raised toward the heavens, directing the eyes of his companions to a point, where the mystery was immediately explained. A ragged oak grew on the right bank of the river, nearly opposite to their position, which, seeking the freedom of the open space, had inclined so far forward that its upper branches overhung that arm of the stream which flowed nearest to its own shore. Among the topmost leaves, which scantily concealed the gnarled and stunted limbs, a savage was nestled, partly concealed by the trunk of the tree, and partly exposed, as though looking down upon them to ascertain the effect produced by his treacherous aim.

"These devils will scale heaven to circumvent us to our ruin," said Hawkeye; "keep him in play, boy, until I can bring 'killdeer' to bear, when we will try his metal on each side of the tree at once."

Uncas delayed his fire until the scout uttered the word.

The rifles flashed, the leaves and bark of the oak flew into the air, and were scattered by the wind, but the Indian answered their assault by a taunting laugh, sending down upon them another bullet in return, that struck the cap of Hawkeye from his head. Once more the savage yells burst out of the woods, and the leaden hail whistled above the heads of the besieged, as if to confine them to a place where they might become easy victims to the enterprise of the warrior who had mounted the tree.

"This must be looked to," said the scout,

glancing about him with an anxious eye. “Uncas, call up your father; we have need of all our we’pons to bring the cunning varmint from his roost.”

The signal was instantly given; and, before Hawkeye had reloaded his rifle, they were joined by Chingachgook. When his son pointed out to the experienced warrior the situation of their dangerous enemy, the usual exclamatory “hugh” burst from his lips; after which, no further expression of surprise or alarm was suffered to escape him. Hawkeye and the Mohicans conversed earnestly together in Delaware for a few moments, when each quietly took his post, in order to execute the plan they had speedily devised.

The warrior in the oak had maintained a quick, though ineffectual fire, from the moment of his discovery. But his aim was interrupted by the vigilance of his enemies, whose rifles instantaneously bore on any part of his person that was left exposed. Still his bullets fell in the center of the crouching party. The clothes of Heyward, which rendered him peculiarly conspicuous, were repeatedly cut, and once blood was drawn from a slight wound in his arm.

At length, emboldened by the long and patient watchfulness of his enemies, the Huron attempted a better and more fatal aim. The quick eyes of the Mohicans caught the dark line of his lower limbs incautiously exposed through the thin foliage, a few inches from the trunk of the tree. Their rifles made a common report, when, sinking on his wounded limb, part of the body of the savage came into view. Swift as thought, Hawkeye seized the advantage, and discharged his fatal weapon into the top of the oak. The leaves were unusually agitated; the dangerous rifle fell from its commanding elevation, and after a few moments of vain struggling, the form of the savage was seen swinging in the wind, while he still grasped a ragged and naked branch of the tree with hands clenched in desperation.

"Give him, in pity, give him the contents of another rifle," cried Duncan, turning away his eyes in horror from the spectacle of a fellow creature in such awful jeopardy.

"Not a karnel!" exclaimed the obdurate Hawkeye; "his death is certain, and we have no powder to spare, for Indian fights sometimes last for days; 'tis their scalps or ours! and God, who made us, has put into our natures the craving to keep the skin on the head."

Against this stern and unyielding morality, supported as it was by such visible policy, there was no appeal. From that moment the yells in the forest once more ceased, the fire was suffered to decline, and all eyes, those of friends as well as enemies, became fixed on the hopeless condition of the wretch who was dangling between heaven and earth. The body yielded to the currents of air, and though no murmur or groan escaped the victim, there were instants when he grimly faced his foes, and the anguish of cold despair might be traced, through the intervening distance, in possession of his swarthy lineaments. Three several times the scout raised his piece in mercy, and as often, prudence getting the better of his intention, it was again silently lowered. At length one hand of the Huron lost its hold, and dropped exhausted to his side. A desperate and fruitless struggle to recover the branch succeeded, and then the savage was seen for a fleeting instant, grasping wildly at the empty air. The lightning is not quicker than was the flame from the rifle of Hawkeye; the limbs of the victim trembled and contracted, the head fell to the bosom, and the body parted the foaming waters like lead, when the element closed above it, in its ceaseless velocity, and every vestige of the unhappy Huron was lost forever.

No shout of triumph succeeded this important advantage, but even the Mohicans gazed at each other in silent horror. A single yell burst from the woods, and all was again still. Hawkeye, who alone appeared to reason on the occasion, shook his head at his own momentary weakness, even uttering his self-disapprobation aloud.

"'Twas the last charge in my horn and the last bullet in my pouch, and 'twas the act of a boy!" he said; "what mattered it whether he struck the rock living or dead! feeling would soon be over. Uncas, lad, go down to the canoe, and bring up the big horn; it is all the powder we have left, and we shall need it to the last grain, or I am ignorant of the Mingo nature."

The young Mohican complied, leaving the scout turning over the useless contents of his pouch, and shaking the empty horn with renewed discontent. From this unsatisfactory examination, however, he was soon called by a loud and piercing exclamation from Uncas, that sounded, even to the unpracticed ears of Duncan, as the signal of some new and unexpected calamity. Every thought filled with apprehension for the previous treasure he had concealed in the cavern, the young man started to his feet, totally regardless of the hazard he incurred by such an exposure. As if actuated by a common impulse, his movement was imitated by his companions, and, together they rushed down the pass to the friendly chasm, with a rapidity that rendered the scattering fire of their enemies perfectly harmless. The unwonted cry had brought the sisters, together with the wounded David, from their place of refuge; and the whole party, at a single glance, was made acquainted with the nature of the disaster that had disturbed even the practiced stoicism of their youthful Indian protector.

At a short distance from the rock, their little bark was to be seen floating across the eddy, toward the swift current of the river, in a manner which proved that its course was directed by some hidden agent. The instant this unwelcome sight caught the eye of the scout, his rifle was leveled as by instinct, but the barrel gave no answer to the bright sparks of the flint.

"'Tis too late, 'tis too late!" Hawkeye exclaimed, dropping the useless piece in bitter disappointment; "the miscreant has struck the rapid; and had we powder, it could hardly send the lead swifter than he now goes!"

The adventurous Huron raised his head above the shelter of the canoe, and, while it glided swiftly down the stream, he waved his hand, and gave forth the shout, which was the known signal of success. His cry was answered by a yell and a laugh from the woods, as tauntingly exulting as if fifty demons were uttering their blasphemies at the fall of some Christian soul.

"Well may you laugh, ye children of the devil!" said the scout, seating himself on a projection of the rock, and suffering his gun to fall neglected at his feet, "for the three quickest and truest rifles in these woods are no better than so many stalks of mullein, or the last year's horns of a buck!"

"What is to be done?" demanded Duncan, losing the first feeling of disappointment in a more manly desire for exertion; "what will become of us?"

Hawkeye made no other reply than by passing his finger around the crown of his head, in a manner so significant, that none who witnessed the action could mistake its meaning.

"Surely, surely, our case is not so desperate!" exclaimed the youth; "the Hurons are not here; we may make good the caverns, we may oppose their landing."

"With what?" coolly demanded the scout. "The arrows of Uncas, or such tears as women shed! No, no; you are young, and rich, and have friends, and at such an age I know it is hard to die! But," glancing his eyes at the Mohicans, "let us remember we are men without a cross, and let us teach these natives of the forest that white blood can run as freely as red, when the appointed hour is come."

Duncan turned quickly in the direction indicated by the other's eyes, and read a confirmation of his worst apprehensions in the conduct of the Indians. Chingachgook, placing himself in a dignified posture on another fragment of the rock, had already laid aside his knife and tomahawk, and was in the act of taking the eagle's plume from his head, and smoothing the solitary tuft of hair in readiness to perform its last and revolting office. His countenance was composed, though thoughtful, while his dark, gleaming eyes were gradually losing the fierceness of the combat in an expression better suited to the change he expected momentarily to undergo.

"Our case is not, cannot be so hopeless!" said Duncan; "even at this very moment succor may be at hand. I see no enemies! They have sickened of a struggle in which they risk so much with so little prospect of gain!"

"It may be a minute, or it may be an hour, afore the wily sarpents steal upon us, and it is quite in natur' for them to be lying within hearing at this very moment," said Hawkeye; "but come they will, and in such a fashion as will leave us nothing to hope! Chingachgook" – he spoke in Delaware – "my brother, we have fought our last battle together, and the Maquas will triumph in the death of the sage man of the Mohicans, and of the pale face, whose eyes can make night as day, and level the clouds to the mists of the springs!"

"Let the Mingo women go weep over the slain!" returned the Indian, with characteristic pride and unmoved firmness; "the Great Snake of the Mohicans has coiled himself in their wigwams, and has poisoned their triumph with the wailings of children, whose fathers have not returned! Eleven warriors lie hid from the graves of their tribes since the snows have melted, and none will tell where to find them when the tongue of Chingachgook shall be silent! Let them draw the sharpest knife, and whirl the swiftest tomahawk, for their bitterest enemy is in their hands. Uncas, topmost branch of a noble trunk, call on the cowards to hasten, or their hearts will soften, and they will change to women!"

"They look among the fishes for their dead!" returned the low, soft voice of the youthful chieftain; "the Hurons float with the slimy eels! They drop from the oaks like fruit that is ready to be eaten! and the Delawares laugh!"

"Ay, ay," muttered the scout, who had listened to this peculiar burst of the natives with deep attention; "they have warmed their Indian feelings, and they'll soon provoke the Maquas to give them a speedy end. As for me, who am of the whole blood of the whites, it is befitting that I should die as becomes my color, with no words of scoffing in my mouth, and without bitterness at the heart!"

"Why die at all!" said Cora, advancing from the place where natural horror had, until this moment, held her riveted to the rock; "the path is open on every side; fly, then, to the woods, and call on God for succor. Go, brave men, we owe you too much already; let us no longer involve you in our hapless fortunes!"

"You but little know the craft of the Iroquois, lady, if you judge they have left the path open to the woods!" returned Hawkeye, who, however, immediately added in his simplicity, "the down stream current, it is certain, might soon sweep us beyond the reach of their rifles or the sound of their voices."

"Then try the river. Why linger to add to the number of the victims of our merciless enemies?"

"Why," repeated the scout, looking about him proudly; "because it is better for a man to die at peace with himself than to live haunted by an evil conscience! What answer could we give Munro, when he asked us where and how we left his children?"

"Go to him, and say that you left them with a message to hasten to their aid," returned Cora, advancing nigher to the scout in her generous ardor; "that the Hurons bear them into the northern wilds, but that by vigilance and speed they may yet be rescued; and if, after all, it should please heaven that his assistance come too late, bear to him," she continued, her voice gradually lowering, until it seemed nearly choked, "the love, the blessings, the final prayers of his daughters, and bid him not mourn their early fate, but to look forward with humble confidence to the Christian's goal to meet his children." The hard, weather-beaten features of the scout began to work, and when she had ended, he dropped his chin to his hand, like a man musing profoundly on the nature of the proposal.

"There is reason in her words!" at length broke from his compressed and trembling lips; "ay, and they bear the spirit of Christianity; what might be right and proper in a red-skin, may be sinful in a man who has not even a cross in blood to plead for his ignorance. Chingachgook! Uncas! hear you the talk of the dark-eyed woman?"

He now spoke in Delaware to his companions, and his address, though calm and deliberate, seemed very decided. The elder Mohican heard with deep gravity, and appeared to ponder on his words, as though he felt the importance of their import. After a moment of hesitation, he waved his hand in assent, and uttered the English word "Good!" with the peculiar emphasis of his people. Then, replacing his knife and tomahawk in his girdle, the warrior moved silently to the edge of the rock which was most concealed from the banks of the river. Here he paused a moment, pointed significantly to the woods below, and saying a few words in his own language, as if indicating his intended route, he dropped into the water, and sank from before the eyes of the witnesses of his movements.

The scout delayed his departure to speak to the generous girl, whose breathing became lighter as she saw the success of her remonstrance.

"Wisdom is sometimes given to the young, as well as to the old," he said; "and what you have spoken is wise, not to call it by a better word. If you are led into the woods, that is such of you as may be spared for awhile, break the twigs on the bushes as you pass, and make the marks of your trail as broad as you can, when, if mortal eyes can see them, depend on having a friend who will follow to the ends of the 'arth afore he desarts you."

He gave Cora an affectionate shake of the hand, lifted his rifle, and after regarding it a moment with melancholy solicitude, laid it carefully aside, and descended to the place where Chingachgook had just disappeared. For an instant he hung suspended by the rock, and looking about him, with a countenance of peculiar care, he added bitterly, "Had the powder held out, this disgrace could never have befallen!" then, loosening his hold, the water closed above his head, and he also became lost to view.

All eyes now were turned on Uncas, who stood leaning against the ragged rock, in immovable composure. After waiting a short time, Cora pointed down the river, and said:

"Your friends have not been seen, and are now, most probably, in safety. Is it not time for you to follow?"

"Uncas will stay," the young Mohican calmly answered in English.

"To increase the horror of our capture, and to diminish the chances of our release! Go, generous young man," Cora continued, lowering her eyes under the gaze of the Mohican, and perhaps, with an intuitive consciousness of her power; "go to my father, as I have said, and be the most confidential of my messengers. Tell him to trust you with the means to buy the freedom of his daughters. Go! 'tis my wish, 'tis my prayer, that you will go!"

The settled, calm look of the young chief changed to an expression of gloom, but he no longer hesitated. With a noiseless step he crossed the rock, and dropped into the troubled stream. Hardly a breath was drawn by those he left behind, until they caught a glimpse of his head emerging for air, far down the current, when he again sank, and was seen no more.

These sudden and apparently successful experiments had all taken place in a few minutes of that time which had now become so precious. After a last look at Uncas, Cora turned and with a quivering lip, addressed herself to Heyward:

"I have heard of your boasted skill in the water, too, Duncan," she said; "follow, then, the wise example set you by these simple and faithful beings."

"Is such the faith that Cora Munro would exact from her protector?" said the young man, smiling mournfully, but with bitterness.

"This is not a time for idle subtleties and false opinions," she answered; "but a moment when every duty should be equally considered. To us you can be of no further service here, but your precious life may be saved for other and nearer friends."

He made no reply, though his eye fell wistfully on the beautiful form of Alice, who was clinging to his arm with the dependency of an infant.

"Consider," continued Cora, after a pause, during which she seemed to struggle with a pang even more acute than any that her fears had excited, "that the worst to us can be but death; a tribute that all must pay at the good time of God's appointment."

"There are evils worse than death," said Duncan, speaking hoarsely, and as if fretful at her importunity, "but which the presence of one who would die in your behalf may avert."

Cora ceased her entreaties; and veiling her face in her shawl, drew the nearly insensible Alice after her into the deepest recess of the inner cavern.

Chapter Nine

“Be gay securely;
Dispel, my fair, with smiles, the tim’rous
clouds,
That hang on thy clear brow.”
– Death of Agrippina

THE SUDDEN AND ALMOST magical change, from the stirring incidents of the combat to the stillness that now reigned around him, acted on the heated imagination of Heyward like some exciting dream. While all the images and events he had witnessed remained deeply impressed on his memory, he felt a difficulty in persuading him of their truth. Still ignorant of the fate of those who had trusted to the aid of the swift current, he at first listened intently to any signal or sounds of alarm, which might announce the good or evil fortune of their hazardous undertaking. His attention was, however, bestowed in vain; for with the disappearance of Uncas, every sign of the adventurers had been lost, leaving him in total uncertainty of their fate.

In a moment of such painful doubt, Duncan did not hesitate to look around him, without consulting that protection from the rocks which just before had been so necessary to his safety. Every effort, however, to detect the least evidence of the approach of their hidden enemies was as fruitless as the inquiry after his late companions. The wooded banks of the river seemed again deserted by everything possessing animal life. The uproar which had so lately echoed through the vaults of the forest was gone, leaving the rush of the waters to swell and sink on the currents of the air, in the unmingled sweetness of nature. A fish-hawk, which, secure on the topmost branches of a dead pine, had been a distant spectator of the fray, now swooped from his high and ragged perch, and soared, in wide sweeps, above his prey; while a jay, whose noisy voice had been stilled by the hoarser cries of the savages, ventured again to open his discordant throat, as though once more in undisturbed possession of his wild domains. Duncan caught from these natural accompaniments of the solitary scene a glimmering of hope; and he began to rally his faculties to renewed exertions, with something like a reviving confidence of success.

"The Hurons are not to be seen," he said, addressing David, who had by no means recovered from the effects of the stunning blow he had received; "let us conceal ourselves in the cavern, and trust the rest to Providence."

"I remember to have united with two comely maidens, in lifting up our voices in praise and thanksgiving," returned the bewildered singing-master; "since which time I have been visited by a heavy judgment for my sins. I have been mocked with the likeness of sleep, while sounds of discord have rent my ears, such as might manifest the fullness of time, and that nature had forgotten her harmony."

"Poor fellow! thine own period was, in truth, near its accomplishment! But arouse, and come with me; I will lead you where all other sounds but those of your own psalmody shall be excluded."

"There is melody in the fall of the cataract, and the rushing of many waters is sweet to the senses!" said David, pressing his hand confusedly on his brow. "Is not the air yet filled with shrieks and cries, as though the departed spirits of the damned – "

"Not now, not now," interrupted the impatient Heyward, "they have ceased, and they who raised them, I trust in God, they are gone, too! everything but the water is still and at peace; in, then, where you may create those sounds you love so well to hear."

David smiled sadly, though not without a momentary gleam of pleasure, at this allusion to his beloved vocation. He no longer hesitated to be led to a spot which promised such unalloyed gratification to his wearied senses; and leaning on the arm of his companion, he entered the narrow mouth of the cave. Duncan seized a pile of the sassafras, which he drew before the passage, studiously concealing every appearance of an aperture. Within this fragile barrier he arranged the blankets abandoned by the foresters, darkening the inner extremity of the cavern, while its outer received a chastened light from the narrow ravine, through which one arm of the river rushed to form the junction with its sister branch a few rods below.

"I like not the principle of the natives, which teaches them to submit without a struggle, in emergencies that appear desperate," he said, while busied in this employment; "our own maxim, which says, 'while life remains there is hope', is more consoling, and better suited to a soldier's temperament. To you, Cora, I will urge no words of idle encouragement; your own fortitude and undisturbed reason will teach you all that may become your sex; but cannot we dry the tears of that trembling weeper on your bosom?"

"I am calmer, Duncan," said Alice, raising herself from the arms of her sister, and forcing an appearance of composure through her tears; "much calmer, now. Surely, in this hidden spot we are safe, we are secret, free from injury; we will hope everything from those generous men who have risked so much already in our behalf."

"Now does our gentle Alice speak like a daughter of Munro!" said Heyward, pausing to press her hand as he passed toward the outer entrance of the cavern. "With two such examples of courage before him, a man would be ashamed to prove other than a hero." He then seated himself in the center of the cavern, grasping his remaining pistol with a hand convulsively clenched, while his contracted and frowning eye announced the sullen desperation of his purpose. "The Hurons, if they come, may not gain our position so easily as they think," he slowly muttered; and propping his head back against the rock, he seemed to await the result in patience, though his gaze was unceasingly bent on the open avenue to their place of retreat.

With the last sound of his voice, a deep, a long, and almost breathless silence succeeded. The fresh air of the morning had penetrated the recess, and its influence was gradually felt on the spirits of its inmates. As minute after minute passed by, leaving them in undisturbed security, the insinuating feeling of hope was gradually gaining possession of every bosom, though each one felt reluctant to give utterance to expectations that the next moment might so fearfully destroy.

David alone formed an exception to these varying emotions. A gleam of light from the opening crossed his wan countenance, and fell upon the pages of the little volume, whose leaves he was again occupied in turning, as if searching for some song more fitted to their condition than any that had yet met their eye. He was, most probably, acting all this time under a confused recollection of the promised consolation of Duncan. At length, it would seem, his patient industry found its reward; for, without explanation or apology, he pronounced aloud the words "Isle of Wight," drew a long, sweet sound from his pitch-pipe, and then ran through the preliminary modulations of the air whose name he had just mentioned, with the sweeter tones of his own musical voice.

"May not this prove dangerous?" asked

Cora, glancing her dark eye at Major Heyward.

"Poor fellow! his voice is too feeble to be heard above the din of the falls," was the answer; "beside, the cavern will prove his friend. Let him indulge his passions since it may be done without hazard."

"Isle of Wight!" repeated David, looking about him with that dignity with which he had long been wont to silence the whispering echoes of his school; "'tis a brave tune, and set to solemn words! let it be sung with meet respect!"

After allowing a moment of stillness to enforce his discipline, the voice of the singer was heard, in low, murmuring syllables, gradually stealing on the ear, until it filled the narrow vault with sounds rendered trebly thrilling by the feeble and tremulous utterance produced by his debility. The melody, which no weakness could destroy, gradually wrought its sweet influence on the senses of those who heard it. It even prevailed over the miserable travesty of the song of David which the singer had selected from a volume of similar effusions, and caused the sense to be forgotten in the insinuating harmony of the sounds. Alice unconsciously dried her tears, and bent her melting eyes on the pallid features of Gamut, with an expression of chastened delight that she neither affected or wished to conceal. Cora bestowed an approving smile on the pious efforts of the namesake of the Jewish prince, and Heyward soon turned his steady, stern look from the outlet of the cavern, to fasten it, with a milder character, on the face of David, or to meet the wandering beams which at moments strayed from the humid eyes of Alice. The open sympathy of the listeners stirred the spirit of the votary of music, whose voice regained its richness and volume, without losing that touching softness which proved its secret charm. Exerting his renovated powers to their utmost, he was yet filling the arches of the cave with long and full tones, when a yell burst into the air without, that instantly stilled his pious strains, choking his voice suddenly, as though his heart had literally bounded into the passage of his throat.

"We are lost!" exclaimed Alice, throwing herself into the arms of Cora.

"Not yet, not yet," returned the agitated but undaunted Heyward: "the sound came from the center of the island, and it has been produced by the sight of their dead companions. We are not yet discovered, and there is still hope."

Faint and almost despairing as was the prospect of escape, the words of Duncan were not thrown away, for it awakened the powers of the sisters in such a manner that they awaited the results in silence. A second yell soon followed the first, when a rush of voices was heard pouring down the island, from its upper to its lower extremity, until they reached the naked rock above the caverns, where, after a shout of savage triumph, the air continued full of horrible cries and screams, such as man alone can utter, and he only when in a state of the fiercest barbarity.

The sounds quickly spread around them in every direction. Some called to their fellows from the water's edge, and were answered from the heights above. Cries were heard in the startling vicinity of the chasm between the two caves, which mingled with hoarser yells that arose out of the abyss of the deep ravine. In short, so rapidly had the savage sounds diffused themselves over the barren rock, that it was not difficult for the anxious listeners to imagine they could be heard beneath, as in truth they were above on every side of them.

In the midst of this tumult, a triumphant yell was raised within a few yards of the hidden entrance to the cave. Heyward abandoned every hope, with the belief it was the signal that they were discovered. Again the impression passed away, as he heard the voices collect near the spot where the white man had so reluctantly abandoned his rifle. Amid the jargon of Indian dialects that he now plainly heard, it was easy to distinguish not only words, but sentences, in the patois of the Canadas. A burst of voices had shouted simultaneously, “La Longue Carabine!” causing the opposite woods to re-echo with a name which, Heyward well remembered, had been given by his enemies to a celebrated hunter and scout of the English camp, and who, he now learned for the first time, had been his late companion.

“La Longue Carabine! La Longue Carabine!” passed from mouth to mouth, until the whole band appeared to be collected around a trophy which would seem to announce the death of its formidable owner. After a vociferous consultation, which was, at times, deafened by bursts of savage joy, they again separated, filling the air with the name of a foe, whose body, Heywood could collect from their expressions, they hoped to find concealed in some crevice of the island.

"Now," he whispered to the trembling sisters, "now is the moment of uncertainty! if our place of retreat escape this scrutiny, we are still safe! In every event, we are assured, by what has fallen from our enemies, that our friends have escaped, and in two short hours we may look for succor from Webb."

There were now a few minutes of fearful stillness, during which Heyward well knew that the savages conducted their search with greater vigilance and method. More than once he could distinguish their footsteps, as they brushed the sassafras, causing the faded leaves to rustle, and the branches to snap. At length, the pile yielded a little, a corner of a blanket fell, and a faint ray of light gleamed into the inner part of the cave. Cora folded Alice to her bosom in agony, and Duncan sprang to his feet. A shout was at that moment heard, as if issuing from the center of the rock, announcing that the neighboring cavern had at length been entered. In a minute, the number and loudness of the voices indicated that the whole party was collected in and around that secret place.

As the inner passages to the two caves were so close to each other, Duncan, believing that escape was no longer possible, passed David and the sisters, to place himself between the latter and the first onset of the terrible meeting. Grown desperate by his situation, he drew nigh the slight barrier which separated him only by a few feet from his relentless pursuers, and placing his face to the casual opening, he even looked out with a sort of desperate indifference, on their movements.

Within reach of his arm was the brawny shoulder of a gigantic Indian, whose deep and authoritative voice appeared to give directions to the proceedings of his fellows. Beyond him again, Duncan could look into the vault opposite, which was filled with savages, upturning and rifling the humble furniture of the scout. The wound of David had dyed the leaves of sassafras with a color that the native well knew as anticipating the season. Over this sign of their success, they sent up a howl, like an opening from so many hounds who had recovered a lost trail. After this yell of victory, they tore up the fragrant bed of the cavern, and bore the branches into the chasm, scattering the boughs, as if they suspected them of concealing the person of the man they had so long hated and feared. One fierce and wild-looking warrior approached the chief, bearing a load of the brush, and pointing exultingly to the deep red stains with which it was sprinkled, uttered his joy in Indian yells, whose meaning Heyward was only enabled to comprehend by the frequent repetition of the name "La Longue Carabine!" When his triumph had ceased, he cast the brush on the slight heap Duncan had made before the entrance of the second cavern, and closed the view. His example was followed by others, who, as they drew the branches from the cave of the scout, threw them into one pile, adding, unconsciously, to the security of those they sought. The very slightness of the defense was its chief merit, for no one thought of disturbing a mass of brush, which all of them believed, in that moment of hurry and confusion, had been accidentally raised by the hands of their own party.

As the blankets yielded before the outward pressure, and the branches settled in the fissure of the rock by their own weight, forming a compact body, Duncan once more breathed freely. With a light step and lighter heart, he returned to the center of the cave, and took the place he had left, where he could command a view of the opening next the river. While he was in the act of making this movement, the Indians, as if changing their purpose by a common impulse, broke away from the chasm in a body, and were heard rushing up the island again, toward the point whence they had originally descended. Here another wailing cry betrayed that they were again collected around the bodies of their dead comrades.

Duncan now ventured to look at his companions; for, during the most critical moments of their danger, he had been apprehensive that the anxiety of his countenance might communicate some additional alarm to those who were so little able to sustain it.

"They are gone, Cora!" he whispered; "Alice, they are returned whence they came, and we are saved! To Heaven, that has alone delivered us from the grasp of so merciless an enemy, be all the praise!"

"Then to Heaven will I return my thanks!" exclaimed the younger sister, rising from the encircling arm of Cora, and casting herself with enthusiastic gratitude on the naked rock; "to that Heaven who has spared the tears of a gray-headed father;

has saved the lives of those I so much love."

Both Heyward and the more temperate Cora witnessed the act of involuntary emotion with powerful sympathy, the former secretly believing that piety had never worn a form so lovely as it had now assumed in the youthful person of Alice. Her eyes were radiant with the glow of grateful feelings; the flush of her beauty was again seated on her cheeks, and her whole soul seemed ready and anxious to pour out its thanksgivings through the medium of her eloquent features. But when her lips moved, the words they should have uttered appeared frozen by some new and sudden chill. Her bloom gave place to the paleness of death; her soft and melting eyes grew hard, and seemed contracting with horror; while those hands, which she had raised, clasped in each other, toward heaven, dropped in horizontal lines before her, the fingers pointed forward in convulsed motion. Heyward turned the instant she gave a direction to his suspicions, and peering just above the ledge which formed the threshold of the open outlet of the cavern, he beheld the malignant, fierce and savage features of Le Renard Subtil.

In that moment of surprise, the self-possession of Heyward did not desert him. He observed by the vacant expression of the Indian's countenance, that his eye, accustomed to the open air had not yet been able to penetrate the dusky light which pervaded the depth of the cavern. He had even thought of retreating beyond a curvature in the natural wall, which might still conceal him and his companions, when by the sudden gleam of intelligence that shot across the features of the savage, he saw it was too late, and that they were betrayed.

The look of exultation and brutal triumph which announced this terrible truth was irresistibly irritating. Forgetful of everything but the impulses of his hot blood, Duncan leveled his pistol and fired. The report of the weapon made the cavern bellow like an eruption from a volcano; and when the smoke it vomited had been driven away before the current of air which issued from the ravine the place so lately occupied by the features of his treacherous guide was vacant. Rushing to the outlet, Heyward caught a glimpse of his dark figure stealing around a low and narrow ledge, which soon hid him entirely from sight.

Among the savages a frightful stillness succeeded the explosion, which had just been heard bursting from the bowels of the rock. But when Le Renard raised his voice in a long and intelligible whoop, it was answered by a spontaneous yell from the mouth of every Indian within hearing of the sound.

The clamorous noises again rushed down the island; and before Duncan had time to recover from the shock, his feeble barrier of brush was scattered to the winds, the cavern was entered at both its extremities, and he and his companions were dragged from their shelter and borne into the day, where they stood surrounded by the whole band of the triumphant Hurons.

Chapter Ten

"I fear we shall outsleep the coming morn
As much as we this night have overwatched!"
– Midsummer Night's Dream

THE INSTANT THE SHOCK of this sudden misfortune had abated, Duncan began to make his observations on the appearance and proceedings of their captors. Contrary to the usages of the natives in the wantonness of their success they had respected, not only the persons of the trembling sisters, but his own. The rich ornaments of his military attire had indeed been repeatedly handled by different individuals of the tribes with eyes expressing a savage longing to possess the baubles; but before the customary violence could be resorted to, a mandate in the authoritative voice of the large warrior, already mentioned, stayed the uplifted hand, and convinced Heyward that they were to be reserved for some object of particular moment.

While, however, these manifestations of weakness were exhibited by the young and vain of the party, the more experienced warriors continued their search throughout both caverns, with an activity that denoted they were far from being satisfied with those fruits of their conquest which had already been brought to light. Unable to discover any new victim, these diligent workers of vengeance soon approached their male prisoners, pronouncing the name "La Longue Carabine," with a fierceness that could not be easily mistaken. Duncan affected not to comprehend the meaning of their repeated and violent interrogatories, while his companion was spared the effort of a similar deception by his ignorance of French. Wearied at length by their importunities, and apprehensive of irritating his captors by too stubborn a silence, the former looked about him in quest of Magua, who might interpret his answers to questions which were at each moment becoming more earnest and threatening.

The conduct of this savage had formed a solitary exception to that of all his fellows. While the others were busily occupied in seeking to gratify their childish passion for finery, by plundering even the miserable effects of the scout, or had been searching with such bloodthirsty vengeance in their looks for their absent owner, Le Renard had stood at a little distance from the prisoners, with a demeanor so quiet and satisfied, as to betray that he had already effected the grand purpose of his treachery. When the eyes of Heyward first met those of his recent guide, he turned them away in horror at the sinister though calm look he encountered. Conquering his disgust, however, he was able, with an averted face, to address his successful enemy.

"Le Renard Subtil is too much of a warrior," said the reluctant Heyward, "to refuse telling an unarmed man what his conquerors say."

"They ask for the hunter who knows the paths through the woods," returned Magua, in his broken English, laying his hand, at the same time, with a ferocious smile, on the bundle of leaves with which a wound on his own shoulder was bandaged. "'La Longue Carabine'! His rifle is good, and his eye never shut; but, like the short gun of the white chief, it is nothing against the life of Le Subtil."

"Le Renard is too brave to remember the hurts received in war, or the hands that gave them."

"Was it war, when the tired Indian rested at the sugartree to taste his corn! who filled the bushes with creeping enemies! who drew the knife, whose tongue was peace, while his heart was colored with blood! Did Magua say that the hatchet was out of the ground, and that his hand had dug it up?"

As Duncan dared not retort upon his accuser by reminding him of his own premeditated treachery, and disdained to deprecate his resentment by any words of apology, he remained silent. Magua seemed also content to rest the controversy as well as all further communication there, for he resumed the leaning attitude against the rock from which, in momentary energy, he had arisen. But the cry of "La Longue Carabine" was renewed the instant the impatient savages perceived that the short dialogue was ended.

"You hear," said Magua, with stubborn indifference: "the red Hurons call for the life of 'The Long Rifle', or they will have the blood of him that keep him hid!"

"He is gone – escaped; he is far beyond

their reach."

Renard smiled with cold contempt, as he answered:

"When the white man dies, he thinks he is at peace; but the red men know how to torture even the ghosts of their enemies. Where is his body? Let the Hurons see his scalp."

"He is not dead, but escaped."

Magua shook his head incredulously.

"Is he a bird, to spread his wings; or is he a fish, to swim without air! The white chief read in his books, and he believes the Hurons are fools!"

"Though no fish, 'The Long Rifle' can swim. He floated down the stream when the powder was all burned, and when the eyes of the Hurons were behind a cloud."

"And why did the white chief stay?" demanded the still incredulous Indian. "Is he a stone that goes to the bottom, or does the scalp burn his head?"

"That I am not stone, your dead comrade,

who fell into the falls, might answer, were the life still in him," said the provoked young man, using, in his anger, that boastful language which was most likely to excite the admiration of an Indian. "The white man thinks none but cowards desert their women."

Magua muttered a few words, inaudibly, between his teeth, before he continued, aloud:

"Can the Delawares swim, too, as well as crawl in the bushes? Where is 'Le Gros Serpent'?"

Duncan, who perceived by the use of these Canadian appellations, that his late companions were much better known to his enemies than to himself, answered, reluctantly: "He also is gone down with the water."

"'Le Cerf Agile' is not here?"

"I know not whom you call 'The Nimble Deer'," said Duncan gladly profiting by any excuse to create delay.

"Uncas," returned Magua, pronouncing the Delaware name with even greater difficulty than he spoke his English words. "'Bounding Elk' is what the white man says, when he calls to the young Mohican."

"Here is some confusion in names between us, Le Renard," said Duncan, hoping to provoke a discussion. "Daim is the French for deer, and cerf for stag; elan is the true term, when one would speak of an elk."

"Yes," muttered the Indian, in his native tongue; "the pale faces are prattling women! they have two words for each thing, while a red-skin will make the sound of his voice speak to him." Then, changing his language, he continued, adhering to the imperfect nomenclature of his provincial instructors. "The deer is swift, but weak; the elk is swift, but strong; and the son of 'Le Serpent' is 'Le Cerf Agile.' Has he leaped the river to the woods?"

"If you mean the younger Delaware, he,

too, has gone down with the water."

As there was nothing improbable to an Indian in the manner of the escape, Magua admitted the truth of what he had heard, with a readiness that afforded additional evidence how little he would prize such worthless captives. With his companions, however, the feeling was manifestly different.

The Hurons had awaited the result of this short dialogue with characteristic patience, and with a silence that increased until there was a general stillness in the band. When Heyward ceased to speak, they turned their eyes, as one man, on Magua, demanding, in this expressive manner, an explanation of what had been said. Their interpreter pointed to the river, and made them acquainted with the result, as much by the action as by the few words he uttered. When the fact was generally understood, the savages raised a frightful yell, which declared the extent of their disappointment. Some ran furiously to the water's edge, beating the air with frantic gestures, while others spat upon the element, to resent the supposed treason it had committed against their acknowledged rights as conquerors. A few, and they not the least powerful and terrific of the band, threw lowering looks, in which the fiercest passion was only tempered by habitual self-command, at those captives who still remained in their power, while one or two even gave vent to their malignant feelings by the most menacing gestures, against which neither the sex nor the beauty of the sisters was any protection. The young soldier made a desperate but fruitless effort to spring to the side of Alice, when he saw the dark hand of a savage twisted in the rich tresses which were flowing in volumes over her shoulders, while a knife was passed around the head from which they fell, as if to denote the horrid manner in which it was about to be robbed of its beautiful ornament. But his hands were bound; and at the first movement he made, he felt the grasp of the powerful Indian who directed the band, pressing his shoulder like a vise. Immediately conscious how unavailing any struggle against such an overwhelming force must prove, he submitted to his fate, encouraging his gentle companions by a few low and tender assurances, that the natives seldom failed to threaten more than they performed.

But while Duncan resorted to these words of consolation to quiet the apprehensions of the sisters, he was not so weak as to deceive himself. He well knew that the authority of an Indian chief was so little conventional, that it was oftener maintained by physical superiority than by any moral supremacy he might possess. The danger was, therefore, magnified exactly in proportion to the number of the savage spirits by which they were surrounded. The most positive mandate from him who seemed the acknowledged leader, was liable to be violated at each moment by any rash hand that might choose to sacrifice a victim to the manes of some dead friend or relative. While, therefore, he sustained an outward appearance of calmness and fortitude, his heart leaped into his throat, whenever any of their fierce captors drew nearer than common to the helpless sisters, or fastened one of their sullen, wandering looks on those fragile forms which were so little able to resist the slightest assault.

His apprehensions were, however, greatly relieved, when he saw that the leader had summoned his warriors to himself in counsel. Their deliberations were short, and it would seem, by the silence of most of the party, the decision unanimous. By the frequency with which the few speakers pointed in the direction of the encampment of Webb, it was apparent they dreaded the approach of danger from that quarter. This consideration probably hastened their determination, and quickened the subsequent movements.

Chapter Ten

During his short conference, Heyward, finding a respite from his gravest fears, had leisure to admire the cautious manner in which the Hurons had made their approaches, even after hostilities had ceased.

It has already been stated that the upper half of the island was a naked rock, and destitute of any other defenses than a few scattered logs of driftwood. They had selected this point to make their descent, having borne the canoe through the wood around the cataract for that purpose. Placing their arms in the little vessel a dozen men clinging to its sides had trusted themselves to the direction of the canoe, which was controlled by two of the most skillful warriors, in attitudes that enabled them to command a view of the dangerous passage. Favored by this arrangement, they touched the head of the island at that point which had proved so fatal to their first adventurers, but with the advantages of superior numbers, and the possession of firearms. That such had been the manner of their descent was rendered quite apparent to Duncan; for they now bore the light bark from the upper end of the rock, and placed it in the water, near the mouth of the outer cavern. As soon as this change was made, the leader made signs to the prisoners to descend and enter.

As resistance was impossible, and remonstrance useless, Heyward set the example of submission, by leading the way into the canoe, where he was soon seated with the sisters and the still wondering David. Notwithstanding the Hurons were necessarily ignorant of the little channels among the eddies and rapids of the stream, they knew the common signs of such a navigation too well to commit any material blunder. When the pilot chosen for the task of guiding the canoe had taken his station, the whole band plunged again into the river, the vessel glided down the current, and in a few moments the captives found themselves on the south bank of the stream, nearly opposite to the point where they had struck it the preceding evening.

Here was held another short but earnest consultation, during which the horses, to whose panic their owners ascribed their heaviest misfortune, were led from the cover of the woods, and brought to the sheltered spot. The band now divided. The great chief, so often mentioned, mounting the charger of Heyward, led the way directly across the river, followed by most of his people, and disappeared in the woods, leaving the prisoners in charge of six savages, at whose head was Le Renard Subtil. Duncan witnessed all their movements with renewed uneasiness.

He had been fond of believing, from the uncommon forbearance of the savages, that he was reserved as a prisoner to be delivered to Montcalm. As the thoughts of those who are in misery seldom slumber, and the invention is never more lively than when it is stimulated by hope, however feeble and remote, he had even imagined that the parental feelings of Munro were to be made instrumental in seducing him from his duty to the king. For though the French commander bore a high character for courage and enterprise, he was also thought to be expert in those political practises which do not always respect the nicer obligations of morality, and which so generally disgraced the European diplomacy of that period.

All those busy and ingenious speculations were now annihilated by the conduct of his captors. That portion of the band who had followed the huge warrior took the route toward the foot of the Horican, and no other expectation was left for himself and companions, than that they were to be retained as hopeless captives by their savage conquerors. Anxious to know the worst, and willing, in such an emergency, to try the potency of gold he overcame his reluctance to speak to Magua. Addressing himself to his former guide, who had now assumed the authority and manner of one who was to direct the future movements of the party, he said, in tones as friendly and confiding as he could assume:

"I would speak to Magua, what is fit only for so great a chief to hear."

The Indian turned his eyes on the young soldier scornfully, as he answered:

"Speak; trees have no ears."

"But the red Hurons are not deaf; and counsel that is fit for the great men of a nation would make the young warriors drunk. If Magua will not listen, the officer of the king knows how to be silent."

The savage spoke carelessly to his comrades, who were busied, after their awkward manner, in preparing the horses for the reception of the sisters, and moved a little to one side, whither by a cautious gesture he induced Heyward to follow.

"Now, speak," he said; "if the words are such as Magua should hear."

"Le Renard Subtil has proved himself worthy of the honorable name given to him by his Canada fathers," commenced Heyward; "I see his wisdom, and all that he has done for us, and shall remember it when the hour to reward him arrives. Yes! Renard has proved that he is not only a great chief in council, but one who knows how to deceive his enemies!"

"What has Renard done?" coldly demanded the Indian.

"What! has he not seen that the woods were filled with outlying parties of the enemies, and that the serpent could not steal through them without being seen? Then, did he not lose his path to blind the eyes of the Hurons? Did he not pretend to go back to his tribe, who had treated him ill, and driven him from their wigwams like a dog? And when he saw what he wished to do, did we not aid him, by making a false face, that the Hurons might think the white man believed that his friend was his enemy? Is not all this true? And when Le Subtil had shut the eyes and stopped the ears of his nation by his wisdom, did they not forget that they had once done him wrong, and forced him to flee to the Mohawks? And did they not leave him on the south side of the river, with their prisoners, while they have gone foolishly on the north? Does not Renard mean to turn like a fox on his footsteps, and to carry to the rich and gray-headed Scotchman his daughters? Yes, Magua, I see it all, and I have already been thinking how so much wisdom and honesty should be repaid. First, the chief of William Henry will give as a great chief should for such a service. The medal[13] of Magua will no longer be of tin, but of beaten gold; his horn will run over with powder; dollars will be as plenty in his pouch as pebbles on the shore of Horican; and the deer will lick his hand, for they will know it to be vain to fly from the rifle he will carry! As for myself, I know not how to exceed the gratitude of the Scotchman, but I – yes, I will – "

"What will the young chief, who comes from toward the sun, give?" demanded the Huron, observing that Heyward hesitated in his desire to end the enumeration of benefits with that which might form the climax of an Indian's wishes.

"He will make the fire-water from the islands

---

13 It has long been a practice with the whites to conciliate the important men of the Indians by presenting medals, which are worn in the place of their own rude ornaments. Those given by the English generally bear the impression of the reigning king, and those given by the Americans that of the president.

in the salt lake flow before the wigwam of Magua, until the heart of the Indian shall be lighter than the feathers of the humming-bird, and his breath sweeter than the wild honeysuckle."

Le Renard had listened gravely as Heyward slowly proceeded in this subtle speech. When the young man mentioned the artifice he supposed the Indian to have practised on his own nation, the countenance of the listener was veiled in an expression of cautious gravity. At the allusion to the injury which Duncan affected to believe had driven the Huron from his native tribe, a gleam of such ungovernable ferocity flashed from the other's eyes, as induced the adventurous speaker to believe he had struck the proper chord. And by the time he reached the part where he so artfully blended the thirst of vengeance with the desire of gain, he had, at least, obtained a command of the deepest attention of the savage. The question put by Le Renard had been calm, and with all the dignity of an Indian; but it was quite apparent, by the thoughtful expression of the listener's countenance, that the answer was most cunningly devised. The Huron mused a few moments, and then laying his hand on the rude bandages of his wounded shoulder, he said, with some energy:

"Do friends make such marks?"

"Would 'La Longue Carbine' cut one so slight on an enemy?"

"Do the Delawares crawl upon those they love like snakes, twisting themselves to strike?"

"Would 'Le Gros Serpent' have been heard by the ears of one he wished to be deaf?"

"Does the white chief burn his powder in the faces of his brothers?"

"Does he ever miss his aim, when seriously bent to kill?" returned Duncan, smiling with well acted sincerity.

Another long and deliberate pause succeeded these sententious questions and ready replies. Duncan saw that the Indian hesitated. In order to complete his victory, he was in the act of recommencing the enumeration of the rewards, when Magua made an expressive gesture and said:

"Enough; Le Renard is a wise chief, and what he does will be seen. Go, and keep the mouth shut. When Magua speaks, it will be the time to answer."

Heyward, perceiving that the eyes of his companion were warily fastened on the rest of the band, fell back immediately, in order to avoid the appearance of any suspicious confederacy with their leader. Magua approached the horses, and affected to be well pleased with the diligence and ingenuity of his comrades. He then signed to Heyward to assist the sisters into the saddles, for he seldom deigned to use the English tongue, unless urged by some motive of more than usual moment.

There was no longer any plausible pretext for delay; and Duncan was obliged, however reluctantly, to comply. As he performed this office, he whispered his reviving hopes in the ears of the trembling females, who, through dread of encountering the savage countenances of their captors, seldom raised their eyes from the ground. The mare of David had been taken with the followers of the large chief; in consequence, its owner, as well as Duncan, was compelled to journey on foot. The latter did not, however, so much regret this circumstance, as it might enable him to retard the speed of the party; for he still turned his longing looks in the direction of Fort Edward, in the vain expectation of catching some sound from that quarter of the forest, which might denote the approach of succor. When all were prepared, Magua made the signal to proceed, advancing in front to lead the party in person. Next followed David, who was gradually coming to a true sense of his condition, as the effects of the wound became less and less apparent. The sisters rode in his rear, with Heyward at their side, while the Indians flanked the party, and brought up the close of the march, with a caution that seemed never to tire.

In this manner they proceeded in uninterrupted silence, except when Heyward addressed some solitary word of comfort to the females, or David gave vent to the moanings of his spirit, in piteous exclamations, which he intended should express the humility of resignation. Their direction lay toward the south, and in a course nearly opposite to the road to William Henry. Notwithstanding this apparent adherence in Magua to the original determination of his conquerors, Heyward could not believe his tempting bait was so soon forgotten; and he knew the windings of an Indian's path too well to suppose that its apparent course led directly to its object, when artifice was at all necessary. Mile after mile was, however, passed through the boundless woods, in this painful manner, without any prospect of a termination to their journey. Heyward watched the sun, as he darted his meridian rays through the branches of the trees, and pined for the moment when the policy of Magua should change their route to one more favorable to his hopes. Sometimes he fancied the wary savage, despairing of passing the army of Montcalm in safety, was holding his way toward a well-known border settlement, where a distinguished officer of the crown, and a favored friend of the Six Nations, held his large possessions, as well as his usual residence. To be delivered into the hands of Sir William Johnson was far preferable to being led into the wilds of Canada; but in order to effect even the former, it would be necessary to traverse the forest for many weary leagues, each step of which was carrying him further from the scene of the war, and, consequently, from the post, not only of honor, but of duty.

Cora alone remembered the parting injunctions of the scout, and whenever an opportunity offered, she stretched forth her arm to bend aside the twigs that met her hands. But the vigilance of the Indians rendered this act of precaution both difficult and dangerous. She was often defeated in her purpose, by encountering their watchful eyes, when it became necessary to feign an alarm she did not feel, and occupy the limb by some gesture of feminine apprehension. Once, and once only, was she completely successful; when she broke down the bough of a large sumach, and by a sudden thought, let her glove fall at the same instant. This sign, intended for those that might follow, was observed by one of her conductors, who restored the glove, broke the remaining branches of the bush in such a manner that it appeared to proceed from the struggling of some beast in its branches, and then laid his hand on his tomahawk, with a look so significant, that it put an effectual end to these stolen memorials of their passage.

As there were horses, to leave the prints of their footsteps, in both bands of the Indians, this interruption cut off any probable hopes of assistance being conveyed through the means of their trail.

Heyward would have ventured a remonstrance had there been anything encouraging in the gloomy reserve of Magua. But the savage, during all this time, seldom turned to look at his followers, and never spoke. With the sun for his only guide, or aided by such blind marks as are only known to the sagacity of a native, he held his way along the barrens of pine, through occasional little fertile vales, across brooks and rivulets, and over undulating hills, with the accuracy of instinct, and nearly with the directness of a bird. He never seemed to hesitate. Whether the path was hardly distinguishable, whether it disappeared, or whether it lay beaten and plain before him, made no sensible difference in his speed or certainty. It seemed as if fatigue could not affect him. Whenever the eyes of the wearied travelers rose from the decayed leaves over which they trod, his dark form was to be seen glancing among the stems of the trees in front, his head immovably fastened in a forward position, with the light plume on his crest fluttering in a current of air, made solely by the swiftness of his own motion.

But all this diligence and speed were not without an object. After crossing a low vale, through which a gushing brook meandered, he suddenly ascended a hill, so steep and difficult of ascent, that the sisters were compelled to alight in order to follow. When the summit was gained, they found themselves on a level spot, but thinly covered with trees, under one of which Magua had thrown his dark form, as if willing and ready to seek that rest which was so much needed by the whole party.

Chapter Eleven

> **"Cursed be my tribe If I forgive him."**
> **– Shylock**

THE INDIAN HAD SELECTED for this desirable purpose one of those steep, pyramidal hills, which bear a strong resemblance to artificial mounds, and which so frequently occur in the valleys of America. The one in question was high and precipitous; its top flattened, as usual; but with one of its sides more than ordinarily irregular. It possessed no other apparent advantage for a resting place, than in its elevation and form, which might render defense easy, and surprise nearly impossible. As Heyward, however, no longer expected that rescue which time and distance now rendered so improbable, he regarded these little peculiarities with an eye devoid of interest, devoting himself entirely to the comfort and condolence of his feebler companions. The Narragansetts were suffered to browse on the branches of the trees and shrubs that were thinly scattered over the summit of the hill, while the remains of their provisions were spread under the shade of a beech, that stretched its horizontal limbs like a canopy above them.

Notwithstanding the swiftness of their flight, one of the Indians had found an opportunity to strike a straggling fawn with an arrow, and had borne the more preferable fragments of the victim, patiently on his shoulders, to the stopping place. Without any aid from the science of cookery, he was immediately employed, in common with his fellows, in gorging himself with this digestible sustenance. Magua alone sat apart, without participating in the revolting meal, and apparently buried in the deepest thought.

This abstinence, so remarkable in an Indian, when he possessed the means of satisfying hunger, at length attracted the notice of Heyward. The young man willingly believed that the Huron deliberated on the most eligible manner of eluding the vigilance of his associates. With a view to assist his plans by any suggestion of his own, and to strengthen the temptation, he left the beech, and straggled, as if without an object, to the spot where Le Renard was seated.

"Has not Magua kept the sun in his face long enough to escape all danger from the Canadians?" he asked, as though no longer doubtful of the good intelligence established between them; "and will not the chief of William Henry be better pleased to see his daughters before another night may have hardened his heart to their loss, to make him less liberal in his reward?"

"Do the pale faces love their children less in the morning than at night?" asked the Indian, coldly.

"By no means," returned Heyward, anxious to recall his error, if he had made one; "the white man may, and does often, forget the burial place of his fathers; he sometimes ceases to remember those he should love, and has promised to cherish; but the affection of a parent for his child is never permitted to die."

"And is the heart of the white-headed chief soft, and will he think of the babes that his squaws have given him? He is hard on his warriors and his eyes are made of stone?"

"He is severe to the idle and wicked, but to the sober and deserving he is a leader, both just and humane. I have known many fond and tender parents, but never have I seen a man whose heart was softer toward his child. You have seen the gray-head in front of his warriors, Magua; but I have seen his eyes swimming in water, when he spoke of those children who are now in your power!"

Heyward paused, for he knew not how to construe the remarkable expression that gleamed across the swarthy features of the attentive Indian. At first it seemed as if the remembrance of the promised reward grew vivid in his mind, while he listened to the sources of parental feeling which were to assure its possession; but, as Duncan proceeded, the expression of joy became so fiercely malignant that it was impossible not to apprehend it proceeded from some passion more sinister than avarice.

"Go," said the Huron, suppressing the alarming exhibition in an instant, in a death-like calmness of countenance; "go to the dark-haired daughter, and say, 'Magua waits to speak' The father will remember what the child promises."

Duncan, who interpreted this speech to

express a wish for some additional pledge that the promised gifts should not be withheld, slowly and reluctantly repaired to the place where the sisters were now resting from their fatigue, to communicate its purport to Cora.

"You understand the nature of an Indian's wishes," he concluded, as he led her toward the place where she was expected, "and must be prodigal of your offers of powder and blankets. Ardent spirits are, however, the most prized by such as he; nor would it be amiss to add some boon from your own hand, with that grace you so well know how to practise. Remember, Cora, that on your presence of mind and ingenuity, even your life, as well as that of Alice, may in some measure depend."

"Heyward, and yours!"

"Mine is of little moment; it is already sold to my king, and is a prize to be seized by any enemy who may possess the power. I have no father to expect me, and but few friends to lament a fate which I have courted with the insatiable longings of youth after distinction. But hush! we approach the Indian. Magua, the lady with whom you wish to speak, is here."

The Indian rose slowly from his seat, and stood for near a minute silent and motionless. He then signed with his hand for Heyward to retire, saying, coldly:

"When the Huron talks to the women, his tribe shut their ears."

Duncan, still lingering, as if refusing to comply, Cora said, with a calm smile:

"You hear, Heyward, and delicacy at least should urge you to retire. Go to Alice, and comfort her with our reviving prospects."

She waited until he had departed, and then turning to the native, with the dignity of her sex in her voice and manner, she added: "What would Le Renard say to the daughter of Munro?"

"Listen," said the Indian, laying his hand firmly upon her arm, as if willing to draw her utmost attention to his words; a movement that Cora as firmly but quietly repulsed, by extricating the limb from his grasp: "Magua was born a chief and a warrior among the red Hurons of the lakes; he saw the suns of twenty summers make the snows of twenty winters run off in the streams before he saw a pale face; and he was happy! Then his Canada fathers came into the woods, and taught him to drink the fire-water, and he became a rascal. The Hurons drove him from the graves of his fathers, as they would chase the hunted buffalo. He ran down the shores of the lakes, and followed their outlet to the 'city of cannon' There he hunted and fished, till the people chased him again through the woods into the arms of his enemies. The chief, who was born a Huron, was at last a warrior among the Mohawks!"

"Something like this I had heard before," said Cora, observing that he paused to suppress those passions which began to burn with too bright a flame, as he recalled the recollection of his supposed injuries.

"Was it the fault of Le Renard that his head was not made of rock? Who gave him the fire-water? who made him a villain? 'Twas the pale faces, the people of your own color."

"And am I answerable that thoughtless and unprincipled men exist, whose shades of countenance may resemble mine?" Cora calmly demanded of the excited savage.

"No; Magua is a man, and not a fool; such as you never open their lips to the burning stream: the Great Spirit has given you wisdom!"

"What, then, have I do to, or say, in the matter of your misfortunes, not to say of your errors?"

"Listen," repeated the Indian, resuming his earnest attitude; "when his English and French fathers dug up the hatchet, Le Renard struck the war-post of the Mohawks, and went out against his own nation. The pale faces have driven the red-skins from their hunting grounds, and now when they fight, a white man leads the way. The old chief at Horican, your father, was the great captain of our war-party. He said to the Mohawks do this, and do that, and he was minded. He made a law, that if an Indian swallowed the fire-water, and came into the cloth wigwams of his warriors, it should not be forgotten. Magua foolishly opened his mouth, and the hot liquor led him into the cabin of Munro. What did the gray-head? let his daughter say."

"He forgot not his words, and did justice, by punishing the offender," said the undaunted daughter.

"Justice!" repeated the Indian, casting an oblique glance of the most ferocious expression at her unyielding countenance; "is it justice to make evil and then punish for it? Magua was not himself; it was the fire-water that spoke and acted for him! but Munro did believe it. The Huron chief was tied up before all the pale-faced warriors, and whipped like a dog."

Cora remained silent, for she knew not

how to palliate this imprudent severity on the part of her father in a manner to suit the comprehension of an Indian.

"See!" continued Magua, tearing aside the slight calico that very imperfectly concealed his painted breast; "here are scars given by knives and bullets – of these a warrior may boast before his nation; but the gray-head has left marks on the back of the Huron chief that he must hide like a squaw, under this painted cloth of the whites."

"I had thought," resumed Cora, "that an Indian warrior was patient, and that his spirit felt not and knew not the pain his body suffered."

"When the Chippewas tied Magua to the stake, and cut this gash," said the other, laying his finger on a deep scar, "the Huron laughed in their faces, and told them, Women struck so light! His spirit was then in the clouds! But when he felt the blows of Munro, his spirit lay under the birch. The spirit of a Huron is never drunk; it remembers forever!"

"But it may be appeased. If my father has done you this injustice, show him how an Indian can forgive an injury, and take back his daughters. You have heard from Major Heyward – "

Magua shook his head, forbidding the repetition of offers he so much despised.

"What would you have?" continued Cora, after a most painful pause, while the conviction forced itself on her mind that the too sanguine and generous Duncan had been cruelly deceived by the cunning of the savage.

"What a Huron loves – good for good; bad for bad!"

"You would, then, revenge the injury inflicted by Munro on his helpless daughters. Would it not be more like a man to go before his face, and take the satisfaction of a warrior?"

"The arms of the pale faces are long, and their knives sharp!" returned the savage, with a malignant laugh: "why should Le Renard go among the muskets of his warriors, when he holds the spirit of the gray-head in his hand?"

"Name your intention, Magua," said Cora, struggling with herself to speak with steady calmness. "Is it to lead us prisoners to the woods, or do you contemplate even some greater evil? Is there no reward, no means of palliating the injury, and of softening your heart? At least, release my gentle sister, and pour out all your malice on me. Purchase wealth by her safety and satisfy your revenge with a single victim. The loss of both his daughters might bring the aged man to his grave, and where would then be the satisfaction of Le Renard?"

"Listen," said the Indian again. "The light eyes can go back to the Horican, and tell the old chief what has been done, if the dark-haired woman will swear by the Great Spirit of her fathers to tell no lie."

"What must I promise?" demanded Cora, still maintaining a secret ascendancy over the fierce native by the collected and feminine dignity of her presence.

"When Magua left his people his wife was given to another chief; he has now made friends with the Hurons, and will go back to the graves of his tribe, on the shores of the great lake. Let the daughter of the English chief follow, and live in his wigwam forever."

However revolting a proposal of such a character might prove to Cora, she retained, notwithstanding her powerful disgust, sufficient self-command to reply, without betraying the weakness.

"And what pleasure would Magua find in sharing his cabin with a wife he did not love; one who would be of a nation and color different from his own? It would be better to take the gold of Munro, and buy the heart of some Huron maid with his gifts."

The Indian made no reply for near a minute, but bent his fierce looks on the countenance of Cora, in such wavering glances, that her eyes sank with shame, under an impression that for the first time they had encountered an expression that no chaste female might endure. While she was shrinking within herself, in dread of having her ears wounded by some proposal still more shocking than the last, the voice of Magua answered, in its tones of deepest malignancy:

"When the blows scorched the back of the Huron, he would know where to find a woman to feel the smart. The daughter of Munro would draw his water, hoe his corn, and cook his venison. The body of the gray-head would sleep among his cannon, but his heart would lie within reach of the knife of Le Subtil."

"Monster! well dost thou deserve thy treacherous name," cried Cora, in an ungovernable burst of filial indignation. "None but a fiend could meditate such a vengeance. But thou overratest thy power! You shall find it is, in truth, the heart of Munro you hold, and that it will defy your utmost malice!"

The Indian answered this bold defiance by

a ghastly smile, that showed an unaltered purpose, while he motioned her away, as if to close the conference forever. Cora, already regretting her precipitation, was obliged to comply, for Magua instantly left the spot, and approached his gluttonous comrades. Heyward flew to the side of the agitated female, and demanded the result of a dialogue that he had watched at a distance with so much interest. But, unwilling to alarm the fears of Alice, she evaded a direct reply, betraying only by her anxious looks fastened on the slightest movements of her captors. To the reiterated and earnest questions of her sister concerning their probable destination, she made no other answer than by pointing toward the dark group, with an agitation she could not control, and murmuring as she folded Alice to her bosom.

"There, there; read our fortunes in their faces; we shall see; we shall see!"

The action, and the choked utterance of

Cora, spoke more impressively than any words, and quickly drew the attention of her companions on that spot where her own was riveted with an intenseness that nothing but the importance of the stake could create.

When Magua reached the cluster of lolling savages, who, gorged with their disgusting meal, lay stretched on the earth in brutal indulgence, he commenced speaking with the dignity of an Indian chief. The first syllables he uttered had the effect to cause his listeners to raise themselves in attitudes of respectful attention. As the Huron used his native language, the prisoners, notwithstanding the caution of the natives had kept them within the swing of their tomahawks, could only conjecture the substance of his harangue from the nature of those significant gestures with which an Indian always illustrates his eloquence.

At first, the language, as well as the action of Magua, appeared calm and deliberative. When he had succeeded in sufficiently awakening the attention of his comrades, Heyward fancied, by his pointing so frequently toward the direction of the great lakes, that he spoke of the land of their fathers, and of their distant tribe. Frequent indications of applause escaped the listeners, who, as they uttered the expressive "Hugh!" looked at each other in commendation of the speaker. Le Renard was too skillful to neglect his advantage. He now spoke of the long and painful route by which they had left those spacious grounds and happy villages, to come and battle against the enemies of their Canadian fathers. He enumerated the warriors of the party; their several merits; their frequent services to the nation; their wounds, and the number of the scalps they had taken. Whenever he alluded to any present (and the subtle Indian neglected none), the dark countenance of the flattered individual gleamed with exultation, nor did he even hesitate to assert the truth of the words, by gestures of applause and confirmation. Then the voice of the speaker fell, and lost the loud, animated tones of triumph with which he had enumerated their deeds of success and victory. He described the cataract of Glenn's; the impregnable position of its rocky island, with its caverns and its numerous rapids and whirlpools; he named the name of "La Longue Carabine," and paused until the forest beneath them had sent up the last echo of a loud and long yell, with which the hated appellation was received. He pointed toward the youthful military captive, and described the death of a favorite warrior, who had been precipitated into the deep ravine by his hand. He not only mentioned the fate of him who, hanging between heaven and earth, had presented such a spectacle of horror to the whole band, but he acted anew the terrors of his situation, his resolution and his death, on the branches of a sapling; and, finally, he rapidly recounted the manner in which each of their friends had fallen, never failing to touch upon their courage, and their most acknowledged virtues. When this recital of events was ended, his voice once more changed, and became plaintive and even musical, in its low guttural sounds. He now spoke of the wives and children of the slain; their destitution; their misery, both physical and moral; their distance; and, at last, of their unavenged wrongs. Then suddenly lifting his voice to a pitch of terrific energy, he concluded by demanding:

"Are the Hurons dogs to bear this? Who shall say to the wife of Menowgua that the fishes have his scalp, and that his nation have not taken revenge! Who will dare meet the mother of Wassawattimie, that scornful woman, with his hands clean! What shall be said to the old men when they ask us for scalps, and we have not a hair from a white head to give them! The women will point their fingers at us. There is a dark spot on the names of the Hurons, and it must be hid in blood!" His voice was no longer audible in the burst of rage which now broke into the air, as if the wood, instead of containing so small a band, was filled with the nation. During the foregoing address the progress of the speaker was too plainly read by those most interested in his success through the medium of the countenances of the men he addressed. They had answered his melancholy and mourning by sympathy and sorrow; his assertions, by gestures of confirmation; and his boasting, with the exultation of savages. When he spoke of courage, their looks were firm and responsive; when he alluded to their injuries, their eyes kindled with fury; when he mentioned the taunts of the women, they dropped their heads in shame; but when he pointed out their means of vengeance, he struck a chord which never failed to thrill in the breast of an Indian. With the first intimation that it was within their reach, the whole band sprang upon their feet as one man; giving utterance to their rage in the most frantic cries, they rushed upon their prisoners in a body with drawn knives and uplifted tomahawks. Heyward threw himself between the sisters and the foremost, whom he grappled with a desperate strength that for a moment checked his violence. This unexpected resistance gave Magua time to interpose, and with rapid enunciation and animated gesture, he drew the attention of the band again to himself. In that language he knew so well how to assume, he diverted his comrades from their instant purpose, and invited them to prolong the misery of their victims. His proposal was received with acclamations, and executed with the swiftness of thought.

Two powerful warriors cast themselves on Heyward, while another was occupied in securing the less active singing-master. Neither of the captives, however, submitted without a desperate, though fruitless, struggle. Even David hurled his assailant to the earth; nor was Heyward secured until the victory over his companion enabled the Indians to direct their united force to that object. He was then bound and fastened to the body of the sapling, on whose branches Magua had acted the pantomime of the falling Huron. When the young soldier regained his recollection, he had the painful certainty before his eyes that a common fate was intended for the whole party. On his right was Cora in a durance similar to his own, pale and agitated, but with an eye whose steady look still read the proceedings of their enemies. On his left, the withes which bound her to a pine, performed that office for Alice which her trembling limbs refused, and alone kept her fragile form from sinking. Her hands were clasped before her in prayer, but instead of looking upward toward that power which alone could rescue them, her unconscious looks wandered to the countenance of Duncan with infantile dependency. David had contended, and the novelty of the circumstance held him silent, in deliberation on the propriety of the unusual occurrence.

The vengeance of the Hurons had now taken a new direction, and they prepared to execute it with that barbarous ingenuity with which they were familiarized by the practise of centuries. Some sought knots, to raise the blazing pile; one was riving the splinters of pine, in order to pierce the flesh of their captives with the burning fragments; and others bent the tops of two saplings to the earth, in order to suspend Heyward by the arms between the recoiling branches. But the vengeance of Magua sought a deeper and more malignant enjoyment.

While the less refined monsters of the band prepared, before the eyes of those who were to suffer, these well-known and vulgar means of torture, he approached Cora, and pointed out, with the most malign expression of countenance, the speedy fate that awaited her:

"Ha!" he added, "what says the daughter of Munro? Her head is too good to find a pillow in the wigwam of Le Renard; will she like it better when it rolls about this hill a plaything for the wolves? Her bosom cannot nurse the children of a Huron; she will see it spit upon by Indians!"

"What means the monster!" demanded the astonished Heyward.

"Nothing!" was the firm reply. "He is a savage, a barbarous and ignorant savage, and knows not what he does. Let us find leisure, with our dying breath, to ask for him penitence and pardon."

"Pardon!" echoed the fierce Huron, mistaking in his anger, the meaning of her words; "the memory of an Indian is no longer than the arm of the pale faces; his mercy shorter than their justice! Say; shall I send the yellow hair to her father, and will you follow Magua to the great lakes, to carry his water, and feed him with corn?"

Cora beckoned him away, with an emotion of disgust she could not control.

"Leave me," she said, with a solemnity that for a moment checked the barbarity of the Indian; "you mingle bitterness in my prayers; you stand between me and my God!"

The slight impression produced on the savage was, however, soon forgotten, and he continued pointing, with taunting irony, toward Alice.

"Look! the child weeps! She is too young to die! Send her to Munro, to comb his gray hairs, and keep life in the heart of the old man."

Cora could not resist the desire to look upon her youthful sister, in whose eyes she met an imploring glance, that betrayed the longings of nature.

"What says he, dearest Cora?" asked the trembling voice of Alice. "Did he speak of sending me to our father?"

For many moments the elder sister looked upon the younger, with a countenance that wavered with powerful and contending emotions. At length she spoke, though her tones had lost their rich and calm fullness, in an expression of tenderness that seemed maternal.

"Alice," she said, "the Huron offers us both life, nay, more than both; he offers to restore Duncan, our invaluable Duncan, as well as you, to our friends – to our father – to our heart-stricken, childless father, if I will bow down this rebellious, stubborn pride of mine, and consent – "

Her voice became choked, and clasping her hands, she looked upward, as if seeking, in her agony, intelligence from a wisdom that was infinite.

"Say on," cried Alice; "to what, dearest Cora? Oh! that the proffer were made to me! to save you, to cheer our aged father, to restore Duncan, how cheerfully could I die!"

"Die!" repeated Cora, with a calmer and firmer voice, "that were easy! Perhaps the alternative may not be less so. He would have me," she continued, her accents sinking under a deep consciousness of the degradation of the proposal, "follow him to the wilderness; go to the habitations of the Hurons; to remain there; in short, to become his wife! Speak, then, Alice; child of my affections! sister of my love! And you, too, Major Heyward, aid my weak reason with your counsel. Is life to be purchased by such a sacrifice? Will you, Alice, receive it at my hands at such a price? And you, Duncan, guide me; control me between you; for I am wholly yours!"

"Would I!" echoed the indignant and astonished youth. "Cora! Cora! you jest with our misery! Name not the horrid alternative again; the thought itself is worse than a thousand deaths."

"That such would be your answer, I well knew!" exclaimed Cora, her cheeks flushing, and her dark eyes once more sparkling with the lingering emotions of a woman. "What says my Alice? for her will I submit without another murmur."

Although both Heyward and Cora listened with painful suspense and the deepest attention, no sounds were heard in reply. It appeared as if the delicate and sensitive form of Alice would shrink into itself, as she listened to this proposal. Her arms had fallen lengthwise before her, the fingers moving in slight convulsions; her head dropped upon her bosom, and her whole person seemed suspended against the tree, looking like some beautiful emblem of the wounded delicacy of her sex, devoid of animation and yet keenly conscious. In a few moments, however, her head began to move slowly, in a sign of deep, unconquerable disapprobation.

"No, no, no; better that we die as we have lived, together!"

"Then die!" shouted Magua, hurling his tomahawk with violence at the unresisting speaker, and gnashing his teeth with a rage that could no longer be bridled at this sudden exhibition of firmness in the one he believed the weakest of the party. The axe cleaved the air in front of Heyward, and cutting some of the flowing ringlets of Alice, quivered in the tree above her head. The sight maddened Duncan to desperation. Collecting all his energies in one effort he snapped the twigs which bound him and rushed upon another savage, who was preparing, with loud yells and a more deliberate aim, to repeat the blow. They encountered, grappled, and fell to the earth together. The naked body of his antagonist afforded Heyward no means of holding his adversary, who glided from his grasp, and rose again with one knee on his chest, pressing him down with the weight of a giant. Duncan already saw the knife gleaming in the air, when a whistling sound swept past him, and was rather accompanied than followed by the sharp crack of a rifle. He felt his breast relieved from the load it had endured; he saw the savage expression of his adversary's countenance change to a look of vacant wildness, when the Indian fell dead on the faded leaves by his side.

Chapter Twelve

"Clo. – I am gone, sire,
And anon, sire, I'll be with you again."
– Twelfth Night

THE HURONS STOOD AGHAST at this sudden visitation of death on one of their band. But as they regarded the fatal accuracy of an aim which had dared to immolate an enemy at so much hazard to a friend, the name of "La Longue Carabine" burst simultaneously from every lip, and was succeeded by a wild and a sort of plaintive howl. The cry was answered by a loud shout from a little thicket, where the incautious party had piled their arms; and at the next moment, Hawkeye, too eager to load the rifle he had regained, was seen advancing upon them, brandishing the clubbed weapon, and cutting the air with wide and powerful sweeps. Bold and rapid as was the progress of the scout, it was exceeded by that of a light and vigorous form which, bounding past him, leaped, with incredible activity and daring, into the very center of the Hurons, where it stood, whirling a tomahawk, and flourishing a glittering knife, with fearful menaces, in front of Cora. Quicker than the thoughts could follow those unexpected and audacious movements, an image, armed in the emblematic panoply of death, glided before their eyes, and assumed a threatening attitude at the other's side. The savage tormentors recoiled before these warlike intruders, and uttered, as they appeared in such quick succession, the often repeated and peculiar exclamations of surprise, followed by the well-known and dreaded appellations of:

"Le Cerf Agile! Le Gros Serpent!"

But the wary and vigilant leader of the Hurons was not so easily disconcerted. Casting his keen eyes around the little plain, he comprehended the nature of the assault at a glance, and encouraging his followers by his voice as well as by his example, he unsheathed his long and dangerous knife, and rushed with a loud whoop upon the expected Chingachgook. It was the signal for a general combat. Neither party had firearms, and the contest was to be decided in the deadliest manner, hand to hand, with weapons of offense, and none of defense.

Uncas answered the whoop, and leaping on an enemy, with a single, well-directed blow of his tomahawk, cleft him to the brain. Heyward tore the weapon of Magua from the sapling, and rushed eagerly toward the fray. As the combatants were now equal in number, each singled an opponent from the adverse band. The rush and blows passed with the fury of a whirlwind, and the swiftness of lightning. Hawkeye soon got another enemy within reach of his arm, and with one sweep of his formidable weapon he beat down the slight and inartificial defenses of his antagonist, crushing him to the earth with the blow. Heyward ventured to hurl the tomahawk he had seized, too ardent to await the moment of closing. It struck the Indian he had selected on the forehead, and checked for an instant his onward rush. Encouraged by this slight advantage, the impetuous young man continued his onset, and sprang upon his enemy with naked hands. A single instant was enough to assure him of the rashness of the measure, for he immediately found himself fully engaged, with all his activity and courage, in endeavoring to ward the desperate thrusts made with the knife of the Huron. Unable longer to foil an enemy so alert and vigilant, he threw his arms about him, and succeeded in pinning the limbs of the other to his side, with an iron grasp, but one that was far too exhausting to himself to continue long. In this extremity he heard a voice near him, shouting:

"Extarminate the varlets! no quarter to an accursed Mingo!"

At the next moment, the breech of Hawkeye's rifle fell on the naked head of his adversary, whose muscles appeared to wither under the shock, as he sank from the arms of Duncan, flexible and motionless.

When Uncas had brained his first antagonist, he turned, like a hungry lion, to seek another. The fifth and only Huron disengaged at the first onset had paused a moment, and then seeing that all around him were employed in the deadly strife, he had sought, with hellish vengeance, to complete the baffled work of revenge. Raising a shout of triumph, he sprang toward the defenseless Cora, sending his keen axe as the dreadful precursor of his approach. The tomahawk grazed her shoulder, and cutting the withes which bound her to the tree, left the maiden at liberty to fly. She eluded the grasp of the savage, and reckless of her own safety, threw herself on the bosom of Alice, striving with convulsed and ill-directed fingers, to tear asunder the twigs which confined the person of her sister. Any other than a monster would have relented at such an act of generous devotion to the best and purest affection; but the breast of the Huron was a stranger to sympathy. Seizing Cora by the rich tresses which fell in confusion about her form, he tore her from her frantic hold, and bowed her down with brutal violence to her knees. The savage drew the flowing curls through his hand, and raising them on high with an outstretched arm, he passed the knife around the exquisitely molded head of his victim, with a taunting and exulting laugh. But he purchased this moment of fierce gratification with the loss of the fatal opportunity. It was just then the sight caught the eye of Uncas. Bounding from his footsteps he appeared for an instant darting through the air and descending in a ball he fell on the chest of his enemy, driving him many yards from the spot, headlong and prostrate. The violence of the exertion cast the young Mohican at his side. They arose together, fought, and bled, each in his turn. But the conflict was soon decided; the tomahawk of Heyward and the rifle of Hawkeye descended on the skull of the Huron, at the same moment that the knife of Uncas reached his heart.

The battle was now entirely terminated with the exception of the protracted struggle between "Le Renard Subtil" and "Le Gros Serpent." Well did these barbarous warriors prove that they deserved those significant names which had been bestowed for deeds in former wars. When they engaged, some little time was lost in eluding the quick and vigorous thrusts which had been aimed at their lives. Suddenly darting on each other, they closed, and came to the earth, twisted together like twining serpents, in pliant and subtle folds. At the moment when the victors found themselves unoccupied, the spot where these experienced and desperate combatants lay could only be distinguished by a cloud of dust and leaves, which moved from the center of the little plain toward its boundary, as if raised by the passage of a whirlwind. Urged by the different motives of filial affection, friendship and gratitude, Heyward and his companions rushed with one accord to the place, encircling the little canopy of dust which hung above the warriors. In vain did Uncas dart around the cloud, with a wish to strike his knife into the heart of his father's foe; the threatening rifle of Hawkeye was raised and suspended in vain, while Duncan endeavored to seize the limbs of the Huron with hands that appeared to have lost their power. Covered as they were with dust and blood, the swift evolutions of the combatants seemed to incorporate their bodies into one. The death-like looking figure of the Mohican, and the dark form of the Huron, gleamed before their eyes in such quick and confused succession, that the friends of the former knew not where to plant the succoring blow. It is true there were short and fleeting moments, when the fiery eyes of Magua were seen glittering, like the fabled organs of the basilisk through the dusty wreath by which he was enveloped, and he read by those short and deadly glances the fate of the combat in the presence of his enemies; ere, however, any hostile hand could descend on his devoted head, its place was filled by the scowling visage of Chingachgook. In this manner the scene of the combat was removed from the center of the little plain to its verge. The Mohican now found an opportunity to make a powerful thrust with his knife; Magua suddenly relinquished his grasp, and fell backward without motion, and seemingly without life. His adversary leaped on his feet, making the arches of the forest ring with the sounds of triumph.

"Well done for the Delawares! victory to the Mohicans!" cried Hawkeye, once more elevating the butt of the long and fatal rifle; "a finishing blow from a man without a cross will never tell against his honor, nor rob him of his right to the scalp."

But at the very moment when the dangerous weapon was in the act of descending, the subtle Huron rolled swiftly from beneath the danger, over the edge of the precipice, and falling on his feet, was seen leaping, with a single bound, into the center of a thicket of low bushes, which clung along its sides. The Delawares, who had believed their enemy dead, uttered their exclamation of surprise, and were following with speed and clamor, like hounds in open view of the deer, when a shrill and peculiar cry from the scout instantly changed their purpose, and recalled them to the summit of the hill.

"'Twas like himself!" cried the inveterate forester, whose prejudices contributed so largely to veil his natural sense of justice in all matters which concerned the Mingoes; "a lying and deceitful varlet as he is. An honest Delaware now, being fairly vanquished, would have lain still, and been knocked on the head, but these knavish Maquas cling to life like so many cats-o'-the-mountain. Let him go – let him go; 'tis but one man, and he without rifle or bow, many a long mile from his French commerades; and like a rattler that lost his fangs, he can do no further mischief, until such time as he, and we too, may leave the prints of our moccasins over a long reach of sandy plain. See, Uncas," he added, in Delaware, "your father is flaying the scalps already. It may be well to go round and feel the vagabonds that are left, or we may have another of them loping through the woods, and screeching like a jay that has been winged."

So saying the honest but implacable scout made the circuit of the dead, into whose senseless bosoms he thrust his long knife, with as much coolness as though they had been so many brute carcasses. He had, however, been anticipated by the elder Mohican, who had already torn the emblems of victory from the unresisting heads of the slain.

But Uncas, denying his habits, we had almost said his nature, flew with instinctive delicacy, accompanied by Heyward, to the assistance of the females, and quickly releasing Alice, placed her in the arms of Cora. We shall not attempt to describe the gratitude to the Almighty Disposer of Events which glowed in the bosoms of the sisters, who were thus unexpectedly restored to life and to each other. Their thanksgivings were deep and silent; the offerings of their gentle spirits burning brightest and purest on the secret altars of their hearts; and their renovated and more earthly feelings exhibiting themselves in long and fervent though speechless caresses. As Alice rose from her knees, where she had sunk by the side of Cora, she threw herself on the bosom of the latter, and sobbed aloud the name of their aged father, while her soft, dove-like eyes, sparkled with the rays of hope.

"We are saved! we are saved!" she murmured; "to return to the arms of our dear, dear father, and his heart will not be broken with grief. And you, too, Cora, my sister, my more than sister, my mother; you, too, are spared. And Duncan," she added, looking round upon the youth with a smile of ineffable innocence, "even our own brave and noble Duncan has escaped without a hurt."

To these ardent and nearly innocent words Cora made no other answer than by straining the youthful speaker to her heart, as she bent over her in melting tenderness. The manhood of Heyward felt no shame in dropping tears over this spectacle of affectionate rapture; and Uncas stood, fresh and blood-stained from the combat, a calm, and, apparently, an unmoved looker-on, it is true, but with eyes that had already lost their fierceness, and were beaming with a sympathy that elevated him far above the intelligence, and advanced him probably centuries before, the practises of his nation.

During this display of emotions so natural in their situation, Hawkeye, whose vigilant distrust had satisfied itself that the Hurons, who disfigured the heavenly scene, no longer possessed the power to interrupt its harmony, approached David, and liberated him from the bonds he had, until that moment, endured with the most exemplary patience.

"There," exclaimed the scout, casting the last withe behind him, "you are once more master of your own limbs, though you seem not to use them with much greater judgment than that in which they were first fashioned. If advice from one who is not older than yourself, but who, having lived most of his time in the wilderness, may be said to have experience beyond his years, will give no offense, you are welcome to my thoughts;

and these are, to part with the little tooting instrument in your jacket to the first fool you meet with, and buy some we'pon with the money, if it be only the barrel of a horseman's pistol. By industry and care, you might thus come to some prefarment; for by this time, I should think, your eyes would plainly tell you that a carrion crow is a better bird than a mocking-thresher. The one will, at least, remove foul sights from before the face of man, while the other is only good to brew disturbances in the woods, by cheating the ears of all that hear them."

"Arms and the clarion for the battle, but the song of thanksgiving to the victory!" answered the liberated David. "Friend," he added, thrusting forth his lean, delicate hand toward Hawkeye, in kindness, while his eyes twinkled and grew moist, "I thank thee that the hairs of my head still grow where they were first rooted by Providence; for, though those of other men may be more glossy and curling, I have ever found mine own well suited to the brain they shelter. That I did not join myself to the battle, was less owing to disinclination, than to the bonds of the heathen. Valiant and skillful hast thou proved thyself in the conflict, and I hereby thank thee, before proceeding to discharge other and more important duties, because thou hast proved thyself well worthy of a Christian's praise."

"The thing is but a trifle, and what you may often see if you tarry long among us," returned the scout, a good deal softened toward the man of song, by this unequivocal expression of gratitude. "I have got back my old companion, 'killdeer'," he added, striking his hand on the breech of his rifle; "and that in itself is a victory. These Iroquois are cunning, but they outwitted themselves when they placed their firearms out of reach; and had Uncas or his father been gifted with only their common Indian patience, we should have come in upon the knaves with three bullets instead of one, and that would have made a finish of the whole pack; yon loping varlet, as well as his commerades. But 'twas all fore-ordered, and for the best."

"Thou sayest well," returned David, "and hast caught the true spirit of Christianity. He that is to be saved will be saved, and he that is predestined to be damned will be damned. This is the doctrine of truth, and most consoling and refreshing it is to the true believer."

The scout, who by this time was seated, examining into the state of his rifle with a species of parental assiduity, now looked up at the other in a displeasure that he did not affect to conceal, roughly interrupting further speech.

"Doctrine or no doctrine," said the sturdy woodsman, "'tis the belief of knaves, and the curse of an honest man. I can credit that yonder Huron was to fall by my hand, for with my own eyes I have seen it; but nothing short of being a witness will cause me to think he has met with any reward, or that

Chingachgook there will be condemned at the final day."

"You have no warranty for such an audacious doctrine, nor any covenant to support it," cried David who was deeply tinctured with the subtle distinctions which, in his time, and more especially in his province, had been drawn around the beautiful simplicity of revelation, by endeavoring to penetrate the awful mystery of the divine nature, supplying faith by self-sufficiency, and by consequence, involving those who reasoned from such human dogmas in absurdities and doubt; "your temple is reared on the sands, and the first tempest will wash away its foundation. I demand your authorities for such an uncharitable assertion (like other advocates of a system, David was not always accurate in his use of terms). Name chapter and verse; in which of the holy books do you find language to support you?"

"Book!" repeated Hawkeye, with singular

and ill-concealed disdain; "do you take me for a whimpering boy at the apronstring of one of your old gals; and this good rifle on my knee for the feather of a goose's wing, my ox's horn for a bottle of ink, and my leathern pouch for a cross-barred handkercher to carry my dinner? Book! what have such as I, who am a warrior of the wilderness, though a man without a cross, to do with books? I never read but in one, and the words that are written there are too simple and too plain to need much schooling; though I may boast that of forty long and hard-working years."

"What call you the volume?" said David, misconceiving the other's meaning.

"'Tis open before your eyes," returned the scout; "and he who owns it is not a niggard of its use. I have heard it said that there are men who read in books to convince themselves there is a God. I know not but man may so deform his works in the settlement, as to leave that which is so clear in the wilderness a matter of doubt among traders and priests.

If any such there be, and he will follow me from sun to sun, through the windings of the forest, he shall see enough to teach him that he is a fool, and that the greatest of his folly lies in striving to rise to the level of One he can never equal, be it in goodness, or be it in power."

The instant David discovered that he battled with a disputant who imbibed his faith from the lights of nature, eschewing all subtleties of doctrine, he willingly abandoned a controversy from which he believed neither profit nor credit was to be derived. While the scout was speaking, he had also seated himself, and producing the ready little volume and the iron-rimmed spectacles, he prepared to discharge a duty, which nothing but the unexpected assault he had received in his orthodoxy could have so long suspended. He was, in truth, a minstrel of the western continent – of a much later day, certainly, than those gifted bards, who formerly sang the profane renown of baron and prince, but after the spirit of his own age and country; and he was now prepared to exercise the cunning of his craft, in celebration of, or rather in thanksgiving for, the recent victory. He waited patiently for Hawkeye to cease, then lifting his eyes, together with his voice, he said, aloud:

"I invite you, friends, to join in praise for this signal deliverance from the hands of barbarians and infidels, to the comfortable and solemn tones of the tune called 'Northampton'."

He next named the page and verse where the rhymes selected were to be found, and applied the pitch-pipe to his lips, with the decent gravity that he had been wont to use in the temple. This time he was, however, without any accompaniment, for the sisters were just then pouring out those tender effusions of affection which have been already alluded to. Nothing deterred by the smallness of his audience, which, in truth, consisted only of the discontented scout, he raised his voice, commencing and ending the sacred song without accident or interruption of any kind.

Hawkeye listened while he coolly adjusted his flint and reloaded his rifle; but the sounds, wanting the extraneous assistance of scene and sympathy, failed to awaken his slumbering emotions. Never minstrel, or by whatever more suitable name David should be known, drew upon his talents in the presence of more insensible auditors; though considering the singleness and sincerity of his motive, it is probable that no bard of profane song ever uttered notes that ascended so near to that throne where all homage and praise is due. The scout shook his head, and muttering some unintelligible words, among which “throat” and “Iroquois” were alone audible, he walked away, to collect and to examine into the state of the captured arsenal of the Hurons. In this office he was now joined by Chingachgook, who found his own, as well as the rifle of his son, among the arms. Even Heyward and David were furnished with weapons; nor was ammunition wanting to render them all effectual.

When the foresters had made their selection, and distributed their prizes, the scout announced that the hour had arrived when it was necessary to move. By this time the song of Gamut had ceased, and the sisters had learned to still the exhibition of their emotions. Aided by Duncan and the younger Mohican, the two latter descended the precipitous sides of that hill which they had so lately ascended under so very different auspices, and whose summit had so nearly proved the scene of their massacre. At the foot they found the Narragansetts browsing the herbage of the bushes, and having mounted, they followed the movements of a guide, who, in the most deadly straits, had so often proved himself their friend. The journey was, however, short. Hawkeye, leaving the blind path that the Hurons had followed, turned short to his right, and entering the thicket, he crossed a babbling brook, and halted in a narrow dell, under the shade of a few water elms. Their distance from the base of the fatal hill was but a few rods, and the steeds had been serviceable only in crossing the shallow stream.

The scout and the Indians appeared to be familiar with the sequestered place where they now were; for, leaning their rifle against the trees, they commenced throwing aside the dried leaves, and opening the blue clay, out of which a clear and sparkling spring of bright, glancing water, quickly bubbled. The white man then looked about him, as though seeking for some object, which was not to be found as readily as he expected.

"Them careless imps, the Mohawks, with their Tuscarora and Onondaga brethren, have been here slaking their thirst," he muttered, "and the vagabonds have thrown away the gourd! This is the way with benefits, when they are bestowed on such disremembering hounds! Here has the Lord laid his hand, in the midst of the howling wilderness, for their good, and raised a fountain of water from the bowels of the ‘arth, that might laugh at the richest shop of apothecary’s ware in all the colonies; and see! the knaves have trodden in the clay, and deformed the cleanliness of the place, as though they were brute beasts, instead of human men.”

Uncas silently extended toward him the desired gourd, which the spleen of Hawkeye had hitherto prevented him from observing on a branch of an elm. Filling it with water, he retired a short distance, to a place where the ground was more firm and dry; here he coolly seated himself, and after taking a long, and, apparently, a grateful draught, he commenced a very strict examination of the fragments of food left by the Hurons, which had hung in a wallet on his arm.

“Thank you, lad!” he continued, returning the empty gourd to Uncas; “now we will see how these rampaging Hurons lived, when outlying in ambushments. Look at this! The varlets know the better pieces of the deer; and one would think they might carve and roast a saddle, equal to the best cook in the land! But everything is raw, for the Iroquois are thorough savages. Uncas, take my steel and kindle a fire; a mouthful of a tender broil will give natur' a helping hand, after so long a trail."

Heyward, perceiving that their guides now set about their repast in sober earnest, assisted the ladies to alight, and placed himself at their side, not unwilling to enjoy a few moments of grateful rest, after the bloody scene he had just gone through. While the culinary process was in hand, curiosity induced him to inquire into the circumstances which had led to their timely and unexpected rescue:

"How is it that we see you so soon, my generous friend," he asked, "and without aid from the garrison of Edward?"

“Had we gone to the bend in the river, we might have been in time to rake the leaves over your bodies, but too late to have saved your scalps,” coolly answered the scout. “No, no; instead of throwing away strength and opportunity by crossing to the fort, we lay by, under the bank of the Hudson, waiting to watch the movements of the Hurons.”

“You were, then, witnesses of all that passed?”

“Not of all; for Indian sight is too keen to be easily cheated, and we kept close. A difficult matter it was, too, to keep this Mohican boy snug in the ambushment. Ah! Uncas, Uncas, your behavior was more like that of a curious woman than of a warrior on his scent.”

Uncas permitted his eyes to turn for an instant on the sturdy countenance of the speaker, but he neither spoke nor gave any indication of repentance. On the contrary, Heyward thought the manner of the young Mohican was disdainful, if not a little fierce, and that he suppressed passions that were ready to explode, as much in compliment to the listeners, as from the deference he usually paid to his white associate.

"You saw our capture?" Heyward next demanded.

"We heard it," was the significant answer. "An Indian yell is plain language to men who have passed their days in the woods. But when you landed, we were driven to crawl like sarpents, beneath the leaves; and then we lost sight of you entirely, until we placed eyes on you again trussed to the trees, and ready bound for an Indian massacre."

"Our rescue was the deed of Providence. It was nearly a miracle that you did not mistake the path, for the Hurons divided, and each band had its horses."

"Ay! there we were thrown off the scent, and might, indeed, have lost the trail, had it not been for Uncas; we took the path, however, that led into the wilderness; for we judged, and judged rightly, that the savages would hold that course with their prisoners. But when we had followed it for many miles, without finding a single twig broken, as I had advised, my mind misgave me; especially as all the footsteps had the prints of moccasins."

"Our captors had the precaution to see us shod like themselves," said Duncan, raising a foot, and exhibiting the buckskin he wore.

"Aye, 'twas judgmatical and like themselves; though we were too expart to be thrown from a trail by so common an invention."

"To what, then, are we indebted for our safety?"

"To what, as a white man who has no taint of Indian blood, I should be ashamed to own; to the judgment of the young Mohican, in matters which I should know better than he, but which I can now hardly believe to be true, though my own eyes tell me it is so."

"'Tis extraordinary! will you not name the reason?"

"Uncas was bold enough to say, that the beasts ridden by the gentle ones," continued

Hawkeye, glancing his eyes, not without curious interest, on the fillies of the ladies, "planted the legs of one side on the ground at the same time, which is contrary to the movements of all trotting four-footed animals of my knowledge, except the bear. And yet here are horses that always journey in this manner, as my own eyes have seen, and as their trail has shown for twenty long miles."

"'Tis the merit of the animal! They come from the shores of Narragansett Bay, in the small province of Providence Plantations, and are celebrated for their hardihood, and the ease of this peculiar movement; though other horses are not unfrequently trained to the same."

"It may be – it may be," said Hawkeye, who had listened with singular attention to this explanation; "though I am a man who has the full blood of the whites, my judgment in deer and beaver is greater than in beasts of burden. Major Effingham has many noble chargers, but I have never seen one travel after such a sidling gait."

"True; for he would value the animals for very different properties. Still is this a breed highly esteemed and, as you witness, much honored with the burdens it is often destined to bear."

The Mohicans had suspended their operations about the glimmering fire to listen; and, when Duncan had done, they looked at each other significantly, the father uttering the never-failing exclamation of surprise. The scout ruminated, like a man digesting his newly-acquired knowledge, and once more stole a glance at the horses.

"I dare to say there are even stranger sights to be seen in the settlements!" he said, at length. "Natur' is sadly abused by man, when he once gets the mastery. But, go sidling or go straight, Uncas had seen the movement, and their trail led us on to the broken bush. The outer branch, near the prints of one of the horses, was bent upward, as a lady breaks a flower from its stem, but all the rest were ragged and broken down, as if the strong hand of a man had been tearing them! So I concluded that the cunning varments had seen the twig bent, and had torn the rest, to make us believe a buck had been feeling the boughs with his antlers."

"I do believe your sagacity did not deceive you; for some such thing occurred!"

"That was easy to see," added the scout, in no degree conscious of having exhibited any extraordinary sagacity; "and a very different matter it was from a waddling horse! It then struck me the Mingoes would push for this spring, for the knaves well know the vartue of its waters!"

"Is it, then, so famous?" demanded Heyward, examining, with a more curious eye, the secluded dell, with its bubbling fountain, surrounded, as it was, by earth of a deep, dingy brown.

"Few red-skins, who travel south and east of the great lakes but have heard of its qualities. Will you taste for yourself?"

Heyward took the gourd, and after swallowing a little of the water, threw it aside with grimaces of discontent. The scout laughed in his silent but heartfelt manner, and shook his head with vast satisfaction.

"Ah! you want the flavor that one gets by habit; the time was when I liked it as little as yourself; but I have come to my taste, and I now crave it, as a deer does the licks.[14] Your

---

14 Many of the animals of the American forests resort to those spots where salt springs are found. These are called "licks" or "salt licks," in the language of the country, from

high-spiced wines are not better liked than a red-skin relishes this water; especially when his natur' is ailing. But Uncas has made his fire, and it is time we think of eating, for our journey is long, and all before us."

Interrupting the dialogue by this abrupt transition, the scout had instant recourse to the fragments of food which had escaped the voracity of the Hurons. A very summary process completed the simple cookery, when he and the Mohicans commenced their humble meal, with the silence and characteristic diligence of men who ate in order to enable themselves to endure great and unremitting toil.

When this necessary, and, happily, grateful duty had been performed, each of the foresters stooped and took a long

---

the circumstance that the quadruped is often obliged to lick the earth, in order to obtain the saline particles. These licks are great places of resort with the hunters, who waylay their game near the paths that lead to them.

and parting draught at that solitary and silent spring,[15] around which and its sister fountains, within fifty years, the wealth, beauty and talents of a hemisphere were to assemble in throngs, in pursuit of health and pleasure. Then Hawkeye announced his determination to proceed. The sisters resumed their saddles; Duncan and David grapsed their rifles, and followed on footsteps; the scout leading the advance, and the Mohicans bringing up the rear. The whole party moved swiftly through the narrow path, toward the north, leaving the healing waters to mingle unheeded with the adjacent brooks and the bodies of the dead to fester on the neighboring mount, without the rites of sepulture; a fate but too common to the warriors of the woods to excite either commiseration or comment.

---

15 The scene of the foregoing incidents is on the spot where the village of Ballston now stands; one of the two principal watering places of America.

Chapter Thirteen

"I'll seek a readier path."
– Parnell

THE ROUTE TAKEN BY Hawkeye lay across those sandy plains, relived by occasional valleys and swells of land, which had been traversed by their party on the morning of the same day, with the baffled Magua for their guide. The sun had now fallen low toward the distant mountains; and as their journey lay through the interminable forest, the heat was no longer oppressive. Their progress, in consequence, was proportionate; and long before the twilight gathered about them, they had made good many toilsome miles on their return.

The hunter, like the savage whose place he filled, seemed to select among the blind signs of their wild route, with a species of instinct, seldom abating his speed, and never pausing to deliberate. A rapid and oblique glance at the moss on the trees, with an occasional upward gaze toward the setting sun, or a steady but passing look at the direction of the numerous water courses, through which he waded, were sufficient to determine his path, and remove his greatest difficulties. In the meantime, the forest began to change its hues, losing that lively green which had embellished its arches, in the graver light which is the usual precursor of the close of day.

While the eyes of the sisters were endeavoring to catch glimpses through the trees, of the flood of golden glory which formed a glittering halo around the sun, tinging here and there with ruby streaks, or bordering with narrow edgings of shining yellow, a mass of clouds that lay piled at no great distance above the western hills, Hawkeye turned suddenly and pointing upward toward the gorgeous heavens, he spoke:

"Yonder is the signal given to man to seek his food and natural rest," he said; "better and wiser would it be, if he could understand the signs of nature, and take a lesson from the fowls of the air and the beasts of the field! Our night, however, will soon be over, for with the moon we must be up and moving again. I remember to have fou't the Maquas, hereaways, in the first war in which I ever drew blood from man; and we threw up a work of blocks, to keep the ravenous varmints from handling our scalps. If my marks do not fail me, we shall find the place a few rods further to our left."

Without waiting for an assent, or, indeed, for any reply, the sturdy hunter moved boldly into a dense thicket of young chestnuts, shoving aside the branches of the exuberant shoots which nearly covered the ground, like a man who expected, at each step, to discover some object he had formerly known. The recollection of the scout did not deceive him. After penetrating through the brush, matted as it was with briars, for a few hundred feet, he entered an open space, that surrounded a low, green hillock, which was crowned by the decayed blockhouse in question. This rude and neglected building was one of those deserted works, which, having been thrown up on an emergency, had been abandoned with the disappearance of danger, and was now quietly crumbling in the solitude of the forest, neglected and nearly forgotten, like the circumstances which had caused it to be reared. Such memorials of the passage and struggles of man are yet frequent throughout the broad barrier of wilderness which once separated the hostile provinces, and form a species of ruins that are intimately associated with the recollections of colonial history, and which are in appropriate keeping with the gloomy character of the surrounding scenery. The roof of bark had long since fallen, and mingled with the soil, but the huge logs of pine, which had been hastily thrown together, still preserved their relative positions, though one angle of the work had given way under the pressure, and threatened a speedy downfall to the remainder of the rustic edifice. While Heyward and his companions hesitated to approach a building so decayed, Hawkeye and the Indians entered within the low walls, not only without fear, but with obvious interest. While the former surveyed the ruins, both internally and externally, with the curiosity of one whose recollections were reviving at each moment, Chingachgook related to his son, in the language of the Delawares, and with the pride of a conqueror, the brief history of the skirmish which had been fought, in his youth, in that secluded spot. A strain of melancholy, however, blended with his triumph, rendering his voice, as usual, soft and musical.

In the meantime, the sisters gladly dismounted, and prepared to enjoy their halt in the coolness of the evening, and in a security which they believed nothing but the beasts of the forest could invade.

"Would not our resting-place have been more retired, my worthy friend," demanded the more vigilant Duncan, perceiving that the scout had already finished his short survey, "had we chosen a spot less known, and one more rarely visited than this?"

"Few live who know the blockhouse was ever raised," was the slow and musing answer; "'tis not often that books are made, and narratives written of such a scrimmage as was here fou't atween the Mohicans and the Mohawks, in a war of their own waging. I was then a younker, and went out with the Delawares, because I know'd they were a scandalized and wronged race. Forty days and forty nights did the imps crave our blood around this pile of logs, which I designed and partly reared, being, as you'll remember, no Indian myself, but a man without a cross. The Delawares lent themselves to the work, and we made it good, ten to twenty, until our numbers were nearly equal, and then we sallied out upon the hounds, and not a man of them ever got back to tell the fate of his party. Yes, yes; I was then young, and new to the sight of blood; and not relishing the thought that creatures who had spirits like myself should lay on the naked ground, to be torn asunder by beasts, or to bleach in the rains, I buried the dead with my own hands, under that very little hillock where you have placed yourselves; and no bad seat does it make neither, though it be raised by the bones of mortal men."

Heyward and the sisters arose, on the instant, from the grassy sepulcher; nor could the two latter, notwithstanding the terrific scenes they had so recently passed through, entirely suppress an emotion of natural horror, when they found themselves in such familiar contact with the grave of the dead Mohawks. The gray light, the gloomy little area of dark grass, surrounded by its border of brush, beyond which the pines rose, in breathing silence, apparently into the very clouds, and the deathlike stillness of the vast forest, were all in unison to deepen such a sensation. "They are gone, and they are harmless," continued Hawkeye, waving his hand, with a melancholy smile at their manifest alarm; "they'll never shout the war-whoop nor strike a blow with the tomahawk again! And of all those who aided in placing them where they lie, Chingachgook and I only are living! The brothers and family of the Mohican formed our war party; and you see before you all that are now left of his race."

The eyes of the listeners involuntarily sought the forms of the Indians, with a compassionate interest in their desolate fortune. Their dark persons were still to be seen within the shadows of the blockhouse, the son listening to the relation of his father with that sort of intenseness which would be created by a narrative that redounded so much to the honor of those whose names he had long revered for their courage and savage virtues.

"I had thought the Delawares a pacific people," said Duncan, "and that they never waged war in person; trusting the defense of their hands to those very Mohawks that you slew!"

"'Tis true in part," returned the scout, "and yet, at the bottom, 'tis a wicked lie. Such a treaty was made in ages gone by, through the deviltries of the Dutchers, who wished to disarm the natives that had the best right to the country, where they had settled themselves. The Mohicans, though a part of the same nation, having to deal with the English, never entered into the silly bargain, but kept to their manhood; as in truth did the Delawares, when their eyes were open to their folly. You see before you a chief of the great Mohican Sagamores! Once his family could chase their deer over tracts of country wider than that which belongs to the Albany Patteroon, without crossing brook or hill that was not their own; but what is left of their descendant? He may find his six feet of earth when God chooses, and keep it in peace, perhaps, if he has a friend who will take the pains to sink his head so low that the plowshares cannot reach it!"

"Enough!" said Heyward, apprehensive that the subject might lead to a discussion that would interrupt the harmony so necessary to the preservation of his fair companions; "we have journeyed far, and few among us are blessed with forms like that of yours, which seems to know neither fatigue nor weakness."

"The sinews and bones of a man carry me through it all," said the hunter, surveying his muscular limbs with a simplicity that betrayed the honest pleasure the compliment afforded him; "there are larger and heavier men to be found in the settlements, but you might travel many days in a city before you could meet one able to walk fifty miles without stopping to take breath, or who has kept the hounds within hearing during a chase of hours. However, as flesh and blood are not always the same, it is quite reasonable to suppose that the gentle ones are willing to rest, after all they have seen and done this day. Uncas, clear out the spring, while your father and I make a cover for their tender heads of these chestnut shoots, and a bed of grass and leaves."

The dialogue ceased, while the hunter and his companions busied themselves in preparations for the comfort and protection of those they guided. A spring, which many long years before had induced the natives to select the place for their temporary fortification, was soon cleared of leaves, and a fountain of crystal gushed from the bed, diffusing its waters over the verdant hillock. A corner of the building was then roofed in such a manner as to exclude the heavy dew of the climate, and piles of sweet shrubs and dried leaves were laid beneath it for the sisters to repose on.

While the diligent woodsmen were employed in this manner, Cora and Alice partook of that refreshment which duty required much more than inclination prompted them to accept. They then retired within the walls, and first offering up their thanksgivings for past mercies, and petitioning for a continuance of the Divine favor throughout the coming night, they laid their tender forms on the fragrant couch, and in spite of recollections and forebodings, soon sank into those slumbers which nature so imperiously demanded, and which were sweetened by hopes for the morrow. Duncan had prepared himself to pass the night in watchfulness near them, just without the ruin, but the scout, perceiving his intention, pointed toward Chingachgook, as he coolly disposed his own person on the grass, and said:

"The eyes of a white man are too heavy and too blind for such a watch as this! The Mohican will be our sentinel, therefore let us sleep."

"I proved myself a sluggard on my post during the past night," said Heyward, "and have less need of repose than you, who did more credit to the character of a soldier. Let all the party seek their rest, then, while I hold the guard."

"If we lay among the white tents of the Sixtieth, and in front of an enemy like the French, I could not ask for a better watchman," returned the scout; "but in the darkness and among the signs of the wilderness your judgment would be like the folly of a child, and your vigilance thrown away. Do then, like Uncas and myself, sleep, and sleep in safety."

Heyward perceived, in truth, that the younger Indian had thrown his form on the side of the hillock while they were talking, like one who sought to make the most of the time allotted to rest, and that his example had been followed by David, whose voice literally "clove to his jaws," with the fever of his wound, heightened, as it was, by their toilsome march. Unwilling to prolong a useless discussion, the young man affected to comply, by posting his back against the logs of the blockhouse, in a half recumbent posture, though resolutely determined, in his own mind, not to close an eye until he had delivered his precious charge into the arms of Munro himself. Hawkeye, believing he had prevailed, soon fell asleep, and a silence as deep as the solitude in which they had found it, pervaded the retired spot.

For many minutes Duncan succeeded in keeping his senses on the alert, and alive to every moaning sound that arose from the forest. His vision became more acute as the shades of evening settled on the place; and even after the stars were glimmering above his head, he was able to distinguish the recumbent forms of his companions, as they lay stretched on the grass, and to note the person of Chingachgook, who sat upright and motionless as one of the trees which formed the dark barrier on every side. He still heard the gentle breathings of the sisters, who lay within a few feet of him, and not a leaf was ruffled by the passing air of which his ear did not detect the whispering sound. At length, however, the mournful notes of a whip-poor-will became blended with the moanings of an owl; his heavy eyes occasionally sought the bright rays of the stars, and he then fancied he saw them through the fallen lids. At instants of momentary wakefulness he mistook a bush for his associate sentinel; his head next sank upon his shoulder, which, in its turn, sought the support of the ground; and, finally, his whole person became relaxed and pliant, and the young man sank into a deep sleep, dreaming that he was a knight of ancient chivalry, holding his midnight vigils before the tent of a recaptured princess, whose favor he did not despair of gaining, by such a proof of devotion and watchfulness.

How long the tired Duncan lay in this insensible state he never knew himself, but his slumbering visions had been long lost in total forgetfulness, when he was awakened by a light tap on the shoulder. Aroused by this signal, slight as it was, he sprang upon his feet with a confused recollection of the self-imposed duty he had assumed with the commencement of the night.

“Who comes?” he demanded, feeling for his sword, at the place where it was usually suspended. “Speak! friend or enemy?”

“Friend,” replied the low voice of Chingachgook; who, pointing upward at the luminary which was shedding its mild light through the opening in the trees, directly in their bivouac, immediately added, in his rude English: "Moon comes and white man's fort far – far off; time to move, when sleep shuts both eyes of the Frenchman!"

"You say true! Call up your friends, and bridle the horses while I prepare my own companions for the march!"

"We are awake, Duncan," said the soft, silvery tones of Alice within the building, "and ready to travel very fast after so refreshing a sleep; but you have watched through the tedious night in our behalf, after having endured so much fatigue the livelong day!"

"Say, rather, I would have watched, but my treacherous eyes betrayed me; twice have I proved myself unfit for the trust I bear."

"Nay, Duncan, deny it not," interrupted the smiling Alice, issuing from the shadows of the building into the light of the moon, in all the loveliness of her freshened beauty; "I know you to be a heedless one, when self is the object of your care, and but too vigilant in favor of others. Can we not tarry here a little longer while you find the rest you need? Cheerfully, most cheerfully, will Cora and I keep the vigils, while you and all these brave men endeavor to snatch a little sleep!"

"If shame could cure me of my drowsiness, I should never close an eye again," said the uneasy youth, gazing at the ingenuous countenance of Alice, where, however, in its sweet solicitude, he read nothing to confirm his half-awakened suspicion. "It is but too true, that after leading you into danger by my heedlessness, I have not even the merit of guarding your pillows as should become a soldier."

"No one but Duncan himself should accuse Duncan of such a weakness. Go, then, and sleep; believe me, neither of us, weak girls as we are, will betray our watch."

The young man was relieved from the awkwardness of making any further protestations of his own demerits, by an exclamation from Chingachgook, and the attitude of riveted attention assumed by his son.

"The Mohicans hear an enemy!" whispered Hawkeye, who, by this time, in common with the whole party, was awake and stirring. "They scent danger in the wind!"

"God forbid!" exclaimed Heyward. "Surely we have had enough of bloodshed!"

While he spoke, however, the young soldier seized his rifle, and advancing toward the front, prepared to atone for his venial remissness, by freely exposing his life in defense of those he attended.

"'Tis some creature of the forest prowling around us in quest of food," he said, in a whisper, as soon as the low, and apparently distant sounds, which had startled the Mohicans, reached his own ears.

"Hist!" returned the attentive scout; "'tis man; even I can now tell his tread, poor as my senses are when compared to an Indian's! That Scampering Huron has fallen in with one of Montcalm's outlying parties, and they have struck upon our trail. I shouldn't like, myself, to spill more human blood in this spot," he added, looking around with anxiety in his features, at the dim objects by which he was surrounded; "but what must be, must! Lead the horses into the blockhouse, Uncas; and, friends, do you follow to the same shelter. Poor and old as it is, it offers a cover, and has rung with the crack of a rifle afore to-night!"

He was instantly obeyed, the Mohicans leading the Narragansetts within the ruin, whither the whole party repaired with the most guarded silence.

The sound of approaching footsteps were now too distinctly audible to leave any doubts as to the nature of the interruption. They were soon mingled with voices calling to each other in an Indian dialect, which the hunter, in a whisper, affirmed to Heyward was the language of the Hurons. When the party reached the point where the horses had entered the thicket which surrounded the blockhouse, they were evidently at fault, having lost those marks which, until that moment, had directed their pursuit.

It would seem by the voices that twenty men were soon collected at that one spot, mingling their different opinions and advice in noisy clamor.

"The knaves know our weakness," whispered Hawkeye, who stood by the side of Heyward, in deep shade, looking through an opening in the logs, "or they wouldn't indulge their idleness in such a squaw's march. Listen to the reptiles! each man among them seems to have two tongues, and but a single leg."

Duncan, brave as he was in the combat, could not, in such a moment of painful suspense, make any reply to the cool and characteristic remark of the scout. He only grasped his rifle more firmly, and fastened his eyes upon the narrow opening, through which he gazed upon the moonlight view with increasing anxiety. The deeper tones of one who spoke as having authority were next heard, amid a silence that denoted the respect with which his orders, or rather advice, was received. After which, by the rustling of leaves, and crackling of dried twigs, it was apparent the savages were separating in pursuit of the lost trail. Fortunately for the pursued, the light of the moon, while it shed a flood of mild luster upon the little area around the ruin, was not sufficiently strong to penetrate the deep arches of the forest, where the objects still lay in deceptive shadow. The search proved fruitless; for so short and sudden had been the passage from the faint path the travelers had journeyed into the thicket, that every trace of their footsteps was lost in the obscurity of the woods.

It was not long, however, before the restless savages were heard beating the brush, and gradually approaching the inner edge of that dense border of young chestnuts which encircled the little area.

"They are coming," muttered Heyward,

endeavoring to thrust his rifle through the chink in the logs; "let us fire on their approach."

"Keep everything in the shade," returned the scout; "the snapping of a flint, or even the smell of a single karnel of the brimstone, would bring the hungry varlets upon us in a body. Should it please God that we must give battle for the scalps, trust to the experience of men who know the ways of the savages, and who are not often backward when the war-whoop is howled."

Duncan cast his eyes behind him, and saw that the trembling sisters were cowering in the far corner of the building, while the Mohicans stood in the shadow, like two upright posts, ready, and apparently willing, to strike when the blow should be needed. Curbing his impatience, he again looked out upon the area, and awaited the result in silence. At that instant the thicket opened, and a tall and armed Huron advanced a few paces into the open space. As he gazed upon the silent blockhouse, the moon fell upon his swarthy countenance, and betrayed its surprise and curiosity. He made the exclamation which usually accompanies the former emotion in an Indian, and, calling in a low voice, soon drew a companion to his side.

These children of the woods stood together for several moments pointing at the crumbling edifice, and conversing in the unintelligible language of their tribe. They then approached, though with slow and cautious steps, pausing every instant to look at the building, like startled deer whose curiosity struggled powerfully with their awakened apprehensions for the mastery. The foot of one of them suddenly rested on the mound, and he stopped to examine its nature. At this moment, Heyward observed that the scout loosened his knife in its sheath, and lowered the muzzle of his rifle. Imitating these movements, the young man prepared himself for the struggle which now seemed inevitable.

The savages were so near, that the least motion in one of the horses, or even a breath louder than common, would have betrayed the fugitives. But in discovering the character of the mound, the attention of the Hurons appeared directed to a different object. They spoke together, and the sounds of their voices were low and solemn, as if influenced by a reverence that was deeply blended with awe. Then they drew warily back, keeping their eyes riveted on the ruin, as if they expected to see the apparitions of the dead issue from its silent walls, until, having reached the boundary of the area, they moved slowly into the thicket and disappeared.

Hawkeye dropped the breech of his rifle to the earth, and drawing a long, free breath, exclaimed, in an audible whisper:

"Ay! they respect the dead, and it has this time saved their own lives, and, it may be, the lives of better men too."

Heyward lent his attention for a single moment to his companion, but without replying, he again turned toward those who just then interested him more. He heard the two Hurons leave the bushes, and it was soon plain that all the pursuers were gathered about them, in deep attention to their report. After a few minutes of earnest and solemn dialogue, altogether different from the noisy clamor with which they had first collected about the spot, the sounds grew fainter and more distant, and finally were lost in the depths of the forest.

Hawkeye waited until a signal from the listening Chingachgook assured him that every sound from the retiring party was completely swallowed by the distance, when he motioned to Heyward to lead forth the horses, and to assist the sisters into their saddles. The instant this was done they issued through the broken gateway, and stealing out by a direction opposite to the one by which they entered, they quitted the spot, the sisters casting furtive glances at the silent, grave and crumbling ruin, as they left the soft light of the moon, to bury themselves in the gloom of the woods.

Chapter Fourteen

"Guard. – Qui est la?
Puc. – Paisans, pauvres gens de France."
– King Henry VI

DURING THE RAPID MOVEMENT from the blockhouse, and until the party was deeply buried in the forest, each individual was too much interested in the escape to hazard a word even in whispers. The scout resumed his post in advance, though his steps, after he had thrown a safe distance between himself and his enemies, were more deliberate than in their previous march, in consequence of his utter ignorance of the localities of the surrounding woods. More than once he halted to consult with his confederates, the Mohicans, pointing upward at the moon, and examining the barks of the trees with care. In these brief pauses, Heyward and the sisters listened, with senses rendered doubly acute by the danger, to detect any symptoms which might announce the proximity of their foes. At such moments, it seemed as if a vast range of country lay buried in eternal sleep; not the least sound arising from the forest, unless it was the distant and scarcely audible rippling of a water-course. Birds, beasts, and man, appeared to slumber alike, if, indeed, any of the latter were to be found in that wide tract of wilderness. But the sounds of the rivulet, feeble and murmuring as they were, relieved the guides at once from no trifling embarrassment, and toward it they immediately held their way.

When the banks of the little stream were

gained, Hawkeye made another halt; and taking the moccasins from his feet, he invited Heyward and Gamut to follow his example. He then entered the water, and for near an hour they traveled in the bed of the brook, leaving no trail. The moon had already sunk into an immense pile of black clouds, which lay impending above the western horizon, when they issued from the low and devious water-course to rise again to the light and level of the sandy but wooded plain. Here the scout seemed to be once more at home, for he held on this way with the certainty and diligence of a man who moved in the security of his own knowledge. The path soon became more uneven, and the travelers could plainly perceive that the mountains drew nigher to them on each hand, and that they were, in truth, about entering one of their gorges. Suddenly, Hawkeye made a pause, and, waiting until he was joined by the whole party, he spoke, though in tones so low and cautious, that they added to the solemnity of his words, in the quiet and darkness of the place.

"It is easy to know the pathways, and to find the licks and water-courses of the wilderness," he said; "but who that saw this spot could venture to say, that a mighty army was at rest among yonder silent trees and barren mountains?"

"We are, then, at no great distance from William Henry?" said Heyward, advancing nigher to the scout.

"It is yet a long and weary path, and when and where to strike it is now our greatest difficulty. See," he said, pointing through the trees toward a spot where a little basin of water reflected the stars from its placid bosom, "here is the 'bloody pond'; and I am on ground that I have not only often traveled, but over which I have fou't the enemy, from the rising to the setting sun."

"Ha! that sheet of dull and dreary water, then, is the sepulcher of the brave men who fell in the contest. I have heard it named, but never have I stood on its banks before."

"Three battles did we make with the Dutch-Frenchman[16] in a day," continued Hawkeye, pursuing the train of his own thoughts, rather than replying to the remark of Duncan. "He met us hard by, in our outward march to ambush his advance, and scattered us, like driven deer, through the defile, to the shores of Horican. Then we rallied behind our fallen trees, and made head against him, under Sir William – who was made Sir William for that very deed; and well did we pay him for the disgrace of the morning! Hundreds of Frenchmen saw the sun that day for the last time; and even their leader, Dieskau himself, fell into our hands, so cut and torn with the lead, that he has gone back to his

---

16 Baron Dieskau, a German, in the service of France. A few years previously to the period of the tale, this officer was defeated by Sir William Johnson, of Johnstown, New York, on the shores of Lake George.

own country, unfit for further acts in war."

"'Twas a noble repulse!" exclaimed Heyward, in the heat of his youthful ardor; "the fame of it reached us early, in our southern army."

"Ay! but it did not end there. I was sent by Major Effingham, at Sir William's own bidding, to outflank the French, and carry the tidings of their disaster across the portage, to the fort on the Hudson. Just hereaway, where you see the trees rise into a mountain swell, I met a party coming down to our aid, and I led them where the enemy were taking their meal, little dreaming that they had not finished the bloody work of the day."

"And you surprised them?"

"If death can be a surprise to men who are thinking only of the cravings of their appetites. We gave them but little breathing time, for they had borne hard upon us in the fight of the morning, and there were few in our party who had not lost friend or relative by their hands."

"When all was over, the dead, and some say the dying, were cast into that little pond. These eyes have seen its waters colored with blood, as natural water never yet flowed from the bowels of the 'arth."

"It was a convenient, and, I trust, will prove a peaceful grave for a soldier. You have then seen much service on this frontier?"

"Ay!" said the scout, erecting his tall person with an air of military pride; "there are not many echoes among these hills that haven't rung with the crack of my rifle, nor is there the space of a square mile atwixt Horican and the river, that 'killdeer' hasn't dropped a living body on, be it an enemy or be it a brute beast. As for the grave there being as quiet as you mention, it is another matter. There are them in the camp who say and think, man, to lie still, should not be buried while the breath is in the body; and certain it is that in the hurry of that evening, the doctors had but little time to say who was living and who was dead. Hist! see you nothing walking on the shore of the pond?"

"'Tis not probable that any are as houseless as ourselves in this dreary forest."

"Such as he may care but little for house or shelter, and night dew can never wet a body that passes its days in the water," returned the scout, grasping the shoulder of Heyward with such convulsive strength as to make the young soldier painfully sensible how much superstitious terror had got the mastery of a man usually so dauntless.

"By heaven, there is a human form, and it approaches! Stand to your arms, my friends; for we know not whom we encounter."

"Qui vive?" demanded a stern, quick voice, which sounded like a challenge from another world, issuing out of that solitary and solemn place.

"What says it?" whispered the scout; "it speaks neither Indian nor English."

"Qui vive?" repeated the same voice, which

was quickly followed by the rattling of arms, and a menacing attitude.

"France!" cried Heyward, advancing from the shadow of the trees to the shore of the pond, within a few yards of the sentinel.

"D'ou venez-vous – ou allez-vous, d'aussi bonne heure?" demanded the grenadier, in the language and with the accent of a man from old France.

"Je viens de la decouverte, et je vais me coucher."

"Etes-vous officier du roi?"

"Sans doute, mon camarade; me prends-tu pour un provincial! Je suis capitaine de chasseurs (Heyward well knew that the other was of a regiment in the line); j'ai ici, avec moi, les filles du commandant de la fortification. Aha! tu en as entendu parler! je les ai fait prisonnieres pres de l'autre fort, et je les conduis au general."

"Ma foi! mesdames; j'en suis fвche pour vous," exclaimed the young soldier, touching his cap with grace; "mais – fortune de guerre!

vous trouverez notre general un brave homme, et bien poli avec les dames."

"C'est le caractere des gens de guerre," said Cora, with admirable self-possession. "Adieu, mon ami; je vous souhaiterais un devoir plus agreable a remplir."

The soldier made a low and humble acknowledgment for her civility; and Heyward adding a "Bonne nuit, mon camarade," they moved deliberately forward, leaving the sentinel pacing the banks of the silent pond, little suspecting an enemy of so much effrontery, and humming to himself those words which were recalled to his mind by the sight of women, and, perhaps, by recollections of his own distant and beautiful France: "Vive le vin, vive l'amour," etc., etc.

"'Tis well you understood the knave!" whispered the scout, when they had gained a little distance from the place, and letting his rifle fall into the hollow of his arm again; "I soon saw that he was one of them uneasy Frenchers; and well for him it was that his speech was friendly and his wishes kind, or a place might have been found for his bones among those of his countrymen."

He was interrupted by a long and heavy groan which arose from the little basin, as though, in truth, the spirits of the departed lingered about their watery sepulcher.

"Surely it was of flesh," continued the scout; "no spirit could handle its arms so steadily."

"It was of flesh; but whether the poor fellow still belongs to this world may well be doubted," said Heyward, glancing his eyes around him, and missing Chingachgook from their little band. Another groan more faint than the former was succeeded by a heavy and sullen plunge into the water, and all was still again as if the borders of the dreary pool had never been awakened from the silence of creation. While they yet hesitated in uncertainty, the form of the Indian was seen gliding out of the thicket. As the chief rejoined them, with one hand he attached the reeking scalp of the unfortunate young Frenchman to his girdle, and with the other he replaced the knife and tomahawk that had drunk his blood. He then took his wonted station, with the air of a man who believed he had done a deed of merit.

The scout dropped one end of his rifle to the earth, and leaning his hands on the other, he stood musing in profound silence. Then, shaking his head in a mournful manner, he muttered:

"'Twould have been a cruel and an unhuman act for a white-skin; but 'tis the gift and natur' of an Indian, and I suppose it should not be denied. I could wish, though, it had befallen an accursed Mingo, rather than that gay young boy from the old countries."

"Enough!" said Heyward, apprehensive the unconscious sisters might comprehend the nature of the detention, and conquering his disgust by a train of reflections very much like that of the hunter; "'tis done; and though better it were left undone, cannot be amended. You see, we are, too obviously within the sentinels of the enemy; what course do you propose to follow?"

"Yes," said Hawkeye, rousing himself again; "'tis as you say, too late to harbor further thoughts about it. Ay, the French have gathered around the fort in good earnest and we have a delicate needle to thread in passing them."

"And but little time to do it in," added Heyward, glancing his eyes upwards, toward the bank of vapor that concealed the setting moon.

"And little time to do it in!" repeated the scout. "The thing may be done in two fashions, by the help of Providence, without which it may not be done at all."

"Name them quickly for time presses."

"One would be to dismount the gentle ones, and let their beasts range the plain, by sending the Mohicans in front, we might then cut a lane through their sentries, and enter the fort over the dead bodies."

"It will not do – it will not do!" interrupted the generous Heyward; "a soldier might force his way in this manner, but never with such a convoy."

"'Twould be, indeed, a bloody path for such tender feet to wade in," returned the equally reluctant scout; "but I thought it befitting my manhood to name it. We must, then, turn in our trail and get without the line of their lookouts, when we will bend short to the west, and enter the mountains; where I can hide you, so that all the devil's hounds in Montcalm's pay would be thrown off the scent for months to come."

"Let it be done, and that instantly."

Further words were unnecessary; for Hawkeye, merely uttering the mandate to "follow," moved along the route by which they had just entered their present critical and even dangerous situation. Their progress, like their late dialogue, was guarded, and without noise; for none knew at what moment a passing patrol, or a crouching picket of the enemy, might rise upon their path. As they held their silent way along the margin of the pond, again Heyward and the scout stole furtive glances at its appalling dreariness. They looked in vain for the form they had so recently seen stalking along in silent shores, while a low and regular wash of the little waves, by announcing that the waters were not yet subsided, furnished a frightful memorial of the deed of blood they had just witnessed. Like all that passing and gloomy scene, the low basin, however, quickly melted in the darkness, and became blended with the mass of black objects in the rear of the travelers.

Hawkeye soon deviated from the line of their retreat, and striking off towards the mountains which form the western boundary of the narrow plain, he led his followers, with swift steps, deep within the shadows that were cast from their high and broken summits. The route was now painful; lying over ground ragged with rocks, and intersected with ravines, and their progress proportionately slow. Bleak and black hills lay on every side of them, compensating in some degree for the additional toil of the march by the sense of security they imparted. At length the party began slowly to rise a steep and rugged ascent, by a path that curiously wound among rocks and trees, avoiding the one and supported by the other, in a manner that showed it had been devised by men long practised in the arts of the wilderness. As they gradually rose from the level of the valleys, the thick darkness which usually precedes the approach of day began to disperse, and objects were seen in the plain and palpable colors with which they had been gifted by nature. When they issued from the stunted woods which clung to the barren sides of the mountain, upon a flat and mossy rock that formed its summit, they met the morning, as it came blushing above the green pines of a hill that lay on the opposite side of the valley of the Horican.

The scout now told the sisters to dismount; and taking the bridles from the mouths, and the saddles off the backs of the jaded beasts, he turned them loose, to glean a scanty subsistence among the shrubs and meager herbage of that elevated region.

"Go," he said, "and seek your food where natur' gives it to you; and beware that you become not food to ravenous wolves yourselves, among these hills."

"Have we no further need of them?" demanded Heyward.

"See, and judge with your own eyes," said the scout, advancing toward the eastern brow of the mountain, whither he beckoned for the whole party to follow; "if it was as easy to look into the heart of man as it is to spy out the nakedness of Montcalm's camp from this spot, hypocrites would grow scarce, and the cunning of a Mingo might prove a losing game, compared to the honesty of a

Delaware."

When the travelers reached the verge of the precipices they saw, at a glance, the truth of the scout's declaration, and the admirable foresight with which he had led them to their commanding station.

The mountain on which they stood, elevated perhaps a thousand feet in the air, was a high cone that rose a little in advance of that range which stretches for miles along the western shores of the lake, until meeting its sisters miles beyond the water, it ran off toward the Canadas, in confused and broken masses of rock, thinly sprinkled with evergreens. Immediately at the feet of the party, the southern shore of the Horican swept in a broad semicircle from mountain to mountain, marking a wide strand, that soon rose into an uneven and somewhat elevated plain. To the north stretched the limpid, and, as it appeared from that dizzy height, the narrow sheet of the "holy lake," indented with numberless bays, embellished by fantastic headlands, and dotted with countless islands. At the distance of a few leagues, the bed of the water became lost among mountains, or was wrapped in the masses of vapor that came slowly rolling along their bosom, before a light morning air. But a narrow opening between the crests of the hills pointed out the passage by which they found their way still further north, to spread their pure and ample sheets again, before pouring out their tribute into the distant Champlain. To the south stretched the defile, or rather broken plain, so often mentioned. For several miles in this direction, the mountains appeared reluctant to yield their dominion, but within reach of the eye they diverged, and finally melted into the level and sandy lands, across which we have accompanied our adventurers in their double journey. Along both ranges of hills, which bounded the opposite sides of the lake and valley, clouds of light vapor were rising in spiral wreaths from the uninhabited woods, looking like the smoke of hidden cottages;

or rolled lazily down the declivities, to mingle with the fogs of the lower land. A single, solitary, snow-white cloud floated above the valley, and marked the spot beneath which lay the silent pool of the "bloody pond."

Directly on the shore of the lake, and nearer to its western than to its eastern margin, lay the extensive earthen ramparts and low buildings of William Henry. Two of the sweeping bastions appeared to rest on the water which washed their bases, while a deep ditch and extensive morasses guarded its other sides and angles. The land had been cleared of wood for a reasonable distance around the work, but every other part of the scene lay in the green livery of nature, except where the limpid water mellowed the view, or the bold rocks thrust their black and naked heads above the undulating outline of the mountain ranges. In its front might be seen the scattered sentinels, who held a weary watch against their numerous foes; and within the walls themselves, the travelers looked down upon men still drowsy with a night of vigilance. Toward the southeast, but in immediate contact with the fort, was an entrenched camp, posted on a rocky eminence, that would have been far more eligible for the work itself, in which Hawkeye pointed out the presence of those auxiliary regiments that had so recently left the Hudson in their company. From the woods, a little further to the south, rose numerous dark and lurid smokes, that were easily to be distinguished from the purer exhalations of the springs, and which the scout also showed to Heyward, as evidences that the enemy lay in force in that direction.

But the spectacle which most concerned the young soldier was on the western bank of the lake, though quite near to its southern termination. On a strip of land, which appeared from his stand too narrow to contain such an army, but which, in truth, extended many hundreds of yards from the shores of the Horican to the base of the mountain, were to be seen the white tents and military engines of an encampment of ten thousand men. Batteries were already thrown up in their front, and even while the spectators above them were looking down, with such different emotions, on a scene which lay like a map beneath their feet, the roar of artillery rose from the valley, and passed off in thundering echoes along the eastern hills.

"Morning is just touching them below," said the deliberate and musing scout, "and the watchers have a mind to wake up the sleepers by the sound of cannon. We are a few hours too late! Montcalm has already filled the woods with his accursed Iroquois."

"The place is, indeed, invested," returned Duncan; "but is there no expedient by which we may enter? capture in the works would be far preferable to falling again into the hands of roving Indians."

"See!" exclaimed the scout, unconsciously

directing the attention of Cora to the quarters of her own father, “how that shot has made the stones fly from the side of the commandant’s house! Ay! these Frenchers will pull it to pieces faster than it was put together, solid and thick though it be!”

“Heyward, I sicken at the sight of danger that I cannot share,” said the undaunted but anxious daughter. “Let us go to Montcalm, and demand admission: he dare not deny a child the boon.”

“You would scarce find the tent of the Frenchman with the hair on your head”; said the blunt scout. “If I had but one of the thousand boats which lie empty along that shore, it might be done! Ha! here will soon be an end of the firing, for yonder comes a fog that will turn day to night, and make an Indian arrow more dangerous than a molded cannon. Now, if you are equal to the work, and will follow, I will make a push; for I long to get down into that camp, if it be only to scatter some Mingo dogs that I see lurking in the skirts of yonder thicket of birch."

"We are equal," said Cora, firmly; "on such an errand we will follow to any danger."

The scout turned to her with a smile of honest and cordial approbation, as he answered:

"I would I had a thousand men, of brawny limbs and quick eyes, that feared death as little as you! I'd send them jabbering Frenchers back into their den again, afore the week was ended, howling like so many fettered hounds or hungry wolves. But, sir," he added, turning from her to the rest of the party, "the fog comes rolling down so fast, we shall have but just the time to meet it on the plain, and use it as a cover. Remember, if any accident should befall me, to keep the air blowing on your left cheeks – or, rather, follow the Mohicans; they'd scent their way, be it in day or be it at night."

He then waved his hand for them to follow, and threw himself down the steep declivity, with free, but careful footsteps. Heyward assisted the sisters to descend, and in a few minutes they were all far down a mountain whose sides they had climbed with so much toil and pain.

The direction taken by Hawkeye soon brought the travelers to the level of the plain, nearly opposite to a sally-port in the western curtain of the fort, which lay itself at the distance of about half a mile from the point where he halted to allow Duncan to come up with his charge. In their eagerness, and favored by the nature of the ground, they had anticipated the fog, which was rolling heavily down the lake, and it became necessary to pause, until the mists had wrapped the camp of the enemy in their fleecy mantle. The Mohicans profited by the delay, to steal out of the woods, and to make a survey of surrounding objects. They were followed at a little distance by the scout, with a view to profit early by their report, and to obtain some faint knowledge for himself of the more immediate localities.

In a very few moments he returned, his face reddened with vexation, while he muttered his disappointment in words of no very gentle import.

“Here has the cunning Frenchman been posting a picket directly in our path,” he said; “red-skins and whites; and we shall be as likely to fall into their midst as to pass them in the fog!”

“Cannot we make a circuit to avoid the danger,” asked Heyward, “and come into our path again when it is passed?”

“Who that once bends from the line of his march in a fog can tell when or how to find it again! The mists of Horican are not like the curls from a peace-pipe, or the smoke which settles above a mosquito fire.”

He was yet speaking, when a crashing sound was heard, and a cannon-ball entered the thicket, striking the body of a sapling, and rebounding to the earth, its force being much expended by previous resistance.

The Indians followed instantly like busy attendants on the terrible messenger, and Uncas commenced speaking earnestly and with much action, in the Delaware tongue.

"It may be so, lad," muttered the scout, when he had ended; "for desperate fevers are not to be treated like a toothache. Come, then, the fog is shutting in."

"Stop!" cried Heyward; "first explain your expectations."

"'Tis soon done, and a small hope it is; but it is better than nothing. This shot that you see," added the scout, kicking the harmless iron with his foot, "has plowed the 'arth in its road from the fort, and we shall hunt for the furrow it has made, when all other signs may fail. No more words, but follow, or the fog may leave us in the middle of our path, a mark for both armies to shoot at."

Heyward perceiving that, in fact, a crisis had arrived, when acts were more required than words, placed himself between the sisters, and drew them swiftly forward, keeping the dim figure of their leader in his eye. It was soon apparent that Hawkeye had not magnified the power of the fog, for before they had proceeded twenty yards, it was difficult for the different individuals of the party to distinguish each other in the vapor.

They had made their little circuit to the left, and were already inclining again toward the right, having, as Heyward thought, got over nearly half the distance to the friendly works, when his ears were saluted with the fierce summons, apparently within twenty feet of them, of:

"Qui va la?"

"Push on!" whispered the scout, once more bending to the left.

"Push on!" repeated Heyward; when the summons was renewed by a dozen voices, each of which seemed charged with menace.

"C'est moi," cried Duncan, dragging rather than leading those he supported swiftly onward.

"Bete! – qui? – moi!"

"Ami de la France."

"Tu m'as plus l'air d'un ennemi de la France; arrete ou pardieu je te ferai ami du diable. Non! feu, camarades, feu!"

The order was instantly obeyed, and the fog was stirred by the explosion of fifty muskets. Happily, the aim was bad, and the bullets cut the air in a direction a little different from that taken by the fugitives; though still so nigh them, that to the unpractised ears of David and the two females, it appeared as if they whistled within a few inches of the organs. The outcry was renewed, and the order, not only to fire again, but to pursue, was too plainly audible. When Heyward briefly explained the meaning of the words they heard, Hawkeye halted and spoke with quick decision and great firmness.

"Let us deliver our fire," he said; "they will believe it a sortie, and give way, or they will wait for reinforcements."

The scheme was well conceived, but failed

in its effects. The instant the French heard the pieces, it seemed as if the plain was alive with men, muskets rattling along its whole extent, from the shores of the lake to the furthest boundary of the woods.

"We shall draw their entire army upon us, and bring on a general assault," said Duncan: "lead on, my friend, for your own life and ours."

The scout seemed willing to comply; but, in the hurry of the moment, and in the change of position, he had lost the direction. In vain he turned either cheek toward the light air; they felt equally cool. In this dilemma, Uncas lighted on the furrow of the cannon ball, where it had cut the ground in three adjacent ant-hills.

"Give me the range!" said Hawkeye, bending to catch a glimpse of the direction, and then instantly moving onward.

Cries, oaths, voices calling to each other, and the reports of muskets, were now quick and incessant, and, apparently, on every side of them. Suddenly a strong glare of light flashed across the scene, the fog rolled upward in thick wreaths, and several cannons belched across the plain, and the roar was thrown heavily back from the bellowing echoes of the mountain.

"'Tis from the fort!" exclaimed Hawkeye, turning short on his tracks; "and we, like stricken fools, were rushing to the woods, under the very knives of the Maquas."

The instant their mistake was rectified, the whole party retraced the error with the utmost diligence. Duncan willingly relinquished the support of Cora to the arm of Uncas and Cora as readily accepted the welcome assistance. Men, hot and angry in pursuit, were evidently on their footsteps, and each instant threatened their capture, if not their destruction.

"Point de quartier aux coquins!" cried an eager pursuer, who seemed to direct the operations of the enemy.

"Stand firm, and be ready, my gallant

Sixtieths!" suddenly exclaimed a voice above them; "wait to see the enemy, fire low and sweep the glacis."

"Father! father!" exclaimed a piercing cry from out the mist: "it is I! Alice! thy own Elsie! Spare, oh! save your daughters!"

"Hold!" shouted the former speaker, in the awful tones of parental agony, the sound reaching even to the woods, and rolling back in solemn echo. "'Tis she! God has restored me to my children! Throw open the sally-port; to the field, Sixtieths, to the field; pull not a trigger, lest ye kill my lambs! Drive off these dogs of France with your steel."

Duncan heard the grating of the rusty hinges, and darting to the spot, directed by the sound, he met a long line of dark red warriors, passing swiftly toward the glacis. He knew them for his own battalion of the Royal Americans, and flying to their head, soon swept every trace of his pursuers from before the works.

For an instant, Cora and Alice had

stood trembling and bewildered by this unexpected desertion; but before either had leisure for speech, or even thought, an officer of gigantic frame, whose locks were bleached with years and service, but whose air of military grandeur had been rather softened than destroyed by time, rushed out of the body of mist, and folded them to his bosom, while large scalding tears rolled down his pale and wrinkled cheeks, and he exclaimed, in the peculiar accent of Scotland:

"For this I thank thee, Lord! Let danger come as it will, thy servant is now prepared!"

Chapter Fifteen

"Then go we in, to know his embassy;
Which I could, with ready guess, declare,
Before the Frenchmen speak a word of it."

– King Henry V

A FEW SUCCEEDING DAYS were passed amid the privations, the uproar, and the dangers of the siege, which was vigorously pressed by a power, against whose approaches Munro possessed no competent means of resistance. It appeared as if Webb, with his army, which lay slumbering on the banks of the Hudson, had utterly forgotten the strait to which his countrymen were reduced. Montcalm had filled the woods of the portage with his savages, every yell and whoop from whom rang through the British encampment, chilling the hearts of men who were already but too much disposed to magnify the danger.

Not so, however, with the besieged. Animated by the words, and stimulated by the examples of their leaders, they had found their courage, and maintained their ancient reputation, with a zeal that did justice to the stern character of their commander. As if satisfied with the toil of marching through the wilderness to encounter his enemy, the French general, though of approved skill, had neglected to seize the adjacent mountains; whence the besieged might have been exterminated with impunity, and which, in the more modern warfare of the country, would not have been neglected for a single hour. This sort of contempt for eminences, or rather dread of the labor of ascending them, might have been termed the besetting weakness of the warfare of the period. It originated in the simplicity of the Indian contests, in which, from the nature of the combats, and the density of the forests, fortresses were rare, and artillery next to useless. The carelessness engendered by these usages descended even to the war of the Revolution and lost the States the important fortress of Ticonderoga opening a way for the army of Burgoyne into what was then the bosom of the country. We look back at this ignorance, or infatuation, whichever it may be called, with wonder, knowing that the neglect of an eminence, whose difficulties, like those of Mount Defiance, have been so greatly exaggerated, would, at the present time, prove fatal to the reputation of the engineer who had planned the works at their base, or to that of the general whose lot it was to defend them.

The tourist, the valetudinarian, or the amateur of the beauties of nature, who, in the train of his four-in-hand, now rolls through the scenes we have attempted to describe, in quest of information, health, or pleasure, or floats steadily toward his object on those artificial waters which have sprung up under the administration of a statesman[17] who has dared to stake his political character on the hazardous issue, is not to suppose that his ancestors traversed those hills, or struggled with the same currents with equal facility. The transportation of a single heavy gun was often considered equal to a victory gained; if happily, the difficulties of the passage had not so far separated it from its necessary concomitant, the ammunition, as to render it no more than a useless tube of unwieldy iron.

The evils of this state of things pressed heavily on the fortunes of the resolute

17 Evidently the late De Witt Clinton, who died governor of New York in 1828.

Scotsman who now defended William Henry. Though his adversary neglected the hills, he had planted his batteries with judgment on the plain, and caused them to be served with vigor and skill. Against this assault, the besieged could only oppose the imperfect and hasty preparations of a fortress in the wilderness.

It was in the afternoon of the fifth day of the siege, and the fourth of his own service in it, that Major Heyward profited by a parley that had just been beaten, by repairing to the ramparts of one of the water bastions, to breathe the cool air from the lake, and to take a survey of the progress of the siege. He was alone, if the solitary sentinel who paced the mound be excepted; for the artillerists had hastened also to profit by the temporary suspension of their arduous duties. The evening was delightfully calm, and the light air from the limpid water fresh and soothing. It seemed as if, with the termination of the roar of artillery and the plunging of shot, nature had also seized the moment to assume her mildest and most captivating form. The sun poured down his parting glory on the scene, without the oppression of those fierce rays that belong to the climate and the season. The mountains looked green, and fresh, and lovely, tempered with the milder light, or softened in shadow, as thin vapors floated between them and the sun. The numerous islands rested on the bosom of the Horican, some low and sunken, as if embedded in the waters, and others appearing to hover about the element, in little hillocks of green velvet; among which the fishermen of the beleaguering army peacefully rowed their skiffs, or floated at rest on the glassy mirror in quiet pursuit of their employment.

The scene was at once animated and still. All that pertained to nature was sweet, or simply grand; while those parts which depended on the temper and movements of man were lively and playful.

Two little spotless flags were abroad,

the one on a salient angle of the fort, and the other on the advanced battery of the besiegers; emblems of the truth which existed, not only to the acts, but it would seem, also, to the enmity of the combatants.

Behind these again swung, heavily opening and closing in silken folds, the rival standards of England and France.

A hundred gay and thoughtless young Frenchmen were drawing a net to the pebbly beach, within dangerous proximity to the sullen but silent cannon of the fort, while the eastern mountain was sending back the loud shouts and gay merriment that attended their sport. Some were rushing eagerly to enjoy the aquatic games of the lake, and others were already toiling their way up the neighboring hills, with the restless curiosity of their nation. To all these sports and pursuits, those of the enemy who watched the besieged, and the besieged themselves, were, however, merely the idle though sympathizing spectators. Here and there a picket had, indeed, raised a song, or mingled in a dance, which had drawn the dusky savages around them, from their lairs in the forest. In short, everything wore rather the appearance of a day of pleasure, than of an hour stolen from the dangers and toil of a bloody and vindictive warfare.

Duncan had stood in a musing attitude, contemplating this scene a few minutes, when his eyes were directed to the glacis in front of the sally-port already mentioned, by the sounds of approaching footsteps. He walked to an angle of the bastion, and beheld the scout advancing, under the custody of a French officer, to the body of the fort. The countenance of Hawkeye was haggard and careworn, and his air dejected, as though he felt the deepest degradation at having fallen into the power of his enemies. He was without his favorite weapon, and his arms were even bound behind him with thongs, made of the skin of a deer. The arrival of flags to cover the messengers of summons, had occurred so often of late, that when Heyward first threw his careless glance on this group, he expected to see another of the officers of the enemy, charged with a similar office but the instant he recognized the tall person and still sturdy though downcast features of his friend, the woodsman, he started with surprise, and turned to descend from the bastion into the bosom of the work.

The sounds of other voices, however, caught his attention, and for a moment caused him to forget his purpose. At the inner angle of the mound he met the sisters, walking along the parapet, in search, like himself, of air and relief from confinement. They had not met from that painful moment when he deserted them on the plain, only to assure their safety. He had parted from them worn with care, and jaded with fatigue; he now saw them refreshed and blooming, though timid and anxious. Under such an inducement it will cause no surprise that the young man lost sight for a time, of other objects in order to address them. He was, however, anticipated by the voice of the ingenuous and youthful Alice.

"Ah! thou tyrant! thou recreant knight! he who abandons his damsels in the very lists," she cried; "here have we been days, nay, ages, expecting you at our feet, imploring mercy and forgetfulness of your craven backsliding, or I should rather say, backrunning – for verily you fled in the manner that no stricken deer, as our worthy friend the scout would say, could equal!"

"You know that Alice means our thanks and our blessings," added the graver and more thoughtful Cora. "In truth, we have a little wonder why you should so rigidly absent yourself from a place where the gratitude of the daughters might receive the support of a parent's thanks."

"Your father himself could tell you, that, though absent from your presence, I have not been altogether forgetful of your safety," returned the young man; "the mastery of yonder village of huts," pointing to the neighboring entrenched camp, "has been keenly disputed; and he who holds it is sure to be possessed of this fort, and that which it contains. My days and nights have all been passed there since we separated, because I thought that duty called me thither. But," he added, with an air of chagrin, which he endeavored, though unsuccessfully, to conceal, "had I been aware that what I then believed a soldier's conduct could be so construed, shame would have been added to the list of reasons."

"Heyward! Duncan!" exclaimed Alice, bending forward to read his half-averted countenance, until a lock of her golden hair rested on her flushed cheek, and nearly concealed the tear that had started to her eye; "did I think this idle tongue of mine had pained you, I would silence it forever. Cora can say, if Cora would, how justly we have prized your services, and how deep – I had almost said, how fervent – is our gratitude."

"And will Cora attest the truth of this?" cried Duncan, suffering the cloud to be chased from his countenance by a smile of open pleasure. "What says our graver sister? Will she find an excuse for the neglect of the knight in the duty of a soldier?"

Cora made no immediate answer, but turned her face toward the water, as if looking on the sheet of the Horican. When she did bend her dark eyes on the young man, they were yet filled with an expression of anguish that at once drove every thought but that of kind solicitude from his mind.

"You are not well, dearest Miss Munro!" he exclaimed; "we have trifled while you are in suffering!"

"'Tis nothing," she answered, refusing his support with feminine reserve. "That I cannot see the sunny side of the picture of life, like this artless but ardent enthusiast," she added, laying her hand lightly, but affectionately, on the arm of her sister, "is the penalty of experience, and, perhaps, the misfortune of my nature. See," she continued, as if determined to shake off infirmity, in a sense of duty; "look around you, Major Heyward, and tell me what a prospect is this for the daughter of a soldier whose greatest happiness is his honor and his military renown."

"Neither ought nor shall be tarnished by circumstances over which he has had no control," Duncan warmly replied. "But your words recall me to my own duty. I go now to your gallant father, to hear his determination in matters of the last moment to the defense. God bless you in every fortune, noble – Cora – I may and must call you." She frankly gave him her hand, though her lip quivered, and her cheeks gradually became of ashly paleness. "In every fortune, I know you will be an ornament and honor to your sex. Alice, adieu" – his voice changed from admiration to tenderness – "adieu, Alice; we shall soon meet again; as conquerors, I trust, and amid rejoicings!"

Without waiting for an answer from either, the young man threw himself down the grassy steps of the bastion, and moving rapidly across the parade, he was quickly in the presence of their father. Munro was pacing his narrow apartment with a disturbed air and gigantic strides as Duncan entered.

"You have anticipated my wishes, Major Heyward," he said; "I was about to request this favor."

"I am sorry to see, sir, that the messenger I so warmly recommended has returned in custody of the French! I hope there is no reason to distrust his fidelity?"

"The fidelity of 'The Long Rifle' is well known to me," returned Munro, "and is above suspicion; though his usual good fortune seems, at last, to have failed. Montcalm has got him, and with the accursed politeness of his nation, he has sent him in with a doleful tale, of 'knowing how I valued the fellow, he could not think of retaining him.' A Jesuitical way that, Major Duncan Heyward, of telling a man of his misfortunes!"

"But the general and his succor?"

"Did ye look to the south as ye entered, and could ye not see them?" said the old soldier, laughing bitterly.

"Hoot! hoot! you're an impatient boy, sir, and cannot give the gentlemen leisure for their march!"

"They are coming, then? The scout has said as much?"

"When? and by what path? for the dunce has omitted to tell me this. There is a letter, it would seem, too; and that is the only agreeable part of the matter. For the customary attentions of your Marquis of Montcalm – I warrant me, Duncan, that he of Lothian would buy a dozen such marquisates – but if the news of the letter were bad, the gentility of this French monsieur would certainly compel him to let us know it."

"He keeps the letter, then, while he releases

the messenger?"

"Ay, that does he, and all for the sake of what you call your 'bonhommie' I would venture, if the truth was known, the fellow's grandfather taught the noble science of dancing."

"But what says the scout? he has eyes and ears, and a tongue. What verbal report does he make?"

"Oh! sir, he is not wanting in natural organs, and he is free to tell all that he has seen and heard. The whole amount is this; there is a fort of his majesty's on the banks of the Hudson, called Edward, in honor of his gracious highness of York, you'll know; and it is well filled with armed men, as such a work should be."

"But was there no movement, no signs of any intention to advance to our relief?"

"There were the morning and evening parades; and when one of the provincial loons – you'll know, Duncan, you're half a Scotsman yourself – when one of them dropped his powder over his porretch, if it touched the coals, it just burned!" Then, suddenly changing his bitter, ironical manner, to one more grave and thoughtful, he continued: "and yet there might, and must be, something in that letter which it would be well to know!"

"Our decision should be speedy," said Duncan, gladly availing himself of this change of humor, to press the more important objects of their interview; "I cannot conceal from you, sir, that the camp will not be much longer tenable; and I am sorry to add, that things appear no better in the fort; more than half the guns are bursted."

"And how should it be otherwise? Some were fished from the bottom of the lake; some have been rusting in woods since the discovery of the country; and some were never guns at all – mere privateersmen's playthings! Do you think, sir, you can have Woolwich Warren in the midst of a wilderness, three thousand miles from Great Britain?"

"The walls are crumbling about our ears, and provisions begin to fail us," continued Heyward, without regarding the new burst of indignation; "even the men show signs of discontent and alarm."

"Major Heyward," said Munro, turning to his youthful associate with the dignity of his years and superior rank; "I should have served his majesty for half a century, and earned these gray hairs in vain, were I ignorant of all you say, and of the pressing nature of our circumstances; still, there is everything due to the honor of the king's arms, and something to ourselves. While there is hope of succor, this fortress will I defend, though it be to be done with pebbles gathered on the lake shore. It is a sight of the letter, therefore, that we want, that we may know the intentions of the man the earl of Loudon has left among us as his substitute."

"And can I be of service in the matter?"

"Sir, you can; the marquis of Montcalm

has, in addition to his other civilities, invited me to a personal interview between the works and his own camp; in order, as he says, to impart some additional information. Now, I think it would not be wise to show any undue solicitude to meet him, and I would employ you, an officer of rank, as my substitute; for it would but ill comport with the honor of Scotland to let it be said one of her gentlemen was outdone in civility by a native of any other country on earth."

Without assuming the supererogatory task of entering into a discussion of the comparative merits of national courtesy, Duncan cheerfully assented to supply the place of the veteran in the approaching interview. A long and confidential communication now succeeded, during which the young man received some additional insight into his duty, from the experience and native acuteness of his commander, and then the former took his leave.

As Duncan could only act as the representative of the commandant of the fort, the ceremonies which should have accompanied a meeting between the heads of the adverse forces were, of course, dispensed with. The truce still existed, and with a roll and beat of the drum, and covered by a little white flag, Duncan left the sally-port, within ten minutes after his instructions were ended. He was received by the French officer in advance with the usual formalities, and immediately accompanied to a distant marquee of the renowned soldier who led the forces of France.

The general of the enemy received the youthful messenger, surrounded by his principal officers, and by a swarthy band of the native chiefs, who had followed him to the field, with the warriors of their several tribes. Heyward paused short, when, in glancing his eyes rapidly over the dark group of the latter, he beheld the malignant countenance of Magua, regarding him with the calm but sullen attention which marked the expression of that subtle savage. A slight exclamation of surprise even burst from the lips of the young man, but instantly, recollecting his errand, and the presence in which he stood, he suppressed every appearance of emotion, and turned to the hostile leader, who had already advanced a step to receive him.

The marquis of Montcalm was, at the period of which we write, in the flower of his age, and, it may be added, in the zenith of his fortunes. But even in that enviable situation, he was affable, and distinguished as much for his attention to the forms of courtesy, as for that chivalrous courage which, only two short years afterward, induced him to throw away his life on the plains of Abraham. Duncan, in turning his eyes from the malign expression of Magua, suffered them to rest with pleasure on the smiling and polished features, and the noble military air, of the French general.

"Monsieur," said the latter, "j'ai beaucoup de plaisir a – bah! – ou est cet interprete?"

"Je crois, monsieur, qu'il ne sear pas necessaire," Heyward modestly replied; "je parle un peu francais."

"Ah! j'en suis bien aise," said Montcalm, taking Duncan familiarly by the arm, and leading him deep into the marquee, a little out of earshot; "je deteste ces fripons-la; on ne sait jamais sur quel pie on est avec eux. Eh, bien! monsieur," he continued still speaking in French; "though I should have been proud of receiving your commandant, I am very happy that he has seen proper to employ an officer so distinguished, and who, I am sure, is so amiable, as yourself."

Duncan bowed low, pleased with the compliment, in spite of a most heroic determination to suffer no artifice to allure him into forgetfulness of the interest of his prince; and Montcalm, after a pause of a moment, as if to collect his thoughts, proceeded:

"Your commandant is a brave man, and well qualified to repel my assault. Mais, monsieur, is it not time to begin to take more counsel of humanity, and less of your courage? The one as strongly characterizes the hero as the other."

"We consider the qualities as inseparable," returned Duncan, smiling; "but while we find in the vigor of your excellency every motive to stimulate the one, we can, as yet, see no particular call for the exercise of the other."

Montcalm, in his turn, slightly bowed, but it was with the air of a man too practised to remember the language of flattery. After musing a moment, he added:

"It is possible my glasses have deceived me, and that your works resist our cannon better than I had supposed. You know our force?"

"Our accounts vary," said Duncan, carelessly; "the highest, however, has not exceeded twenty thousand men."

The Frenchman bit his lip, and fastened his eyes keenly on the other as if to read his thoughts; then, with a readiness peculiar to himself, he continued, as if assenting to the truth of an enumeration which quite doubled his army:

"It is a poor compliment to the vigilance of us soldiers, monsieur, that, do what we will, we never can conceal our numbers. If it were to be done at all, one would believe it might succeed in these woods. Though you think it too soon to listen to the calls of humanity," he added, smiling archly, "I may be permitted to believe that gallantry is not forgotten by one so young as yourself. The daughters of the commandant, I learn, have passed into the fort since it was invested?"

"It is true, monsieur; but, so far from weakening our efforts, they set us an example of courage in their own fortitude. Were nothing but resolution necessary to repel so accomplished a soldier as M. de Montcalm, I would gladly trust the defense of William Henry to the elder of those ladies."

"We have a wise ordinance in our Salique laws, which says, 'The crown of France shall never degrade the lance to the distaff'," said Montcalm, dryly, and with a little hauteur; but instantly adding, with his former frank and easy air: "as all the nobler qualities are hereditary, I can easily credit you; though, as I said before, courage has its limits, and humanity must not be forgotten. I trust, monsieur, you come authorized to treat for the surrender of the place?"

"Has your excellency found our defense so feeble as to believe the measure necessary?"

"I should be sorry to have the defense protracted in such a manner as to irritate my red friends there," continued Montcalm, glancing his eyes at the group of grave and attentive Indians, without attending to the other's questions; "I find it difficult, even now, to limit them to the usages of war."

Heyward was silent; for a painful recollection of the dangers he had so recently escaped came over his mind, and recalled the images of those defenseless beings who had shared in all his sufferings.

"Cesmessieurs-la," said Montcalm, following up the advantage which he conceived he had gained, "are most formidable when baffled; and it is unnecessary to tell you with what difficulty they are restrained in their anger. Eh bien, monsieur! shall we speak of the terms?"

"I fear your excellency has been deceived as to the strength of William Henry, and the resources of its garrison!"

"I have not sat down before Quebec, but an earthen work, that is defended by twenty-three hundred gallant men," was the laconic reply.

"Our mounds are earthen, certainly – nor are they seated on the rocks of Cape Diamond; but they stand on that shore which proved so destructive to Dieskau and his army. There is also a powerful force within a few hours' march of us, which we account upon as a part of our means."

"Some six or eight thousand men," returned Montcalm, with much apparent indifference, "whom their leader wisely judges to be safer in their works than in the field."

It was now Heyward's turn to bite his lip with vexation as the other so coolly alluded to a force which the young man knew to be overrated. Both mused a little while in silence, when Montcalm renewed the conversation, in a way that showed he believed the visit of his guest was solely to propose terms of capitulation. On the other hand, Heyward began to throw sundry inducements in the way of the French general, to betray the discoveries he had made through the intercepted letter. The artifice of neither, however, succeeded; and after a protracted and fruitless interview, Duncan took his leave, favorably impressed with an opinion of the courtesy and talents of the enemy's captain, but as ignorant of what he came to learn as when he arrived. Montcalm followed him as far as the entrance of the marquee, renewing his invitations to the commandant of the fort to give him an immediate meeting in the open ground between the two armies.

There they separated, and Duncan returned to the advanced post of the French, accompanied as before; whence he instantly proceeded to the fort, and to the quarters of his own commander.

Chapter Sixteen

"EDG. – Before you fight the battle ope this letter."

– Lear

MAJOR HEYWARD FOUND MUNRO attended only by his daughters. Alice sat upon his knee, parting the gray hairs on the forehead of the old man with her delicate fingers; and whenever he affected to frown on her trifling, appeasing his assumed anger by pressing her ruby lips fondly on his wrinkled brow. Cora was seated nigh them, a calm and amused looker-on; regarding the wayward movements of her more youthful sister with that species of maternal fondness which characterized her love for Alice. Not only the dangers through which they had passed, but those which still impended above them, appeared to be momentarily forgotten, in the soothing indulgence of such a family meeting. It seemed as if they had profited by the short truce, to devote an instant to the purest and best affection; the daughters forgetting their fears, and the veteran his cares, in the security of the moment. Of this scene, Duncan, who, in his eagerness to report his arrival, had entered unannounced, stood many moments an unobserved and a delighted spectator. But the quick and dancing eyes of Alice soon caught a glimpse of his figure reflected from a glass, and she sprang blushing from her father's knee, exclaiming aloud:

"Major Heyward!"

"What of the lad?" demanded her father; "I have sent him to crack a little with the Frenchman. Ha, sir, you are young, and you're nimble! Away with you, ye baggage; as if there were not troubles enough for a soldier, without having his camp filled with such prattling hussies as yourself!"

Alice laughingly followed her sister, who instantly led the way from an apartment where she perceived their presence was no longer desirable. Munro, instead of demanding the result of the young man's mission, paced the room for a few moments, with his hands behind his back, and his head inclined toward the floor, like a man lost in thought. At length he raised his eyes, glistening with a father's fondness, and exclaimed:

"They are a pair of excellent girls, Heyward, and such as any one may boast of."

"You are not now to learn my opinion of your daughters, Colonel Munro."

"True, lad, true," interrupted the impatient old man; "you were about opening your mind more fully on that matter the day you got in, but I did not think it becoming in an old soldier to be talking of nuptial blessings and wedding jokes when the enemies of his king were likely to be unbidden guests at the feast. But I was wrong, Duncan, boy, I was wrong there; and I am now ready to hear what you have to say."

"Notwithstanding the pleasure your assurance gives me, dear sir, I have just now, a message from Montcalm – "

"Let the Frenchman and all his host go to the devil, sir!" exclaimed the hasty veteran. "He is not yet master of William Henry, nor shall he ever be, provided Webb proves himself the man he should. No, sir, thank Heaven we are not yet in such a strait that it can be said Munro is too much pressed to discharge the little domestic duties of his own family. Your mother was the only child of my bosom friend, Duncan; and I'll just give you a hearing, though all the knights of St. Louis were in a body at the sally-port, with the French saint at their head, crying to speak a word under favor. A pretty degree of knighthood, sir, is that which can be bought with sugar hogsheads! and then your twopenny marquisates. The thistle is the order for dignity and antiquity; the veritable 'nemo me impune lacessit' of chivalry. Ye had ancestors in that degree, Duncan, and they were an ornament to the nobles of Scotland."

Heyward, who perceived that his superior took a malicious pleasure in exhibiting his contempt for the message of the French general, was fain to humor a spleen that he knew would be short-lived; he therefore, replied with as much indifference as he could assume on such a subject:

"My request, as you know, sir, went so far as to presume to the honor of being your son."

"Ay, boy, you found words to make yourself very plainly comprehended. But, let me ask ye, sir, have you been as intelligible to the girl?"

"On my honor, no," exclaimed Duncan, warmly; "there would have been an abuse of a confided trust, had I taken advantage of my situation for such a purpose."

"Your notions are those of a gentleman, Major Heyward, and well enough in their place. But Cora Munro is a maiden too discreet, and of a mind too elevated and improved, to need the guardianship even of a father."

"Cora!"

"Ay – Cora! we are talking of your pretensions to Miss Munro, are we not, sir?"

"I – I – I was not conscious of having mentioned her name," said Duncan, stammering.

"And to marry whom, then, did you wish my consent, Major Heyward?" demanded the old soldier, erecting himself in the dignity of offended feeling.

"You have another, and not less lovely child."

"Alice!" exclaimed the father, in an astonishment equal to that with which Duncan had just repeated the name of her sister.

"Such was the direction of my wishes, sir."

The young man awaited in silence the result of the extraordinary effect produced by a communication, which, as it now appeared, was so unexpected. For several minutes Munro paced the chamber with long and rapid strides, his rigid features working convulsively, and every faculty seemingly absorbed in the musings of his own mind. At length, he paused directly in front of Heyward, and riveting his eyes upon those of the other, he said, with a lip that quivered violently:

"Duncan Heyward, I have loved you for the sake of him whose blood is in your veins; I have loved you for your own good qualities; and I have loved you, because I thought you would contribute to the happiness of my child. But all this love would turn to hatred, were I assured that what I so much apprehend is true."

"God forbid that any act or thought of mine should lead to such a change!" exclaimed the young man, whose eye never quailed under the penetrating look it encountered. Without adverting to the impossibility of the other's comprehending those feelings which were hid in his own bosom, Munro suffered himself to be appeased by the unaltered countenance he met, and with a voice sensibly softened, he continued:

"You would be my son, Duncan, and you're ignorant of the history of the man you wish to call your father. Sit ye down, young man, and I will open to you the wounds of a seared heart, in as few words as may be suitable."

By this time, the message of Montcalm was as much forgotten by him who bore it as by the man for whose ears it was intended. Each drew a chair, and while the veteran communed a few moments with his own thoughts, apparently in sadness, the youth suppressed his impatience in a look and attitude of respectful attention. At length, the former spoke:

"You'll know, already, Major Heyward, that my family was both ancient and honorable," commenced the Scotsman; "though it might not altogether be endowed with that amount of wealth that should correspond with its degree. I was, maybe, such an one as yourself when I plighted my faith to Alice Graham, the only child of a neighboring laird of some estate. But the connection was disagreeable to her father, on more accounts than my poverty. I did, therefore, what an honest man should – restored the maiden her troth, and departed the country in the service of my king. I had seen many regions, and had shed much blood in different lands, before duty called me to the islands of the West Indies. There it was my lot to form a connection with one who in time became my wife, and the mother of Cora. She was the daughter of a gentleman of those isles, by a lady whose misfortune it was, if you will," said the old man, proudly, "to be descended, remotely, from that unfortunate class who are so basely enslaved to administer to the wants of a luxurious people. Ay, sir, that is a curse, entailed on Scotland by her unnatural union with a foreign and trading people. But could I find a man among them who would dare to reflect on my child, he should feel the weight of a father's anger! Ha! Major Heyward, you are yourself born at the south, where these unfortunate beings are considered of a race inferior to your own."

"'Tis most unfortunately true, sir," said Duncan, unable any longer to prevent his eyes from sinking to the floor in embarrassment.

"And you cast it on my child as a reproach! You scorn to mingle the blood of the Heywards with one so degraded – lovely and virtuous though she be?" fiercely demanded the jealous parent.

"Heaven protect me from a prejudice so unworthy of my reason!" returned Duncan, at the same time conscious of such a feeling, and that as deeply rooted as if it had been ingrafted in his nature. "The sweetness, the beauty, the witchery of your younger daughter, Colonel Munro, might explain my motives without imputing to me this injustice."

"Ye are right, sir," returned the old man, again changing his tones to those of gentleness, or rather softness; "the girl is the image of what her mother was at her years, and before she had become acquainted with grief. When death deprived me of my wife I returned to Scotland, enriched by the marriage; and, would you think it, Duncan! the suffering angel had remained in the heartless state of celibacy twenty long years, and that for the sake of a man who could forget her! She did more, sir; she overlooked my want of faith, and, all difficulties being now removed, she took me for her husband."

"And became the mother of Alice?" exclaimed Duncan, with an eagerness that might have proved dangerous at a moment when the thoughts of Munro were less occupied that at present.

"She did, indeed," said the old man, "and dearly did she pay for the blessing she bestowed. But she is a saint in heaven, sir; and it ill becomes one whose foot rests on the grave to mourn a lot so blessed. I had her but a single year, though; a short term of happiness for one who had seen her youth fade in hopeless pining."

There was something so commanding in the distress of the old man, that Heyward did not dare to venture a syllable of consolation. Munro sat utterly unconscious of the other's presence, his features exposed and working with the anguish of his regrets, while heavy tears fell from his eyes, and rolled unheeded from his cheeks to the floor. At length he moved, and as if suddenly recovering his recollection; when he arose, and taking a single turn across the room, he approached his companion with an air of military grandeur, and demanded:

"Have you not, Major Heyward, some communication that I should hear from the marquis de Montcalm?"

Duncan started in his turn, and immediately commenced in an embarrassed voice, the half-forgotten message. It is unnecessary to dwell upon the evasive though polite manner with which the French general had eluded every attempt of Heyward to worm from him the purport of the communication he had proposed making, or on the decided, though still polished message, by which he now gave his enemy to understand, that, unless he chose to receive it in person, he should not receive it at all. As Munro listened to the detail of Duncan, the excited feelings of the father gradually gave way before the obligations of his station, and when the other was done, he saw before him nothing but the veteran, swelling with the wounded feelings of a soldier.

"You have said enough, Major Heyward," exclaimed the angry old man; "enough to make a volume of commentary on French civility. Here has this gentleman invited me to a conference, and when I send him a capable substitute, for ye're all that, Duncan, though your years are but few, he answers me with a riddle."

"He may have thought less favorably of the substitute, my dear sir; and you will remember that the invitation, which he now repeats, was to the commandant of the works, and not to his second."

"Well, sir, is not a substitute clothed with all the power and dignity of him who grants the commission? He wishes to confer with Munro! Faith, sir, I have much inclination to indulge the man, if it should only be to let him behold the firm countenance we maintain in spite of his numbers and his summons. There might be not bad policy in such a stroke, young man."

Duncan, who believed it of the last importance that they should speedily come to the contents of the letter borne by the scout, gladly encouraged this idea.

"Without doubt, he could gather no confidence by witnessing our indifference," he said.

"You never said truer word. I could wish, sir, that he would visit the works in open day, and in the form of a storming party; that is the least failing method of proving the countenance of an enemy, and would be far preferable to the battering system he has chosen. The beauty and manliness of warfare has been much deformed, Major Heyward, by the arts of your Monsieur Vauban. Our ancestors were far above such scientific cowardice!"

"It may be very true, sir; but we are now obliged to repel art by art. What is your pleasure in the matter of the interview?"

"I will meet the Frenchman, and that without fear or delay; promptly, sir, as becomes a servant of my royal master. Go, Major Heyward, and give them a flourish of the music; and send out a messenger to let them know who is coming. We will follow with a small guard, for such respect is due to one who holds the honor of his king in keeping; and hark'ee, Duncan," he added, in a half whisper, though they were alone, "it may be prudent to have some aid at hand, in case there should be treachery at the bottom of it all."

The young man availed himself of this order to quit the apartment; and, as the day was fast coming to a close, he hastened without delay, to make the necessary arrangements. A very few minutes only were necessary to parade a few files, and to dispatch an orderly with a flag to announce the approach of the commandant of the fort. When Duncan had done both these, he led the guard to the sally-port, near which he found his superior ready, waiting his appearance. As soon as the usual ceremonials of a military departure were observed, the veteran and his more youthful companion left the fortress, attended by the escort.

They had proceeded only a hundred yards from the works, when the little array which attended the French general to the conference was seen issuing from the hollow way which formed the bed of a brook that ran between the batteries of the besiegers and the fort. From the moment that Munro left his own works to appear in front of his enemy's, his air had been grand, and his step and countenance highly military. The instant he caught a glimpse of the white plume that waved in the hat of Montcalm, his eye lighted, and age no longer appeared to possess any influence over his vast and still muscular person.

"Speak to the boys to be watchful, sir," he said, in an undertone, to Duncan; "and to look well to their flints and steel, for one is never safe with a servant of these Louis's; at the same time, we shall show them the front of men in deep security. Ye'll understand me, Major Heyward!"

He was interrupted by the clamor of a drum from the approaching Frenchmen, which was immediately answered, when each party pushed an orderly in advance, bearing a white flag, and the wary Scotsman halted with his guard close at his back. As soon as this slight salutation had passed, Montcalm moved toward them with a quick but graceful step, baring his head to the veteran, and dropping his spotless plume nearly to the earth in courtesy. If the air of Munro was more commanding and manly, it wanted both the ease and insinuating polish of that of the Frenchman. Neither spoke for a few moments, each regarding the other with curious and interested eyes. Then, as became his superior rank and the nature of the interview, Montcalm broke the silence. After uttering the usual words of greeting, he turned to Duncan, and continued, with a smile of recognition, speaking always in French:

"I am rejoiced, monsieur, that you have given us the pleasure of your company on this occasion. There will be no necessity to employ an ordinary interpreter; for, in your hands, I feel the same security as if I spoke your language myself."

Duncan acknowledged the compliment, when Montcalm, turning to his guard, which in imitation of that of their enemies, pressed close upon him, continued:

"En arriere, mes enfants – il fait chaud – -retirez-vous un peu."

Before Major Heyward would imitate this proof of confidence, he glanced his eyes around the plain, and beheld with uneasiness the numerous dusky groups of savages, who looked out from the margin of the surrounding woods, curious spectators of the interview.

"Monsieur de Montcalm will readily acknowledge the difference in our situation," he said, with some embarrassment, pointing at the same time toward those dangerous foes, who were to be seen in almost every direction. "Were we to dismiss our guard, we should stand here at the mercy of our enemies."

"Monsieur, you have the plighted faith of 'un gentilhomme Francais', for your safety," returned Montcalm, laying his hand impressively on his heart; "it should suffice."

"It shall. Fall back," Duncan added to the officer who led the escort; "fall back, sir, beyond hearing, and wait for orders."

Munro witnessed this movement with manifest uneasiness; nor did he fail to demand an instant explanation.

"Is it not our interest, sir, to betray distrust?" retorted Duncan. "Monsieur de Montcalm pledges his word for our safety, and I have ordered the men to withdraw a little, in order to prove how much we depend on his assurance."

"It may be all right, sir, but I have no

overweening reliance on the faith of these marquesses, or marquis, as they call themselves. Their patents of nobility are too common to be certain that they bear the seal of true honor."

"You forget, dear sir, that we confer with an officer, distinguished alike in Europe and America for his deeds. From a soldier of his reputation we can have nothing to apprehend."

The old man made a gesture of resignation, though his rigid features still betrayed his obstinate adherence to a distrust, which he derived from a sort of hereditary contempt of his enemy, rather than from any present signs which might warrant so uncharitable a feeling. Montcalm waited patiently until this little dialogue in demi-voice was ended, when he drew nigher, and opened the subject of their conference.

"I have solicited this interview from your superior, monsieur," he said, "because I believe he will allow himself to be persuaded that he has already done everything which is necessary for the honor of his prince, and will now listen to the admonitions of humanity. I will forever bear testimony that his resistance has been gallant, and was continued as long as there was hope."

When this opening was translated to Munro, he answered with dignity, but with sufficient courtesy:

"However I may prize such testimony from Monsieur Montcalm, it will be more valuable when it shall be better merited."

The French general smiled, as Duncan gave him the purport of this reply, and observed:

"What is now so freely accorded to approved courage, may be refused to useless obstinacy. Monsieur would wish to see my camp, and witness for himself our numbers, and the impossibility of his resisting them with success?"

"I know that the king of France is well served," returned the unmoved Scotsman, as soon as Duncan ended his translation; "but my own royal master has as many and as faithful troops."

"Though not at hand, fortunately for us," said Montcalm, without waiting, in his ardor, for the interpreter. "There is a destiny in war, to which a brave man knows how to submit with the same courage that he faces his foes."

"Had I been conscious that Monsieur Montcalm was master of the English, I should have spared myself the trouble of so awkward a translation," said the vexed Duncan, dryly; remembering instantly his recent by-play with Munro.

"Your pardon, monsieur," rejoined the Frenchman, suffering a slight color to appear on his dark cheek. "There is a vast difference between understanding and speaking a foreign tongue; you will, therefore, please to assist me still." Then, after a short pause, he added: "These hills afford us every opportunity of reconnoitering your works, messieurs, and I am possibly as well acquainted with their weak condition as you can be yourselves."

"Ask the French general if his glasses can reach to the Hudson," said Munro, proudly; "and if he knows when and where to expect the army of Webb."

"Let General Webb be his own interpreter," returned the politic Montcalm, suddenly extending an open letter toward Munro as he spoke; "you will there learn, monsieur, that his movements are not likely to prove embarrassing to my army."

The veteran seized the offered paper, without waiting for Duncan to translate the speech, and with an eagerness that betrayed how important he deemed its contents. As his eye passed hastily over the words, his countenance changed from its look of military pride to one of deep chagrin; his lip began to quiver; and suffering the paper to fall from his hand, his head dropped upon his chest, like that of a man whose hopes were withered at a single blow. Duncan caught the letter from the ground, and without apology for the liberty he took, he read at a glance its cruel purport. Their common superior, so far from encouraging them to resist, advised a speedy surrender, urging in the plainest language, as a reason, the utter impossibility of his sending a single man to their rescue.

"Here is no deception!" exclaimed Duncan, examining the billet both inside and out; "this is the signature of Webb, and must be the captured letter."

"The man has betrayed me!" Munro at length bitterly exclaimed; "he has brought dishonor to the door of one where disgrace was never before known to dwell, and shame has he heaped heavily on my gray hairs."

"Say not so," cried Duncan; "we are yet masters of the fort, and of our honor. Let us, then, sell our lives at such a rate as shall make our enemies believe the purchase too dear."

"Boy, I thank thee," exclaimed the old man, rousing himself from his stupor; "you have, for once, reminded Munro of his duty. We will go back, and dig our graves behind those ramparts."

"Messieurs," said Montcalm, advancing toward them a step, in generous interest, "you little know Louis de St. Veran if you believe him capable of profiting by this letter to humble brave men, or to build up a dishonest reputation for himself. Listen to my terms before you leave me."

"What says the Frenchman?" demanded the veteran, sternly; "does he make a merit of having captured a scout, with a note from headquarters? Sir, he had better raise this siege, to go and sit down before Edward if he wishes to frighten his enemy with words."

Duncan explained the other's meaning.

"Monsieur de Montcalm, we will hear you," the veteran added, more calmly, as Duncan ended.

"To retain the fort is now impossible," said his liberal enemy; "it is necessary to the interests of my master that it should be destroyed; but as for yourselves and your brave comrades, there is no privilege dear to a soldier that shall be denied."

"Our colors?" demanded Heyward.

"Carry them to England, and show them to your king."

"Our arms?"

"Keep them; none can use them better."

"Our march; the surrender of the place?"

"Shall all be done in a way most honorable to yourselves."

Duncan now turned to explain these proposals to his commander, who heard him with amazement, and a sensibility that was deeply touched by so unusual and unexpected generosity.

"Go you, Duncan," he said; "go with this marquess, as, indeed, marquess he should be; go to his marquee and arrange it all.

I have lived to see two things in my old age that never did I expect to behold. An Englishman afraid to support a friend, and a Frenchman too honest to profit by his advantage."

So saying, the veteran again dropped his head to his chest, and returned slowly toward the fort, exhibiting, by the dejection of his air, to the anxious garrison, a harbinger of evil tidings.

From the shock of this unexpected blow the haughty feelings of Munro never recovered; but from that moment there commenced a change in his determined character, which accompanied him to a speedy grave. Duncan remained to settle the terms of the capitulation. He was seen to re-enter the works during the first watches of the night, and immediately after a private conference with the commandant, to leave them again. It was then openly announced that hostilities must cease – Munro having signed a treaty by which the place was to be yielded to the enemy, with the morning; the garrison to retain their arms, the colors and their baggage, and, consequently, according to military opinion, their honor.

Chapter Seventeen

"Weave we the woof.
The thread is spun.
The web is wove.
The work is done."
– Gray

THE HOSTILE ARMIES, which lay in the wilds of the Horican, passed the night of the ninth of August, 1757, much in the manner they would, had they encountered on the fairest field of Europe. While the conquered were still, sullen, and dejected, the victors triumphed. But there are limits alike to grief and joy; and long before the watches of the morning came the stillness of those boundless woods was only broken by a gay call from some exulting young Frenchman of the advanced pickets, or a menacing challenge from the fort, which sternly forbade the approach of any hostile footsteps before the stipulated moment. Even these occasional threatening sounds ceased to be heard in that dull hour which precedes the day, at which period a listener might have sought in vain any evidence of the presence of those armed powers that then slumbered on the shores of the "holy lake."

It was during these moments of deep silence that the canvas which concealed the entrance to a spacious marquee in the French encampment was shoved aside, and a man issued from beneath the drapery into the open air. He was enveloped in a cloak that might have been intended as a protection from the chilling damps of the woods, but which served equally well as a mantle to conceal his person. He was permitted to pass the grenadier, who watched over the slumbers of the French commander, without interruption, the man making the usual salute which betokens military deference, as the other passed swiftly through the little city of tents, in the direction of William Henry. Whenever this unknown individual encountered one of the numberless sentinels who crossed his path, his answer was prompt, and, as it appeared, satisfactory; for he was uniformly allowed to proceed without further interrogation.

With the exception of such repeated but brief interruptions, he had moved silently from the center of the camp to its most advanced outposts, when he drew nigh the soldier who held his watch nearest to the works of the enemy. As he approached he was received with the usual challenge:

"Qui vive?"

"France," was the reply.

"Le mot d'ordre?"

"La victorie," said the other, drawing so

nigh as to be heard in a loud whisper.

"C'est bien," returned the sentinel, throwing his musket from the charge to his shoulder; "vous promenez bien matin, monsieur!"

"Il est necessaire d'etre vigilant, mon enfant," the other observed, dropping a fold of his cloak, and looking the soldier close in the face as he passed him, still continuing his way toward the British fortification. The man started; his arms rattled heavily as he threw them forward in the lowest and most respectful salute; and when he had again recovered his piece, he turned to walk his post, muttering between his teeth:

"Il faut etre vigilant, en verite! je crois que nous avons la, un caporal qui ne dort jamais!"

The officer proceeded, without affecting to hear the words which escaped the sentinel in his surprise; nor did he again pause until he had reached the low strand, and in a somewhat dangerous vicinity to the western water bastion of the fort. The light of an obscure moon was just sufficient to render objects, though dim, perceptible in their outlines. He, therefore, took the precaution to place himself against the trunk of a tree, where he leaned for many minutes, and seemed to contemplate the dark and silent mounds of the English works in profound attention. His gaze at the ramparts was not that of a curious or idle spectator; but his looks wandered from point to point, denoting his knowledge of military usages, and betraying that his search was not unaccompanied by distrust. At length he appeared satisfied; and having cast his eyes impatiently upward toward the summit of the eastern mountain, as if anticipating the approach of the morning, he was in the act of turning on his footsteps, when a light sound on the nearest angle of the bastion caught his ear, and induced him to remain.

Just then a figure was seen to approach the edge of the rampart, where it stood, apparently contemplating in its turn the distant tents of the French encampment. Its head was then turned toward the east, as though equally anxious for the appearance of light, when the form leaned against the mound, and seemed to gaze upon the glassy expanse of the waters, which, like a submarine firmament, glittered with its thousand mimic stars. The melancholy air, the hour, together with the vast frame of the man who thus leaned, musing, against the English ramparts, left no doubt as to his person in the mind of the observant spectator. Delicacy, no less than prudence, now urged him to retire; and he had moved cautiously round the body of the tree for that purpose, when another sound drew his attention, and once more arrested his footsteps. It was a low and almost inaudible movement of the water, and was succeeded by a grating of pebbles one against the other. In a moment he saw a dark form rise, as it were, out of the lake, and steal without further noise to the land, within a few feet of the place where he himself stood. A rifle next slowly rose between his eyes and the watery mirror; but before it could be discharged his own hand was on the lock.

"Hugh!" exclaimed the savage, whose treacherous aim was so singularly and so unexpectedly interrupted.

Without making any reply, the French officer laid his hand on the shoulder of the Indian, and led him in profound silence to a distance from the spot, where their subsequent dialogue might have proved dangerous, and where it seemed that one of them, at least, sought a victim. Then throwing open his cloak, so as to expose his uniform and the cross of St. Louis which was suspended at his breast, Montcalm sternly demanded:

"What means this? Does not my son know that the hatchet is buried between the English and his Canadian Father?"

"What can the Hurons do?" returned the

savage, speaking also, though imperfectly, in the French language.

"Not a warrior has a scalp, and the pale faces make friends!"

"Ha, Le Renard Subtil! Methinks this is an excess of zeal for a friend who was so late an enemy! How many suns have set since Le Renard struck the war-post of the English?"

"Where is that sun?" demanded the sullen savage. "Behind the hill; and it is dark and cold. But when he comes again, it will be bright and warm. Le Subtil is the sun of his tribe. There have been clouds, and many mountains between him and his nation; but now he shines and it is a clear sky!"

"That Le Renard has power with his people, I well know," said Montcalm; "for yesterday he hunted for their scalps, and to-day they hear him at the council-fire."

"Magua is a great chief."

"Let him prove it, by teaching his nation how to conduct themselves toward our new friends."

"Why did the chief of the Canadas bring his young men into the woods, and fire his cannon at the earthen house?" demanded the subtle Indian.

"To subdue it. My master owns the land, and your father was ordered to drive off these English squatters. They have consented to go, and now he calls them enemies no longer."

"'Tis well. Magua took the hatchet to color it with blood. It is now bright; when it is red, it shall be buried."

"But Magua is pledged not to sully the lilies of France. The enemies of the great king across the salt lake are his enemies; his friends, the friends of the Hurons."

"Friends!" repeated the Indian in scorn. "Let his father give Magua a hand."

Montcalm, who felt that his influence over the warlike tribes he had gathered was to be maintained by concession rather than by power, complied reluctantly with the other's request. The savage placed the fingers of the French commander on a deep scar in his bosom, and then exultingly demanded:

"Does my father know that?"

"What warrior does not? 'Tis where a leaden bullet has cut."

"And this?" continued the Indian, who had turned his naked back to the other, his body being without its usual calico mantle.

"This! – my son has been sadly injured here; who has done this?"

"Magua slept hard in the English wigwams, and the sticks have left their mark," returned the savage, with a hollow laugh, which did not conceal the fierce temper that nearly choked him. Then, recollecting himself, with sudden and native dignity, he added: "Go; teach your young men it is peace. Le Renard Subtil knows how to speak to a Huron warrior."

Without deigning to bestow further words, or to wait for any answer, the savage cast his rifle into the hollow of his arm, and moved silently through the encampment toward the woods where his own tribe was known to lie. Every few yards as he proceeded he was challenged by the sentinels; but he stalked sullenly onward, utterly disregarding the summons of the soldiers, who only spared his life because they knew the air and tread no less than the obstinate daring of an Indian.

Montcalm lingered long and melancholy on the strand where he had been left by his companion, brooding deeply on the temper which his ungovernable ally had just discovered. Already had his fair fame been tarnished by one horrid scene, and in circumstances fearfully resembling those under which he now found himself. As he mused he became keenly sensible of the deep responsibility they assume who disregard the means to attain the end, and of all the danger of setting in motion an engine which it exceeds human power to control. Then shaking off a train of reflections that he accounted a weakness in such a moment of triumph, he retraced his steps toward his tent, giving the order as he passed to make the signal that should arouse the army from its slumbers.

The first tap of the French drums was echoed from the bosom of the fort, and presently the valley was filled with the strains of martial music, rising long, thrilling and lively above the rattling accompaniment. The horns of the victors sounded merry and cheerful flourishes, until the last laggard of the camp was at his post; but the instant the British fifes had blown their shrill signal, they became mute. In the meantime the day had dawned, and when the line of the French army was ready to receive its general, the rays of a brilliant sun were glancing along the glittering array. Then that success, which was already so well known, was officially announced; the favored band who were selected to guard the gates of the fort were detailed, and defiled before their chief; the signal of their approach was given, and all the usual preparations for a change of masters were ordered and executed directly under the guns of the contested works.

A very different scene presented itself within the lines of the Anglo-American army. As soon as the warning signal was given, it exhibited all the signs of a hurried and forced departure. The sullen soldiers shouldered their empty tubes and fell into their places, like men whose blood had been heated by the past contest, and who only desired the opportunity to revenge an indignity which was still wounding to their pride, concealed as it was under the observances of military etiquette.

Women and children ran from place to place, some bearing the scanty remnants of their baggage, and others searching in the ranks for those countenances they looked up to for protection.

Munro appeared among his silent troops firm but dejected. It was evident that the unexpected blow had struck deep into his heart, though he struggled to sustain his misfortune with the port of a man.

Duncan was touched at the quiet and impressive exhibition of his grief. He had discharged his own duty, and he now pressed to the side of the old man, to know in what particular he might serve him.

"My daughters," was the brief but expressive reply.

"Good heavens! are not arrangements already made for their convenience?"

"To-day I am only a soldier, Major Heyward," said the veteran. "All that you see here, claim alike to be my children."

Duncan had heard enough. Without losing one of those moments which had now become so precious, he flew toward the quarters of Munro, in quest of the sisters. He found them on the threshold of the low edifice, already prepared to depart, and surrounded by a clamorous and weeping assemblage of their own sex, that had gathered about the place, with a sort of instinctive consciousness that it was the point most likely to be protected. Though the cheeks of Cora were pale and her countenance anxious, she had lost none of her firmness; but the eyes of Alice were inflamed, and betrayed how long and bitterly she had wept. They both, however, received the young man with undisguised pleasure; the former, for a novelty, being the first to speak.

"The fort is lost," she said, with a melancholy smile; "though our good name, I trust, remains."

"'Tis brighter than ever. But, dearest Miss Munro, it is time to think less of others, and to make some provision for yourself. Military usage – pride – that pride on which you so much value yourself, demands that your father and I should for a little while continue with the troops. Then where to seek a proper protector for you against the confusion and chances of such a scene?"

"None is necessary," returned Cora; "who

will dare to injure or insult the daughter of such a father, at a time like this?"

"I would not leave you alone," continued the youth, looking about him in a hurried manner, "for the command of the best regiment in the pay of the king. Remember, our Alice is not gifted with all your firmness, and God only knows the terror she might endure."

"You may be right," Cora replied, smiling again, but far more sadly than before. "Listen! chance has already sent us a friend when he is most needed."

Duncan did listen, and on the instant comprehended her meaning. The low and serious sounds of the sacred music, so well known to the eastern provinces, caught his ear, and instantly drew him to an apartment in an adjacent building, which had already been deserted by its customary tenants. There he found David, pouring out his pious feelings through the only medium in which he ever indulged. Duncan waited, until, by the cessation of the movement of the hand, he believed the strain was ended, when, by touching his shoulder, he drew the attention of the other to himself, and in a few words explained his wishes.

"Even so," replied the single-minded disciple of the King of Israel, when the young man had ended; "I have found much that is comely and melodious in the maidens, and it is fitting that we who have consorted in so much peril, should abide together in peace. I will attend them, when I have completed my morning praise, to which nothing is now wanting but the doxology. Wilt thou bear a part, friend? The meter is common, and the tune 'Southwell'."

Then, extending the little volume, and giving the pitch of the air anew with considerate attention, David recommenced and finished his strains, with a fixedness of manner that it was not easy to interrupt. Heyward was fain to wait until the verse was ended; when, seeing David relieving himself from the spectacles, and replacing the book, he continued.

"It will be your duty to see that none dare to approach the ladies with any rude intention, or to offer insult or taunt at the misfortune of their brave father. In this task you will be seconded by the domestics of their household."

"Even so."

"It is possible that the Indians and stragglers of the enemy may intrude, in which case you will remind them of the terms of the capitulation, and threaten to report their conduct to Montcalm. A word will suffice."

"If not, I have that here which shall," returned David, exhibiting his book, with an air in which meekness and confidence were singularly blended. Here are words which, uttered, or rather thundered, with proper emphasis, and in measured time, shall quiet the most unruly temper:

"'Why rage the heathen furiously'?"

"Enough," said Heyward, interrupting

the burst of his musical invocation; "we understand each other; it is time that we should now assume our respective duties."

Gamut cheerfully assented, and together they sought the females. Cora received her new and somewhat extraordinary protector courteously, at least; and even the pallid features of Alice lighted again with some of their native archness as she thanked Heyward for his care. Duncan took occasion to assure them he had done the best that circumstances permitted, and, as he believed, quite enough for the security of their feelings; of danger there was none. He then spoke gladly of his intention to rejoin them the moment he had led the advance a few miles toward the Hudson, and immediately took his leave.

By this time the signal for departure had been given, and the head of the English column was in motion. The sisters started at the sound, and glancing their eyes around, they saw the white uniforms of the

French grenadiers, who had already taken possession of the gates of the fort. At that moment an enormous cloud seemed to pass suddenly above their heads, and, looking upward, they discovered that they stood beneath the wide folds of the standard of France.

"Let us go," said Cora; "this is no longer a fit place for the children of an English officer."

Alice clung to the arm of her sister, and together they left the parade, accompanied by the moving throng that surrounded them.

As they passed the gates, the French officers, who had learned their rank, bowed often and low, forbearing, however, to intrude those attentions which they saw, with peculiar tact, might not be agreeable. As every vehicle and each beast of burden was occupied by the sick and wounded, Cora had decided to endure the fatigues of a foot march, rather than interfere with their comforts. Indeed, many a maimed and feeble soldier was compelled to drag his exhausted limbs in the rear of the columns, for the want of the necessary means of conveyance in that wilderness. The whole, however, was in motion; the weak and wounded, groaning and in suffering; their comrades silent and sullen; and the women and children in terror, they knew not of what.

As the confused and timid throng left the protecting mounds of the fort, and issued on the open plain, the whole scene was at once presented to their eyes. At a little distance on the right, and somewhat in the rear, the French army stood to their arms, Montcalm having collected his parties, so soon as his guards had possession of the works. They were attentive but silent observers of the proceedings of the vanquished, failing in none of the stipulated military honors, and offering no taunt or insult, in their success, to their less fortunate foes. Living masses of the English, to the amount, in the whole, of near three thousand, were moving slowly across the plain, toward the common center, and gradually approached each other, as they converged to the point of their march, a vista cut through the lofty trees, where the road to the Hudson entered the forest. Along the sweeping borders of the woods hung a dark cloud of savages, eyeing the passage of their enemies, and hovering at a distance, like vultures who were only kept from swooping on their prey by the presence and restraint of a superior army. A few had straggled among the conquered columns, where they stalked in sullen discontent; attentive, though, as yet, passive observers of the moving multitude.

The advance, with Heyward at its head, had already reached the defile, and was slowly disappearing, when the attention of Cora was drawn to a collection of stragglers by the sounds of contention. A truant provincial was paying the forfeit of his disobedience, by being plundered of those very effects which had caused him to desert his place in the ranks. The man was of powerful frame, and too avaricious to part with his goods without a struggle. Individuals from either party interfered; the one side to prevent and the other to aid in the robbery. Voices grew loud and angry, and a hundred savages appeared, as it were, by magic, where a dozen only had been seen a minute before. It was then that Cora saw the form of Magua gliding among his countrymen, and speaking with his fatal and artful eloquence. The mass of women and children stopped, and hovered together like alarmed and fluttering birds. But the cupidity of the Indian was soon gratified, and the different bodies again moved slowly onward.

The savages now fell back, and seemed content to let their enemies advance without further molestation. But, as the female crowd approached them, the gaudy colors of a shawl attracted the eyes of a wild and untutored Huron. He advanced to seize it without the least hesitation. The woman, more in terror than through love of the ornament, wrapped her child in the coveted article, and folded both more closely to her bosom. Cora was in the act of speaking, with an intent to advise the woman to abandon the trifle, when the savage relinquished his hold of the shawl, and tore the screaming infant from her arms. Abandoning everything to the greedy grasp of those around her, the mother darted, with distraction in her mien, to reclaim her child. The Indian smiled grimly, and extended one hand, in sign of a willingness to exchange, while, with the other, he flourished the babe over his head, holding it by the feet as if to enhance the value of the ransom.

"Here–here–there–all–any–everything!" exclaimed the breathless woman, tearing the lighter articles of dress from her person with ill-directed and trembling fingers; "take all, but give me my babe!"

The savage spurned the worthless rags, and perceiving that the shawl had already become a prize to another, his bantering but sullen smile changing to a gleam of ferocity, he dashed the head of the infant against a rock, and cast its quivering remains to her very feet. For an instant the mother stood, like a statue of despair, looking wildly down at the unseemly object, which had so lately nestled in her bosom and smiled in her face; and then she raised her eyes and countenance toward heaven, as if calling on God to curse the perpetrator of the foul deed. She was spared the sin of such a prayer for, maddened at his disappointment, and excited at the sight of blood, the Huron mercifully drove his tomahawk into her own brain. The mother sank under the blow, and fell, grasping at her child, in death, with the same engrossing love that had caused her to cherish it when living.

At that dangerous moment, Magua placed his hands to his mouth, and raised the fatal and appalling whoop. The scattered Indians started at the well-known cry, as coursers bound at the signal to quit the goal; and directly there arose such a yell along the plain, and through the arches of the wood, as seldom burst from human lips before. They who heard it listened with a curdling horror at the heart, little inferior to that dread which may be expected to attend the blasts of the final summons.

More than two thousand raving savages broke from the forest at the signal, and threw themselves across the fatal plain with instinctive alacrity. We shall not dwell on the revolting horrors that succeeded. Death was everywhere, and in his most terrific and disgusting aspects. Resistance only served to inflame the murderers, who inflicted their furious blows long after their victims were beyond the power of their resentment. The flow of blood might be likened to the outbreaking of a torrent; and as the natives became heated and maddened by the sight, many among them even kneeled to the earth, and drank freely, exultingly, hellishly, of the crimson tide.

The trained bodies of the troops threw themselves quickly into solid masses, endeavoring to awe their assailants by the imposing appearance of a military front. The experiment in some measure succeeded, though far too many suffered their unloaded muskets to be torn from their hands, in the vain hope of appeasing the savages.

In such a scene none had leisure to note the fleeting moments. It might have been ten minutes (it seemed an age) that the sisters had stood riveted to one spot, horror-stricken and nearly helpless. When the first blow was struck, their screaming companions had pressed upon them in a body, rendering flight impossible; and now that fear or death had scattered most, if not all, from around them, they saw no avenue open, but such as conducted to the tomahawks of their foes. On every side arose shrieks, groans, exhortations and curses. At this moment, Alice caught a glimpse of the vast form of her father, moving rapidly across the plain, in the direction of the French army. He was, in truth, proceeding to Montcalm, fearless of every danger, to claim the tardy escort for which he had before conditioned. Fifty glittering axes and barbed spears were offered unheeded at his life, but the savages respected his rank and calmness, even in their fury. The dangerous weapons were brushed aside by the still nervous arm of the veteran, or fell of themselves, after menacing an act that it would seem no one had courage to perform. Fortunately, the vindictive Magua was searching for his victim in the very band the veteran had just quitted.

"Father – father – we are here!" shrieked Alice, as he passed, at no great distance, without appearing to heed them. "Come to us, father, or we die!"

The cry was repeated, and in terms and tones that might have melted a heart of stone, but it was unanswered. Once, indeed, the old man appeared to catch the sound, for he paused and listened; but Alice had dropped senseless on the earth, and Cora had sunk at her side, hovering in untiring tenderness over her lifeless form. Munro shook his head in disappointment, and proceeded, bent on the high duty of his station.

"Lady," said Gamut, who, helpless and useless as he was, had not yet dreamed of deserting his trust, "it is the jubilee of the devils, and this is not a meet place for Christians to tarry in. Let us up and fly."

"Go," said Cora, still gazing at her unconscious sister; "save thyself. To me thou canst not be of further use."

David comprehended the unyielding character of her resolution, by the simple but expressive gesture that accompanied her words. He gazed for a moment at the dusky forms that were acting their hellish rites on every side of him, and his tall person grew more erect while his chest heaved, and every feature swelled, and seemed to speak with the power of the feelings by which he was governed.

"If the Jewish boy might tame the great spirit of Saul by the sound of his harp, and the words of sacred song, it may not be amiss," he said, "to try the potency of music here."

Then raising his voice to its highest tone, he poured out a strain so powerful as to be heard even amid the din of that bloody field. More than one savage rushed toward them, thinking to rifle the unprotected sisters of their attire, and bear away their scalps; but when they found this strange and unmoved figure riveted to his post, they paused to listen. Astonishment soon changed to admiration, and they passed on to other and less courageous victims, openly expressing their satisfaction at the firmness with which the white warrior sang his death song. Encouraged and deluded by his success, David exerted all his powers to extend what he believed so holy an influence. The unwonted sounds caught the ears of a distant savage, who flew raging from group to group, like one who, scorning to touch the vulgar herd, hunted for some victim more worthy of his renown. It was Magua, who uttered a yell of pleasure when he beheld his ancient prisoners again at his mercy.

"Come," he said, laying his soiled hands on the dress of Cora, "the wigwam of the Huron is still open. Is it not better than this place?"

"Away!" cried Cora, veiling her eyes from his revolting aspect.

The Indian laughed tauntingly, as he held up his reeking hand, and answered: "It is red, but it comes from white veins!"

"Monster! there is blood, oceans of blood, upon thy soul; thy spirit has moved this scene."

"Magua is a great chief!" returned the exulting savage, "will the dark-hair go to his tribe?"

"Never! strike if thou wilt, and complete

thy revenge." He hesitated a moment, and then catching the light and senseless form of Alice in his arms, the subtle Indian moved swiftly across the plain toward the woods.

"Hold!" shrieked Cora, following wildly on his footsteps; "release the child! wretch! what is't you do?"

But Magua was deaf to her voice; or, rather, he knew his power, and was determined to maintain it.

"Stay – lady – stay," called Gamut, after the unconscious Cora. "The holy charm is beginning to be felt, and soon shalt thou see this horrid tumult stilled."

Perceiving that, in his turn, he was unheeded, the faithful David followed the distracted sister, raising his voice again in sacred song, and sweeping the air to the measure, with his long arm, in diligent accompaniment. In this manner they traversed the plain, through the flying, the wounded and the dead. The fierce Huron was, at any time, sufficient for himself and the victim that he bore; though Cora would have fallen more than once under the blows of her savage enemies, but for the extraordinary being who stalked in her rear, and who now appeared to the astonished natives gifted with the protecting spirit of madness.

Magua, who knew how to avoid the more pressing dangers, and also to elude pursuit, entered the woods through a low ravine, where he quickly found the Narragansetts, which the travelers had abandoned so shortly before, awaiting his appearance, in custody of a savage as fierce and malign in his expression as himself. Laying Alice on one of the horses, he made a sign to Cora to mount the other.

Notwithstanding the horror excited by the presence of her captor, there was a present relief in escaping from the bloody scene enacting on the plain, to which Cora could not be altogether insensible. She took her seat, and held forth her arms for her sister, with an air of entreaty and love that even the Huron could not deny. Placing Alice, then, on the same animal with Cora, he seized the bridle, and commenced his route by plunging deeper into the forest. David, perceiving that he was left alone, utterly disregarded as a subject too worthless even to destroy, threw his long limb across the saddle of the beast they had deserted, and made such progress in the pursuit as the difficulties of the path permitted.

They soon began to ascend; but as the motion had a tendency to revive the dormant faculties of her sister, the attention of Cora was too much divided between the tenderest solicitude in her behalf, and in listening to the cries which were still too audible on the plain, to note the direction in which they journeyed. When, however, they gained the flattened surface of the mountain-top, and approached the eastern precipice, she recognized the spot to which she had once before been led under the more friendly auspices of the scout. Here Magua suffered them to dismount; and notwithstanding their own captivity, the curiosity which seems inseparable from horror, induced them to gaze at the sickening sight below.

The cruel work was still unchecked. On every side the captured were flying before their relentless persecutors, while the armed columns of the Christian king stood fast in an apathy which has never been explained, and which has left an immovable blot on the otherwise fair escutcheon of their leader. Nor was the sword of death stayed until cupidity got the mastery of revenge. Then, indeed, the shrieks of the wounded, and the yells of their murderers grew less frequent, until, finally, the cries of horror were lost to their ear, or were drowned in the loud, long and piercing whoops of the triumphant savages.

CONTINUES IN VOLUME TWO

www.ingramcontent.com/pod-product-compliance
Lightning Source LLC
Chambersburg PA
CBHW020917310726

48980CB00011B/928/J
9781834124216